Valerie S. Malmont

DEATH PAYS *the* ROSE RENT

A Tori Miracle Mystery

SIMON & SCHUSTER

New York London Toronto Sydney Tokyo Singapore

SIMON & SCHUSTER
Rockefeller Center
1230 Avenue of the Americas
New York, New York 10020

SIMON & SCHUSTER and colophon are registered
trademarks of Simon & Schuster Inc.

Designed by Pei Loi Koay
Manufactured in the United States of America

10 9 8 7 6 5 4 3 2 1

Library of Congress Cataloging-in-Publication Data

Malmont, Valerie S.
Death pays the rose rent: a Tori Miracle mystery/Valerie
S. Malmont.
p.   cm.
1. Women detectives—Pennsylvania—Fiction. 2. Serial
murders—Pennsylvania—Fiction. 3. Women novelists,
American—Fiction. I. Title.
PS3563.A43184D4   1994
813'.54—dc20   93–42075 CIP

ISBN 0-671-86967-1

DEATH PAYS the ROSE RENT

Chapter

1

I stood in the green room, waiting for my first two minutes of fame to begin. Never in my entire thirty years had I endured a more humiliating experience than The Makeup Room. My face was now as ageless and devoid of expression as the show's hostess, Jenny Jerome. My short, black, wavy hair had been teased into a mess that even Elizabeth Taylor would have laughed at; my brown eyes were heavy with bright blue eye shadow "to bring them out" and circled with an inch of charcoal; my cheeks were streaked with scarlet to simulate cheekbones; and my lips were puffy with a greasy red lipstick I wouldn't have picked for myself in a million years.

The blond hostess of "Wake Up, New York" finished her interview with the sexy male star of the summer's blockbuster movie. The lights dimmed; he was escorted offstage by a giggling girl in an NYU T-shirt; the blonde had her stiff helmet of hair resprayed; and I was propelled forward by a hand placed firmly between my shoulder blades.

I was on TV!

She smiled at me in the condescending way that tall, perfectly proportioned people often use with short, plump people and began to read from a teleprompter hidden some-where behind my left shoulder. To the viewers at home it would look as though she were speaking directly to me.

"It's now my pleasure to welcome Victoria Miracle, a crime reporter and author of that fascinating new book *The Mark Twain Horror House*. Vicky, as I understand it, you—"

I interrupted her. "Tori. I'm called Tori. That's the name I use when I write."

"Oh, sorry." She continued reading, "Vicky, as I understand it, you were covering the terrible murder of that little girl in the Greenwich Village town house and discovered the house had a history of hauntings dating back to the time when Mark Twain lived there. Vicky, please tell us how you made the transition from newspaper reporter to psychic investigator."

"It's Tori, please." I forced a smile to my lips, which didn't quite reach my eyes. "Jenny, I'm afraid the information you have about me is wrong. I'm not a psychic investigator. I simply wrote a novel using the house and its strange history as background material. The story itself is fiction—completely fabricated, totally made up in my head—an exercise in 'what if' writing. I hope readers will—"

"Thank you, Vicky, for this fascinating glimpse into the world of paranormal research. We certainly appreciate your taking the time away from your exciting investigations of the supernatural." She flashed a relieved smile at the camera, revealing perfect white-capped teeth. "That concludes our interview with Vicky Merkle, a real-life 'ghost buster' and author of *The Mark Twain Horror House*."

"My name is Tori Miracle, and I'm not a ghos—" I started to protest, but it was too late. The lights were off. Jenny removed the microphone from her ample bosom and reached for a water glass, obviously exhausted from the effort of reading off the teleprompter. I was surprised she could read. She certainly hadn't bothered to read my book. I was led away by the NYU T-shirt, through a maze of cables and cameras, to the studio door.

The studio limousine was waiting for me there, but not with the same driver who had picked me up that morning at five A.M. That first one probably didn't want to risk his life again by making a second trip into Hell's Kitchen.

Nestled in the luxurious dove gray plush backseat of the limousine, I wished I could have blamed the publicist who arranged for that stupid interview, but I was the one who'd made a fool of myself in front of several million people. I should have known what to expect, since I'd seen the show before, but my book hadn't been selling well, and I'd said I'd do anything to try to boost sales. This morning's fiasco certainly wasn't going to help, though.

When we stopped on Tenth Avenue, the driver reached back to open my door from the inside. I'd bet he'd never delivered a talk-show guest to this neighborhood before. To him, it must have looked threatening. To me, it was just home—a neighborhood like any other—it had its good points and its bad ones.

It was too early for the bars to be open, so our homeless front-door regular was still asleep under a pile of newspapers on the stoop. I nudged him gently with one foot. "Morning, Sarge," I said when he stuck his head out.

"Hi, Tori. What're you doing out so early?"

"I was on TV."

"Great. What for?"

"I was on 'Wake Up, New York,' being interviewed about my book."

"You wrote a book? Congratulations! Someday I'm going to write one that'll blow the lid off the Vietnam conspiracy. Maybe you'd like me to tell you about it, and you can write it?"

I shook my head. "Sorry, Sarge. I couldn't do it justice."

He nodded in agreement. Over the past four years I'd

heard a number of stories from him; he was a vet suffering post-traumatic stress syndrome, but unable to go to the VA for help because he "knew too much"; he was in the Witness Protection Program; and right after Oliver Stone's movie came out, he was hiding from the mob because he was the mystery man with the umbrella in the Kennedy shooting.

"Well then, maybe you could lend me a couple of bucks for breakfast. I haven't eaten in days," he said pitifully.

I opened my purse and fumbled around until I located my wallet. It held four dollars and a little change. He looked disappointed with the two bills I handed him; enough for something to eat, but not enough for booze.

"Sorry, Sarge. That's all I can part with, now that I, too, have joined the great ranks of the unemployed."

"What happened to your job on the paper?"

"Got pushed out. We were bought by one of those huge multimedia conglomerates. They put their own people in all the good jobs and doled out the crummy ones to the old-timers. I didn't last long after that."

"Hey, I'm real sorry about that. Buy you a cup of coffee? My treat."

"I'll take a rain check. But thanks."

He looked relieved.

Even that early, the downstairs hall smelled of cabbage and urine. Our landlord was "gentrifying" the building to get even more exorbitant rents out of his tenants, but he had started on the top floor and was working down. While my cats and I had two whole rooms, plus a bath, all to ourselves on the fourth floor, the downstairs apartments each housed two or three families. And worst of all, there was only one communal bathroom on each floor, set at the end of the un-lit hallway.

The one advantage to living here, aside from the almost affordable rent, was that I felt safe. No thief in his right mind would ever consider breaking into an apartment in a building that looked and smelled this bad.

I had to stop for a moment on the third floor to catch my breath. I really must lose twenty pounds, I thought. I'll start my diet tomorrow.

Fred and Noel were just beginning to wake up and were indignant that I had left them alone at an hour when we were usually all snuggled up together on my futon.

As big, orange Fred glared at me, it occurred to me that he looked considerably brighter than poor Jenny Jerome of "Wake Up, New York." How long, I wondered, before she was shunted off into bimbo-limbo?

I put the kettle on for coffee and gave each cat a handful of Tasty Tabby Treats. As usual, Fred gobbled his in two seconds and then hovered over Noel, waiting for a chance to steal some of hers. The dainty calico ate leisurely, in a most ladylike manner, ignoring his boorish behavior.

A shave-and-a-haircut-six-bits knock on my door heralded the arrival of my next-door neighbor, the soon-to-be-famous actor slash Italian waiter, Murray Rosenbaum. With typical New York caution, I peered out through the little magnifying-glass hole in the door before unhooking the chain.

"I saw you on TV. Darling, you were marvelous."

"Thanks, Murray. But your Billy Crystal impression needs a little more work."

"That's an actor's life—nothing but work, work, work."

He wore a crimson satin bathrobe and white silk pajamas and smelled like Christmas; Aramis, I guessed.

"Come on in. I was just going to fix coffee."

After pushing the piles of unopened bills and magazines to one side of the table, I poured hot water into two mugs and stirred in instant coffee.

"Want some powdered pretend-cream or artificial sweetener?"

He shuddered. "This is bad enough, thank you. Any luck finding a job?"

I sipped my coffee and shook my head. "Guess I broke the

number one rule—never quit a job until you've got another one lined up."

"You were the best crime reporter on the paper. What happened?"

"They assigned me to cover fashion shows. Fashion shows! Me, who doesn't know the difference between Lamborghini and Lagerfeld."

"One's a car."

"Exactly."

"Something will turn up," said my ever optimistic neighbor. "Look at the bright side. You can get started on that second book. And you can use some of your 'leisure' time to clean up this apartment."

"What's wrong with it?"

I looked around the small living room–kitchen combination, seeing it as if for the first time; the avocado green refrigerator, the harvest gold stove with two nonfunctioning burners, the black and gray tiles on the floor, the single grime-streaked window, the brown sofa with bright orange flowers, covered with a week's worth of laundry, and the blue velour recliner in front of my TV. Papers and books, everywhere and anywhere, on top of chairs, under furniture, stacked in the corners, covering the couch; even my unmade bed had a two-foot-high pile of stuff on the side where I don't sleep. Had I really lived here nine years? It was just supposed to have been a way-stop after college.

"I guess I am a little disorganized," I admitted. "But look at my kitchen counter. I'm quite proud of how clean I keep it."

"That's because you never cook. If the corner deli went out of business, you'd starve." We both laughed at his half-truth.

"Tori, I've known you for a year now—long enough to know you have excellent taste. When we've gone out to dinner, you know gourmet food and which wines are good—

heck, you can even pronounce them. You visit museums frequently. You love concerts, operas, Broadway shows. You always look nice, even though I know most of your things come from secondhand shops. You have all the right instincts for a life of gracious living, but your home is a disaster. Didn't your mother teach you anything about housekeeping . . . or cooking . . . or . . . ?"

"Murray, my dear, nosy friend. I don't usually talk about my past, but for you, I'll make an exception. I grew up in more countries than I can name. My father's a career foreign service officer. He never made much money, but we lived like we were rich, thanks to Uncle Sam. We always had cooks, chauffeurs, gardeners, amahs, maids to wash, maids to iron, maids to scrub floors, you name it—we paid somebody to do it for us. Until I came to this country for college, I'd never stepped foot in a kitchen, scrubbed a toilet, or ironed a dress. When I finally had to, I found I didn't care much for it. In brief, I missed all those normal childhood experiences that should have turned me into your typical domesticated adult."

I tried to sound light and breezy. No need to mention the loneliness, the constant moving, the life empty of friendship and roots. It hurt too much, and I'd learned long ago to avoid the subject of my past.

"Interesting, Tori, but it's never too late to get control of your life. Concentrate on one thing at a time. Let's start with this table, for example. If you go through this great unread pile of mail, you'll find most of it could be pitched. Then you'd be left with a small stack of important things that you could handle. Get me a garbage sack."

I put a paper grocery bag on the floor next to him and watched as he filled it with catalogs, advertising circulars, begging letters from charities, and anything else that didn't have first-class postage on it.

"There," he said with a satisfied sigh. "Here's two issues

of the *Smithsonian.* This pile's your bills. My goodness, dear, three from the phone company, two from the cable company . . ."

"Put those on top." A phone I can do without, but I sure don't want to give up my old late-night movies. There's just nothing like settling down after a hard day's work with a classic like *Plan 9 From Outer Space.*

"Cable's not going to do you a bit of good if you don't pay these electric bills," he said, waving more envelopes at me.

I sighed. "I'll probably be evicted before they get around to turning it off."

"Evicted!" he screeched. "I know you're out of work, but you must have some money saved. And there's your wonderful new book—surely you got an advance for that?"

"All gone."

"You can't mean *all* gone."

I nodded. "It wasn't that large to begin with," I muttered.

"That is totally irresponsible, Tori. You are beyond human help." He tossed two envelopes at me. "Here's a couple that look personal. Is the one with the foreign stamps from your parents?"

"My father. He's the ambassador to a small African country, which changes its name as often as it changes governments." I pushed the letter to one side. Maybe I'd read it later.

I opened the other, postmarked weeks earlier. It came from a fellow journalism-school graduate asking if I knew of any jobs in New York City. If I did, I'd apply for them myself, I thought as I circular-filed his letter.

Murray departed to "get in character" for a soap audition to be held later in the day. Poor Murray, how many more rejections would it take before he went back to Ohio to work in his family's popcorn factory?

I watched Noel stalk a cockroach across the floor. She was making funny little hunting noises that sounded like chirps. "Oh, give me a home, where the cockroaches roam,"

I hummed. The place was a dump, and I was scared to death of losing it.

The phone rang, probably a friend calling to tell me they'd seen me on TV and did I know the camera added ten pounds.

But it was a good telephone call, from Alice-Ann MacKinstrie, my best friend since our freshman year at college. We had a lot of catching up to do, since neither of us was very good about letter writing. It ended with my accepting an invitation to visit Alice-Ann and her husband, Richard, during the last week of July when Richard was to be honored at something called the town's annual Rose Rent Festival. I told her I'd let her know when I could get away. I hated to admit, even to my best friend, that there was nothing, absolutely nothing, keeping me in New York.

After I hung up, I wondered if I really should go. I thought about Richard. He probably didn't like me any better than I liked him. But, Alice-Ann did say he was out most of the time with his real-estate business. It would be wonderful to get out of the city. I could take my typewriter and get started on that second book. Maybe Alice-Ann would even insist I stay with her until it was finished. And my poor cats had never smelled fresh air, never chased butterflies in the sunlight, nor eaten grass until they threw up. I owed them a trip to the country. I called the bus company and learned a bus left for Lickin Creek, Pennsylvania, every morning, arriving there at four in the afternoon.

I fingered my father's letter for a few minutes and finally opened it. Predictably, he thanked me for sending the money to the warehouse where my mother existed (who could call it living?). "You know my salary can't keep up with the constant price increases at The Willows—but it's such an excellent facility that I don't want to move her unless it becomes an absolute necessity. I'm so lucky and proud to have such a loving daughter."

I crumpled up the letter and threw it in the grocery sack

with the rest of the junk mail. Every extra cent I'd ever made had gone to The Willows, including the advance I'd received for my novel. Although, at the time I sent it, I had no idea I was going to be jobless a few weeks later.

My little grimy apartment faded away, and I was once again thirteen years old, living in a small town in northern Thailand. I could smell the heavy perfume of the ginger blossoms in the garden and hear the singsong chatter of the servants inside the sprawling two-story house. It was the amah's day off, and I had begrudgingly agreed to keep an eye on my brother. Billy. Six years old.

I lay on a chaise lounge under a mango tree, indulging in my favorite pastime, reading, when I heard a high-pitched scream. Adults yelling. Confusion.

Billy had wandered down to the klong that ran below our house to watch the fishermen cast their nets. There, a black-and-white-banded krait had bitten him on the ankle. It took two days for him to die. After that, my father withdrew into his work and the arms of a young cultural attaché, and my mother disappeared into a martini-induced fog, from which she never returned. I was left to suffer my grief alone, and always there was the accusation, never stated, that it had been my fault.

I understood the great loss they had suffered, but damn it, they had another child, me, and they had turned against me when I needed them most. It was something I couldn't forgive either of them for. I sent money for mother's care out of guilt, not out of love.

Back in the present again, I dug around in my kitchen utensil drawer until I found a stamp and a battered Amtrak postcard. I addressed it to Alice-Ann telling her I'd be arriving next Tuesday afternoon.

Tuesday

C h a p t e r

2

On Tuesday morning, I emptied my meager bank account, left my key and Alice-Ann's address with Murray, and headed for the bus station with two cat-carriers, a grocery bag containing a litter box and Tasty Tabby Treats, my electric typewriter, and an almost new suitcase from the Goodwill store next door. Most of the clothes in the suitcase had come from the same "boutique." Thank goodness vintage clothing was in vogue. I was wearing comfortable jeans and one of my favorite Oz T-shirts—the one that said RUN, TOTO, RUN. Alice-Ann would get a kick out of it. In college, she'd liked to tease me about my "land of Oz" fixation.

The phone company had made good on its threat. I suspected the electricity would be off before I returned home. At least I didn't have to worry about the apartment for a while. My landlord had agreed to wait for the rent. He knew that I knew that evicting a tenant was an expensive procedure.

The bus was almost empty, and it only cost me ten dollars to bribe the driver into letting me bring the cats on. They amused themselves by waving at each other through their ventilation holes, while I stared out the window at the wastelands of New Jersey, not really seeing anything, and thought about my life.

I'd always wanted to be a writer. Journalism studies taught me my craft, and nine years of reporting sharpened my skills, but my real life began each evening when I sat down at my portable typewriter to produce my novel—my child—perhaps the only one I'd ever have. I really had thought it would be a best-seller; there would be paperback sales, foreign sales, books on tape, movie rights. What happened? My editor assured me it was good, and it wasn't unusual for first books to sell poorly. At least he had the faith in me to sign me to a two-book contract. But it would be a long time before I could support myself by my books, and having a job was essential. I'd worn out some shoe leather job-hunting, but hard times had come to a lot of other journalists, and there were few, if any, jobs available.

Here I was, just turned thirty, living in a dingy flat in New York—no money, no job, no future. I'd even managed to drive my fiancé, Steve, out of my life. I could replay our conversations in my head.

"*Why not get married now, Tori?*"

"*I need to finish my book first, Steve.*"

"*We'll get married, then you can finish it—quit your job if you want.*"

"*Can't you understand, Steve, you're a successful attorney, and I want to come to this marriage as an equal—to do that I have to reach my goal.*"

"*I don't like being alone six nights a week, Tori.*"

"*Last chance—pick a date, Tori.*"

"*Not much longer, Steve.*"

"*Tori, I've met someone else.*"

Well, I wished him and his twenty-two-year-old bride a happy future. No regrets. Except there was this damn ticktocking in my ears—my biological clock reminding me that it would soon be "now or never" time. Murray was right—I had to get my life under control.

I noticed that the bus was out of the urban sprawl that extended between New York and Philadelphia and was now rolling through the lovely, green Pennsylvania countryside. Small, neat farms lined the highway, and every now and then I would catch sight of an Amish farmer, using horses to pull his hay baler.

As we drew near the center of the state, traffic grew even lighter, and I was thrilled to see several black horse-drawn buggies on the road. The fluorescent orange triangles in back optimistically warned the twentieth century to slow down and approach them with caution.

We crossed several mountain ranges. Now we were getting close to the Borough of Lickin Creek where Alice-Ann lived. On my right was a small park, where Alice-Ann and Richard had taken me for a picnic when I had come for their wedding seven years before. That was the day I decided Richard was a one-dimensional, egotistical bore, not worthy of Alice-Ann's hand or any other part of her. There was just no accounting for some people's tastes. A little farther on, a large sign advertised the opening of a play at the Whispering Pines Summer Theatre—"See Stars Under the Stars." It featured Briana Evans, a beautiful young actress who was in a popular TV series. I couldn't help wondering what she was doing in summer stock, but I hoped I'd get a chance to see her.

The highway narrowed to three lanes, the center one for turns, and began its descent into the small valley where Lickin Creek was located. I remembered the approach into the little town as being quite pretty, and it was a terrible disappointment to find it had become junked up with used-car lots, gas stations, strip shopping malls, and a small housing development featuring split-level Taras on quarter-acre lots.

"Sorry, kids," I mumbled to the cats. "It was all country the last time I was here."

After passing a mile or so of fast-food restaurants, we turned off the three-lane highway onto a two-lane road, and suddenly everything seemed to revert in time to a pre–World War II America. Heck, call it pre–Civil War America. The bus slowed down and began to vibrate. The reason, I noticed, was that the street was paved with red bricks.

I enjoyed seeing once more the huge, gracious homes that lined the street and were surrounded by carefully tended gardens and ancient shade trees. Their large front porches all had well-worn outdoor furniture on them, and I could easily imagine residents sitting there on summer evenings enjoying lemonade and calling greetings to strolling friends and neighbors.

What I could see down the side streets indicated that Lickin Creek had more than its share of large Victorian homes. My reporter's instinct told me that there would be ghost stories ripe for the picking in this town.

Just ahead was the square, which was in the heart of the business district. Traffic was diverted here by a fountain in the middle of the street. A bronze mermaid in the center poured water into the large basin from a Grecian-style urn. Sparkling jets of water sprayed into the air and fell back to lightly mist the pots of red geraniums that circled the base. It was hokey, but sincere—Lickin Creek, Pennsylvania— where the last bit of excitement was the Civil War.

Nothing seemed to have changed since my last visit.

We circled the fountain to make a left turn and stopped at the light. The corner buildings were a courthouse, bank, drugstore, and the public library. The whole town always reminded me of the set for an old movie. The buildings were constructed of brick, two and three stories high, with false decorative fronts sometimes making them look taller than they actually were. Wooden window frames were decorated with the gingerbread carving of the Victorian era. Everything had been recently painted in different soft, pastel colors. It would make a great scene for a postcard.

In front of the courthouse was a small, grassy area with old-fashioned park benches set under large shade trees. A couple of lawyer types in seersucker suits, briefcases beside them, were engaged in an animated conversation on one of the benches. On the bench beside them sat a whiskey-befuddled bum, dressed in brown rags, his face turned to the sun like a flower. His eyes were closed and he had a contented smile on his face.

A young woman in a bright sundress walked by, said something with a smile to the bum, and turned into the old-fashioned drugstore. I thought nostalgically of Sarge, snoozing on my stoop. Bet he'd like it here.

The bus passed through the two blocks that made up the business and shopping district of the village, made another left turn and stopped before a small, red-brick building, which, although newly built, blended in perfectly with the eighteenth- and nineteenth- century town houses on the street. Directly across the street was an old-fashioned high school, complete with a row of Corinthian columns along the front and a Latin inscription over the massive front doors. I was beginning to feel as if I were in some strange sort of time warp.

Fred, Noel, and I barely had time to claim our luggage before the bus was gone in a puff of blue smoke. There was no sign of Alice-Ann, so I went inside the station to see about calling her.

A young woman with rosy cheeks, washed-out blond hair, and pink-rimmed, colorless eyes smiled cheerfully. "Hi. I'm Janet," she said. "You'uns must be that writer friend of Alice-Ann's. She called about twenty minutes ago. Starter trouble. If she's not here when I close, I'll give you'uns a ride out. I live near her on Tapeworm Ridge."

The picture that flashed through my mind of what Tapeworm Ridge might look like was too horrible to contemplate. I wanted to ask her how the name had originated, then decided I'd probably be better off not knowing. Poor cats. They might never get outside.

She laughed pleasantly when I suggested I might call a cab.

"Only got one taxi here, Uriah's Heap, and Uriah's usually booked up pretty solid taking old people to the doctor and stuff like that. Besides, here comes Alice-Ann now."

I recognized the clanking sound of her old VW immediately and was out the door before she had the engine turned off.

"Tori! I'm so excited. I can't believe you really came!" she gushed as she extracted herself from the little car. When we hugged, she had to bend down to cover the ten-inch difference in our heights. Some of our classmates who thought they were being funny used to call us Mutt and Jeff.

For a moment I was transported back across a decade to our days in college. We had been assigned to be roommates and had become best friends at our very first meeting, an instant bonding despite the extreme difference in our appearances. She was as tall and blond as I was short and dark. Her athletic body had come to her from Viking ancestors, who had been out discovering the world while my shorter, stockier Celtic forebears were building stone fairy circles in ancient Briton. But we had the same taste in books, movies, and cheap red wine, and in fact just about everything except men. Which was probably the major reason we stayed best friends and roommates until graduation.

She still had a sprinkling of freckles across her nose, and her yellowish brown eyes, which matched her hair exactly, were just as big and shiny as I remembered.

A little boy, about six years old, with streaked blond hair and huge yellow-brown eyes like Alice-Ann's had climbed out of the car and was shyly peering at me from behind her skirt.

"Hi, Aunt Tori," he said, shaking my hand politely.

"Hi, Mark. How are you, honey?"

But he wasn't paying any attention to me at all. "Neat," he exclaimed loudly. "You've got cats in those cages!"

Alice-Ann tilted her head and stared at me. In an exasperated tone of voice, she said, "You didn't bring your cats? What am I thinking of? Of course you brought your cats. I see them. Oh, dear. Richard doesn't believe in allowing animals in the house—he won't let Mark have a pet, not even a guinea pig. Well, nothing we can do about them now. We'll just have to keep them in the laundry room. He can't object too much. After all, it's only for a week."

"I'm sorry," I said contritely.

"It's okay. How could you have known?"

Actually, now I did remember Richard once saying he hated animals, but like most people owned by cats, I was sure he'd be charmed by mine as soon as he met them. I ignored the reference to my staying only for "a week." Figured I had plenty of time to bring up the subject of a longer stay.

Janet helped us load the Volkswagen and waved good-bye to us before we drove on the narrow, one-way street to the highway.

"What country is Janet from?" I asked. "I couldn't understand half of what she was saying."

"She's born and raised in Pennsylvania, Tori. Half the people around here speak with a Pennsylvania Dutch accent, which is really a German accent. But their native tongue is English. You'll get used to it."

I doubted it.

On the phone, Alice-Ann had raved about the beautiful stone home they'd inherited from Richard's father. I stared gloomily at the suburban nightmare on either side of the road, and I imagined "the ancestral home" to be a small stone hut, much like a woodcutter's cottage from Grimms' fairy tales, stuck between a supermarket and a gas station.

Alice-Ann pulled into the center lane of the three-lane highway, where we were in imminent danger of being flattened by a tractor-trailer headed directly at us. Miraculously, both vehicles turned left at exactly the same time and disaster was avoided.

She stopped the car and watched me for a few seconds while I took deep, measured breaths to stop my hyperventilation.

"You scared me when you screamed," she said accusingly.

"I did not scream. I simply swallowed the wrong way and choked a little." I tried to sound calm.

Probably my imagination, but I thought I saw her lips twitch into a tiny smile as she turned away.

After I recovered my dignity, I saw that we had turned onto a one-lane driveway, covered with gravel, not paved. Just ahead of us was a wrought-iron archway, which spanned the drive.

"This is it," Alice-Ann announced cheerfully as she started up the car. As we approached the arch, I could see that its iron scrollwork formed ornate letters. They spelled out SILVERTHORNE.

3

The narrow driveway was flanked on both sides by tall trees, their branches merging overhead to create an eerie, underwaterlike, dark green tunnel. Thick underbrush at the base of the trees hid whatever was behind. Even from the car, I could see the orange berries and dangerous two-inch thorns of pyracantha, the firethorn bush. This shrubbery would be as impenetrable a barrier as barbed wire.

After about a quarter of a mile, the driveway forked in two directions. We took the left branch, which curved up and around a small hill. The gravel crunching under our wheels sounded friendly. As we rounded the bend and approached the top of the hill, I saw a two-story, gray stone house, the kind you see on Pennsylvania postcards. Multi-colored flowers bloomed in abundance everywhere. My mental picture of the woodcutter's hovel was replaced by that of an English country cottage in the Cotswolds. All it lacked was a thatched roof.

The sunlight was almost blinding as we emerged from our leafy tunnel. Windows of old ripply glass sparkled in the light. I climbed out of the car and took a deep breath of the first fresh air I'd inhaled in years. It was even better than I'd hoped for.

Mark immediately scampered off to the side yard where there were a swing set and a sandbox.

"Come on," Alice-Ann said, pushing her streaked blond hair away from her face with a well-remembered gesture. "We've got a lot of catching up to do." She picked up the grocery bag, noticed the cat box protruding from the top, put it down, and picked up my suitcase and typewriter, which were much heavier. I followed behind her, carrying the cats and their belongings.

We entered a long, dim hallway, which extended all the way through the center of the house. A back door opened onto a tree-shaded, screened porch. Cool air moved gently through the house; it was natural air-conditioning at its best.

A chestnut wood staircase curved up to a second-floor landing and then curved again toward what must be the attic. Someone had painted a primitive-style mural on the walls. Here in the first-floor hall, the scene showed a two-story stone house on a hill, just like the one we were in, surrounded by farmland. A blue ribbon, representing a river, flowed through the cornfields, and over by the front door, a tiny covered wagon floated upside down in a small lake. The painted blue sky, dotted with soft white clouds, extended up the staircase as far as I could see.

Alice-Ann waited while I examined the painting. Although it had faded in some places, it was still lovely.

"There were itinerant artists around here in the eighteen hundreds who specialized in this kind of thing," she told me. "They would live with a family for several months while they did the painting, then move on to another house. It was cheaper than importing wallpaper in those days and provided the family with some amusing company. This one's particularly interesting because it not only shows our house, but also depicts the famous 'Scene of the Accident,' where

Richard's great-great-something-or-other fell in the river and decided it was easier to build a town than to replace a broken wagon wheel."

"Do I detect a little sarcasm?" I asked her.

"I do get a little bored with it," she admitted. "It all happened more than two hundred years ago, but the way the locals act, you'd think it was yesterday. I guess I've always felt it was more important to live for the future than the past."

As she spoke, she led me through an arch on the left into the living room. It was a large room, with a ceiling at least fourteen feet high. Tall, curtainless windows across the back let in soft, tree-filtered light.

The furnishings were of that style recently popularized as "country," which meant one or two comfortable, upholstered pieces were combined with awkward wooden benches and rickety chairs. Cracked pottery crocks full of dried weeds sat in every corner. Lamps were made of bean pots, canning jars, and even an old iron water pump. Duck decoys dangled above the windows, while blue and white enameled pots and pans with holes in them hung from the walls. The large stone fireplace, directly across from the entrance, was full of ashes from its last fire, and its front was darkened with soot. A gleaming copper bowl full of flowers sat on a carpenter's bench, which lacked one leg. Since the bench stood before an appallingly spindly wood-framed couch, I deduced that it served as a coffee table. The blue and white braided rugs scattered about on the polished plank floors looked treacherously slippery.

Incredibly, it worked. The room was friendly and cozy.

Alice-Ann got a bottle of wine out of an oak washstand, which had a small bar built inside where the chamber pot used to go. She filled two glasses, but wouldn't let me have mine until I put the cats away.

Actually, the laundry room wasn't bad. It was a converted sunroom, just off the kitchen. The windows had lovely, wide sills, and both cats quickly found sunbeams to sleep in. I put some Tasty Tabby Treats and water down for them and promised them we'd go for a walk later. That soothed my conscience enough so that I could enjoy my wine without guilt.

I sat on a blue-plaid wing chair, which turned out to be more comfortable than it looked, while Alice-Ann, a hand-quilted pillow behind her back, stretched her long legs out on the wooden bench, and we talked and laughed and drank most of the bottle of wine.

"Still into that Wizard of Oz stuff, I see." She smiled, looking at my T-shirt. "I used to think you wished a cyclone would carry you off to Oz."

"Maybe I still do," I said, and changed the subject back to our college days.

Alice-Ann wiped her eyes after we reminisced about the time her date drank too many "purple passions" and jumped off a bridge, yelling, "I'm Crusader Rabbit." We all thought it was hilarious at the time, but it hadn't been so funny later when he had his broken leg set at the hospital.

"You know when I first really decided you were the greatest?" Alice-Ann asked me.

I shook my head.

"When we decided our second semester to pledge a sorority. The first weekend we went over to the house, that obnoxious pledge master, Sally, told you to clean the bathroom."

"I remember that. I took a washcloth and wiped everything with it, and she came in and said it wasn't clean enough, and I asked, 'What should I do?' and she said, 'Use elbow grease.'"

"And you went all over the house asking where they kept the Elbow Grease."

"Because I thought there really was something called Elbow Grease, like Bonami or Pledge. How was I supposed to know? I'd never had to do anything like that before."

"And all the actives went along with the joke and had you chasing around looking for a can of Elbow Grease. Then when you found out, you said, 'Fuck you—who needs this!' and you left."

"And you came running out after me and said, 'Not me!' and that was the end of our careers as Greeks. But I had my first best friend."

"We were a couple of idiots—but nice idiots."

"Do you remember . . . ?"

"I wonder what happened to . . . ?"

Graduation had finally separated us—it had been rough on both of us. I'd left immediately for New York to seek my fortune as a journalist, and Alice-Ann had gone on to graduate school to earn a master's degree in library science. After that she had come to Lickin Creek as the town librarian, met one of the town's most eligible bachelors, and married him. Wryly she told me that some of the older valley residents still considered her an "outsider."

"Still?" I asked incredulously. "You've lived here for eight years. You've been a MacKinstrie for seven."

"That's part of the problem. Richard's family is sort of considered to be the local aristocracy, since it was a great-great-MacKinstrie who founded the town. In a small country town like this that kind of background is even more important than being rich. There were lots of young Pennsylvania girls who had hopes of becoming a MacKinstrie someday. Their families are not about to forgive a foreigner for coming in and marrying their little crown prince."

She glanced at her watch, and I got the impression that she wanted to change the subject. "Tori, I almost forgot. There's something I have to do this afternoon. I've got to deliver a picture frame I repaired to my neighbors, the Thorne sisters. They live in a fabulous mansion, just down the hill from here. I can't wait for you to see it. How about coming with me? They're a couple of real interesting local characters."

I nodded, and she said, "I'll call them and see if we can come over now."

She went into the kitchen to make her phone call. I wandered into the hallway to take another look at the mural and could just hear her saying, "Tonight? I didn't know anything about it. . . . No, no problem. Richard is so busy he probably just forgot to tell me. Do you mind if we bring our house-guest? She's a best-selling novelist. You'll just love her." Pause. "Thanks, Sylvia. We'll see you later."

I moved quietly back to my wing chair. Otherwise she might think I had been eavesdropping, something I would never do intentionally. And naturally, I couldn't tell her that I wasn't a "best-selling novelist," because then she'd know I'd overheard her conversation. Besides, it was great for the ego to be described that way even if it wasn't true.

Alice-Ann came back. "I'm almost sorry I called. It was really embarrassing. When I asked Sylvia Thorne if I could deliver the painting this afternoon, she said she was too busy getting ready for the meeting tonight. She said she expected me to be there, and I could bring the picture with me then. Evidently, Richard was supposed to tell me about it and forgot. Well, there's no harm done, I guess. It's not too late to call my baby-sitter. And Sylvia Thorne wants you to come, too. It's not very often we get a celebrity visiting here. You'll really liven up the meeting."

"What kind of meeting is it?" I asked.

"It's the steering committee for Lickin Creek's annual Rose Rent Festival."

"You mentioned the Rose Rent Festival on the phone. What is it?"

"It's a local celebration—"

"In honor of my late ancestor George MacKinstrie, founder of Lickin Creek," came a masculine voice from the front hall.

Alice-Ann's hand flew up to grab her throat. "Richard, you startled me! I didn't hear you come in."

Richard MacKinstrie, Alice-Ann's husband, appeared in the archway, wearing a black leather jacket over a navy-blue polyester suit. A motorcycle helmet was tucked under his left arm. He looked distinctly displeased at the sight of me. But he boomed heartily, "Victoria. Great to see you. Alice-Ann told me she'd invited you, but I thought you'd be too busy running with the rich and famous to visit a couple of boring old friends like us."

I decided that my initial dislike of him was well grounded and gritted my teeth when he gave me a big, welcoming hug. He didn't have to bend over nearly as far as Alice-Ann because he was no more than five foot six or seven.

Mark had followed his father into the living room. Sand dribbled from his clothes onto the polished wood floor. I smiled at the child over his father's shoulder as I suffered the unpleasant embrace.

Richard turned to see what I was looking at. "Mark," he roared. "You're getting sand everywhere. Go to your room at once."

Alice-Ann's face turned pink and her body stiffened. The Alice-Ann I used to know would have really torn into him. I had the feeling that she was holding back because I was there. Instead, her voice was carefully controlled as she spoke. "Richard. You don't have to be so hard on him all the time. He's a good boy."

Now it was Richard's turn to have a pink face. "Just look at that mess he's made. I'm going to get rid of that damn sandbox." He went over to the washstand bar and poured himself about three inches of Scotch, which he drank in one long swallow. He turned to me with a smile, as though nothing had happened. "Drink?"

"Just wine, thanks," I said, glad that he seemed to have forgotten his son.

Alice-Ann took the little boy by the hand and led him upstairs, telling him that he was going to have a baby-sitter tonight and could stay up until eight to watch TV.

Richard sat stiffly on the wooden bench, as if determined to be uncomfortable, and I settled back into my wing chair. "Put on a little weight, haven't you?" he said.

It was an intentional insult. Anyone who knows me is well aware I could be the poster child for the Yo-yo Dieters Association. I swallowed my angry retort, reminding myself I was, after all, a guest in his home. The stillness in the room was dreadful. Finally, to fill the void, I asked him to tell me about the Rose Rent Festival.

He lit up. I breathed a sigh of relief. I'd asked the right question.

As though he were delivering a lecture before a class of very slow college freshmen, he began, "My ancestor George MacKinstrie, having heard of the beauty of the western part of the country, struck out from Philadelphia into the wilderness in 1745. Luckily for us, his wagon lost a wheel and plunged into what is now known as the Lickin Creek. He immediately realized that the scene of the accident had everything he would need for farming—a mild climate, protected on all sides by mountains, water, and a stream with power enough to operate a gristmill. He made friends with the Indians, obtained permission to settle here, and built a large plantation.

"Within twenty years he had become a rich man, and he decided he would build a town along the banks of the Lickin Creek. He laid it out carefully and then advertised in the Philadelphia newspapers that he would hold a drawing for the lots. Hundreds of people poured into the valley, and in a few years there was a bustling community along the banks of the very creek where he'd had his fortuitous accident.

"My ancestor, according to the news of the times, was a modest and unassuming man who was embarrassed as well as pleased when the newcomers named the town MacKinstrieburg in his honor.

"Rather unfairly, it seems to me, people continued to call the town Lickin Creek, after the stream that runs through the center, and that name was perpetuated by a post office mapping error sometime early in this century."

He paused to sip from his glass.

I wondered if he'd ever get to the Rose Rent part.

"MacKinstrie, like many Scotch-Irish of his time, believed in a hell of fire and brimstone. As he grew older, he worried about what would become of his soul. He had never been a churchgoing man, but decided it was now time to begin.

"He had no way of knowing which church had a direct line to heaven, so he decided to cover all options. He provided three choice lots, downtown near the town square, to three different religious orders: the Presbyterians, which you would expect from a Scotch-Irish, the Catholics, and the Jews. They were to build their churches on these lots and in return pay a small annual rent.

"And for the rent, he specified that the congregations of the three churches would get together once a year and present one red rose each to him or to his oldest living descendant. Naturally my ancestor was the guest of honor at these festive occasions.

"It might have seemed an odd thing to ask, but it proved to be an absolutely brilliant move. The three churches worked together to organize Rose Rent Day, and within a few years it became quite a celebration with the whole town involved. Best of all, this spirit of cooperation extended to other projects as well. Old MacKinstrie died happy, assured of a place in heaven, and the community had the benefit of what could have been rival organizations working together for the benefit of all."

"That's fascinating," I said, half meaning it. "So these congregations have been paying rent in roses to MacKinstries for over two hundred years."

"Not exactly," he said. I groaned inwardly—no more, please!

"When George MacKinstrie died, his descendants received the Rose Rent until 1861. But so many men from MacKinstrieburg left to fight in the Civil War that payment of the Rose Rent was postponed indefinitely. After the war was over, it apparently was forgotten forever, or would have been, if it had not been for Sylvia Thorne."

I interrupted. "That's your neighbor who lives in the mansion?"

He looked surprised. "How did you know that? Well, anyway, she was digging about in the county archives about thirty years ago, looking for a subject to research that would earn her an invitation to join the Lickin Creek Historical Society. She found several references to Rose Rent Day and was intrigued enough to keep searching until she unearthed the whole story, which she then presented to the annual meeting of the Historical Society. Naturally, the Society immediately voted to offer her membership on the basis of her original research. It's considered a great honor to become a member of the Society. It's certainly the most prestigious organization in Lickin Creek, and belonging to it assures one of the highest social standing.

"The president of the Society at that time was my grandfather, David MacKinstrie. He suggested that she approach the present-day leaders of the three congregations to see if they would be interested in resurrecting the Rose Rent ceremony. They were all delighted by the idea and asked Sylvia Thorne to form the new Rose Rent committee.

"With her at the head of the committee, the community rallied round the flag, so to speak. Preparations went on for weeks, and on the last Saturday in July, my grandfather sat on a platform in the town square and was presented with three red roses. After that everyone in town lined up to receive their refreshments, while bands played, flags were waved, and balloons were released. From that first small celebration thirty years ago, the day has mushroomed into a major festival, with just about every civic group in Lickin Creek participating.

"My father succeeded my grandfather as guest of honor, and I, of course, have inherited the honor of receiving the Rose Rent this year." He folded his hands over his stomach (I was pleased to notice a bit of a paunch beginning there) and leaned back, looking as smug as a banker who'd just foreclosed on someone's family farm.

"I suppose you're a member of the hotshot Historical Society," I said.

He ignored the "hotshot" and smirked with unnatural modesty. "Not yet, but I have good reason to believe I will soon be asked to join it."

"I'm sure that will make you very happy."

"It would definitely ensure the success of my business. All the *best* people belong."

As Alice-Ann came back into the living room, Richard glanced at his watch. "I'm sure you two girls have a lot to talk about, and I've got a meeting of the Rose Rent Committee to go to, so if you'll just fix me a quick sandwich, I'll get out of your hair tonight."

Alice-Ann spoke softly, almost apologetically, not like the woman I thought I knew. "Richard, I've been invited to the meeting, too. I had to call Sylvia Thorne today about delivering the frame I fixed for her, and she said she'd told you to bring me. I told her that you've been so busy you probably forgot to tell me."

His nostrils pinched closed as if he smelled something unpleasant.

"Yes, of course I forgot. Sorry, my dear. I'll give her your apologies and tell her you have company."

"Richard, she invited Tori to come, too. Wasn't that nice?"

"You must have asked to bring her, Alice-Ann. What else could she do but invite her? That is what I consider very bad manners on your part, Alice-Ann."

Alice-Ann clenched her fists and sucked in her lips until they were invisible.

Richard seemed to remember I was there and told me,

"Sylvia Thorne is the social and cultural leader of this community. I'm sure you can understand that committing a faux pas with her could just about ruin someone socially. In the real-estate business, one must be very careful not to make any such gaffes."

Why is it, I wondered, the less education people have, the more they like to use French words? Too bad he pronounced it *fox pass*.

"Well, don't worry about me, Richard," I told him. "I promise not to commit a faux pas, and I took lessons in curtsying to royalty in London before I was presented to the queen." I stood up and demonstrated with a deep knee bend. I'd had all of him I could take for now. "Alice-Ann, I'd like to go to my room and unpack."

"Sorry, Tori. I should have shown you your room when you first got here. Come on, you can have a shower while I fix us some sandwiches." She grabbed my suitcase and practically ran up the stairs, while I followed more slowly with my typewriter case. Yes, the diet *must* start tomorrow!

In my room, she sat on the side of the bed.

I stood near the door, hands on my hips. "Well?" I prompted.

"I'm sorry, Tori. I invited you here under false pretenses. I'm going to ask him for a divorce this week, and I didn't want to be alone."

"Are you afraid of him?" I asked, concerned for her safety.

She shook her head. "It's more like I'm afraid of myself. I keep starting to bring it up, then I lose my nerve. You're my Dutch courage."

She hugged me and showed me where the towels and the bathroom were. "I'll tell you the sorry details later," she said before she went back downstairs.

My little bedroom was charming. I was beginning to find country decorating attractive. The walls were a soft, creamy yellow and the furniture was all white wicker, except for the ornate iron double bed, which had been painted white. Through the window, framed with fluffy white curtains, I could see past the end of the gardens and through the weeping willow trees to where a sparkling stream meandered toward an old-fashioned stone bridge. Bucolic. Pretty.

A small table with a lamp on it had been placed in the corner. I figured if I brought up one of those wobbly oak chairs from the living room, it would be a perfect place to work. Which reminded me that I had a book to write. That was something I'd have to get to work on without any more delay. Tomorrow. When I start my diet.

After my shower, I dressed in black slacks and a sleeveless red shell. I put on small gold hoop earrings and a gold chain and checked my image in the mirror. I was pleased with the ladylike gypsy I saw reflected there. Then I stuck my arms straight out to the sides and flapped my hands up and down to see if my upper arms looked flabby. They weren't. Sleeveless was still safe.

I went downstairs to find Richard, Mark, and Alice-Ann talking comfortably in the kitchen. The earlier tension had dissipated, thank God.

While Alice-Ann set the table, I went out to the yard where I had earlier seen the swing and sandbox. I filled two plastic buckets with sand and carried them through the kitchen into the laundry room where both cats were waiting with their legs crossed. I must say I was careful and hardly spilled a grain, but when I came back into the kitchen, Richard's face was bright red.

"Don't worry. I'll clean it up. Alice-Ann, do you have a broom?"

She fetched one out of a narrow closet, and I swept the sand into a little pile in the corner. Richard must have thought I was just going to leave it there because he opened his mouth to say something and the bite of sandwich he had just taken fell onto the table. Alice-Ann caught my eye, and we both started to laugh.

As Richard's face went from red to purple, he looked like a stroke waiting to happen. Wisely, Alice-Ann suggested that Mark take his plate to the living room and watch TV while he ate. The child was thrilled by this unexpected treat.

While Richard gnawed angrily at his tuna salad sandwich, I swept the sand into the dustpan and dumped it outside in a flower bed. When I returned, Richard put his sandwich on the plate, looked across the table at me as though he were going to say something nasty, then apparently changed his mind as he addressed Alice-Ann instead.

"My dear, I may soon have some very exciting news for you."

"That's nice, Richard. What kind of news?"

"There's a very good possibility that I may be invited to join the Lickin Creek Historical Society."

I had the impression that this was meant to impress me. If that was his intention, he sure was mistaken.

Alice-Ann didn't look too impressed either. "I thought you had to present some sort of scholarly research report to be eligible for membership. Digging up some minor historical point out of dusty old books just doesn't sound like you, Richard. Surely, you don't think I'm stupid enough to believe you've been at the library all those nights you've been gone?"

Yippee! The old Alice-Ann was back.

His face grew dark again. "There are people in this town who appreciate what I'm doing. You're in for a big surprise, Alice-Ann. Soon, too. And it's not a minor historical point. It's a major discovery that will bring me a lot more than mere local attention. I might even say it's a discovery of international importance."

"That's nice, dear," Alice-Ann said in the tone of voice one usually uses only with a small child.

Richard finished his meal in silence.

Chapter

After the sitter arrived, we went down the back stairs to the basement where Alice-Ann and I each picked up an end of a six-foot-long rectangular package wrapped in brown paper. "Get my hammer, will you please?" she said to Richard. "I prefer to take my own with me whenever I have a picture to hang," she explained to me. Richard pulled a heavy-duty claw hammer off the Peg-Board and led the way out the back door to a narrow footpath, actually no more than a trail through the trees, which meandered down the hillside. Alice-Ann explained that the MacKinstrie home and the Thorne mansion shared the gravel driveway, but this short-cut was quicker.

"All this land used to be part of the MacKinstrie estate," Richard boasted. "Part of it was sold to the Thorne family by my great-great-grandfather—no maybe it was my great-great-great—"

Alice-Ann had obviously had it. "Nobody really cares about your great-great-anythings, Richard. So, please, just shut up, will you?"

"It would behoove you to take a little more interest in the

history of Lickin Creek," Richard snapped. "You might discover it's not quite the hick town you think it is."

"I'm sorry, Richard. I really am. It's just you take all this local history stuff so seriously."

Richard stormed off ahead of us, while we struggled with the picture frame. The damn thing was heavy and slippery! We had to stop several times to get a better grip on it.

When we emerged from the trees at the bottom of the hill, we crossed the stone bridge I had seen from my window and came to the edge of a small pond. On our left, a sparkling waterfall bubbled out of the side of the hill and splashed into the shining water. In the center of the pond was a tiny island, just large enough to hold a charming Victorian gazebo filled with wicker furniture. A small rowboat was tied up under a weeping willow, and a family of ducks cruised gracefully near the bank where we stood.

Alice-Ann had told me the Thornes lived in a mansion, but that's like describing the Taj Mahal as a cemetery plot. Facing us across the water was a castle. A real one, built of stone, probably as high as my four-story tenement building, with crenellated towers on either side of the entrance. Rows of leaded-glass windows extended for at least a mile in each direction. Words like *majestic* and *romantic* would have described the castle perfectly if it had not been for the countrylike screened porches that had been attached without much thought to various parts of the building.

The white gingerbread trim on the porches lent a humorous, humanizing touch to what would otherwise have been coldly imposing. A light layer of mist hung over the pond, and in the softness of twilight it wasn't hard to imagine beautifully gowned women strolling with their elegant gentlemen friends out onto the porches to enjoy the cool summer breezes coming across the pond. Tall trees and heavy underbrush, including the dangerous firethorn bushes, grew around the castle, hiding it from the road and from the MacKinstries' house. "When old Michael Thorne built his castle, he made sure this place would be his own private kingdom," Alice-Ann said.

"Did I ever tell you I lived in a castle once?" I remarked, admiring the imposing structure. "In Yugoslavia. Castles are vastly overrated as places to live—cold and damp, and the bathroom facilities are invariably dreadful."

Richard turned his glare at me and said sarcastically, "Is there anything you haven't done? Any place you haven't lived, Tori?"

I smiled sweetly. "I was just trying to make conversation."

We walked past a parking area full of cars. Once the castle must have been the site of many grand parties, but the weeds pushing through the gravel attested that those times were long gone. We reached the steps that led up to the front door of the castle, although *front door* was an inadequate term for something this grand. The Gate or The Entry to the Keep or something equally dramatic would be more appropriate. I wanted to use the huge lion-headed door knocker to pound on the wood, but to my disappointment there was a very ordinary doorbell set in the doorframe. Alice-Ann pushed it.

As we stood there, wrapped in uncomfortable silence, I amused myself by imagining a black-cloaked Bela Lugosi answering our ring. Again, I was disappointed, as the woman who opened the door wasn't even Mrs. Danvers, but a rather ordinary-looking middle-aged woman wearing a white net nurse's cap. Her gray hair was pulled straight back in an unbecoming bun and tucked under the hat. She wore a pale green, flowered print dress with an attached, matching cape that came down in a point to cover her chest. Black stockings and Nike running shoes, trimmed in turquoise, completed the ensemble. She was quite pale and had the same kind of colorless eyes as Janet from the bus station.

She frowned when she saw Richard, but broke into a big grin of welcome for Alice-Ann.

"You'uns come on in. They're just gittin' ready ta start."
There was that accent again!

We walked into the great center hall, and she shut the
door behind us. I was stunned. Maybe she wasn't Mrs. Danvers, but I certainly felt like the second Mrs. de Winter stepping into the front hall of Manderley for the first time. The
ceiling must have been sixty feet above us and was decorated with gilded bas-relief angels, their glowing beauty
somewhat dimmed by the dirt of time. A massive stone
staircase rose from the center of the hall to a balcony, where
Gothic arches led to the upper halls of both wings. Centered
at the head of the staircase was an immense stained-glass
window. At first I thought it depicted a biblical scene, but as
my eyes adjusted, I saw that it featured a Michelangelo-type
God, reclining on a cloud that floated above a grape arbor,
beaming like a proud father over an old-fashioned railroad
locomotive. I started to laugh, but changed it to a choking
cough when Alice-Ann gave a small warning shake of her
head.

The nurse mistook my cough for a gasp of admiration.
"People's always surprised the first time they seen it," she
said proudly. "That's the first Mr. Michael Thorne and his
railroad he brought to Lickin Creek. His grandson had it
done by some folks in New York, Tiffenary, or something
like that."

"You mean that's supposed to be a railroad magnate and
not God?" I asked as I stared in disbelief at the Tiffany window. It had to be worth a fortune!

"Yep. Fine-looking man, wasn't he?—though I think he
should of had some clothes on. Made a fortune on the railroad. Then for his beautiful young wife, Sylvia, he built this
castle. Just before the Civil War. Copied it right out of a picture book about England, they say."

"Sylvia? Isn't that the name of the woman who owns this
place?" I asked.

"Named after her beautiful great-grandmother, she is.

Sylvia of the silver hair. You'uns'll see why soon enough. Better follow me."

For once, I couldn't think of anything to say. Alice-Ann and I—Richard would not deign to lift anything heavier than his little finger, it seemed—picked up the painting we were delivering and quietly followed the weirdly dressed nurse down a long, dark hallway toward the sound of muffled conversation.

She led us into an enormous drawing room where about fifty people were sitting on several rows of folding chairs facing a long Jacobean table, upon which sat a crystal vase containing three red rosebuds. A woman standing near the table spotted us and marched regally toward us. She appeared to be in her late sixties and had pure white hair that hung Alice-in-Wonderland style down to her waist. This was a woman who took that "crowning glory" business seriously.

Alice-Ann barely had time to put her end of the picture frame down before the woman swept her into an exuberant embrace. She was at least as tall as Alice-Ann and probably fifty pounds heavier. That was one big woman!

Alice-Ann detached herself and grabbed my arm. "Sylvia, let me introduce my good friend Victoria Miracle. Tori, this is Sylvia Thorne."

I propped my end of the package against my knees and shook her hand. "It's a great pleasure to meet you, Mrs. Thorne."

"It's nice to meet you, too, Miss Miracle, but it's not Mrs. Thorne. I was never fortunate enough to find a man who could put up with my idiosyncrasies long enough to marry me." (Tell me about it, I thought.) "Please call me Sylvia, and I will call you Victoria."

Before I had a chance to say "Tori," she had pulled me with her to the front of the room. When we reached the table, she picked up a gavel as big as a sledgehammer and pounded on the wood three times. The crowd grew still.

"Good evening, dear friends. I am pleased that so many

of you could be here tonight to finalize the plans for this year's Rose Rent Day. Before we start, though, I want to introduce to you our very special guest. Please welcome the famous, best-selling novelist Victoria Miracle." She led the applause.

I could see people whispering to each other as they clapped politely. Probably wondering who the hell Victoria Miracle was—with good reason.

"Victoria, my dear, I am sure our little group would like to hear a few words from you. Could you tell us something about your most recent novel?"

Feeling like a fraud, I tried to smile graciously, but my dry upper lip stuck to my teeth. I hoped it resembled Joan Fontaine's endearing half-smile in *Rebecca,* but I didn't believe it for a minute.

"The title of my book is *The Mark Twain Horror House.* It is a ghost story, based on some occurrences which were supposed to have actually happened in a town house in Greenwich Village. It's something like *The Amityville Horror,* except I don't claim that it's anything but fiction."

I knew I'd lost my audience the instant they heard the title, so I quickly murmured something about being very pleased to be here and looked for a hole to crawl into and die.

Sylvia pointed to a seat at the end of the front row next to an elderly gentleman. She didn't seem to be quite as thrilled to have me as a guest as she had a few minutes ago.

As I sat down, the elderly gentleman whispered, "I liked your book."

I stared at him in awe, not only because he was my one and only fan, but because he wasn't elderly at all. It was his thick white hair that gave that impression. Actually, he was quite gorgeous, around thirty I'd guess, with a dark tan that emphasized the bright blue of his Paul Newman–like eyes. I could actually see muscles rippling under his T-shirt. Things were definitely looking up in Lickin Creek!

Sylvia put another dent in the table with her gavel and glared at us. I pretended she had my total attention.

People began to give their progress reports. It was obvious most of the preparation for Rose Rent Day had already taken place. There would be a parade, of course. The high-school and junior-high-school bands would play in the square throughout the morning. The prize-winning Lickin Creek Cowgirl Drum, Glockenspiel, and Gymnastic Marching Team would perform at eleven, followed by the YMCA women's barbershop quartet. The Scene of the Accident Literary Society would present poetry readings on the front steps of the bank all day, and the Lickin Creek Community Theatre would re-create the fateful day of MacKinstrie's Accident on the exact spot where it had happened.

At noon, Sylvia Thorne would step onto the platform, which was even now being constructed in front of the fountain on the square, and officially start the ceremony. After her remarks, the combined choruses of the two elementary schools would sing the national anthem, and Cub Scout Den Three would raise the flags of the United States and Lickin Creek. That's when Richard MacKinstrie would take his rightful seat on the platform and accept his roses from representatives of the Presbyterian, Jewish, and Catholic religions. After that momentous event, the women's organizations of the three participating congregations would serve coffee and doughnuts to everyone.

And that only touched upon the highlights of the big day—I could hardly wait!

Sylvia, reading from a list, reminded the committee that the doughnuts were the responsibility of the synagogue, coffee would be provided by the Presbyterians, and the Catholics were to take care of the cream and sugar. This brought a protest from the priest in the back row. "That isn't fair, Sylvia. We did cream and sugar last year. It seems to me we should be back to coffee pouring by now."

Sylvia looked at him as if he were an ant at a picnic—not

particularly unpleasant, but a nuisance. "Father Burk-holder, it is too late to make any changes now. If you had thought it important to attend the meeting of the food committee, you could have spoken then."

She directed her next remark to the whole group. "I hope this impresses upon all of you the need to attend every meeting."

The priest sat down, looking embarrassed, and Sylvia went on with the meeting. "Do we have a report from the doughnut committee?"

A short, plump woman in the second row stood and reported that the doughnut mix had arrived and been divided among the two churches and the synagogue. Prisoners had already been released from the county jail to make the doughnuts; they would work right on through Friday night under the supervision of the doughnut committee and would even continue cooking all day Saturday if people wanted more doughnuts to take home.

"Thank you, Mrs. Seligman. I do hope someone is watching the prisoners more carefully this year. Didn't you lose two last year?"

Mrs. Seligman turned pink. "They will all be sleeping in the Community Room at the synagogue. The rabbi is personally taking responsibility for watching them, Miss Thorne." She sat down.

"Coffee committee?"

"All taken care of. We have decided to offer decaffeinated this year as well as our regular blend."

"Wonderful. The insomniacs of Lickin Creek will thank you for that, Mrs. Wright. You will also make sure we have enough paper cups this year, won't you? Remember our population has grown, and it's not unreasonable to expect some tourists to show up."

"We've got enough, but we think the napkins should be the responsibility of the cream and sugar committee since it doesn't have nearly as much to do."

Sylvia looked at Father Burkholder, who nodded.

A short, round man, wearing a wide-lapelled, blue pin-stripe suit of World War II vintage, stood up. He had little dandelion puffs of hair over his ears. Unlike the hunk next to me, this was a genuinely elderly gentleman. He cleared his throat and, when he was sure he had everyone's attention, pronounced, "I think it is time that this committee consider the poor unfortunates of our community—those who are overweight, have diabetes, or other serious health problems, which preclude the use of sugar in their coffee. It seems only fair and just that we provide an artificial sweetener for these people in the event that they should wish to partake of it. Therefore it is my desire to make a motion that—"

"Thank you, Judge Parker," Sylvia interrupted. "I think the matter can be handled by the cream and sugar committee without a formal motion. Right, Father Burkholder?"

The priest stared out the window, but indicated he would accept another duty by a semi-nod of his head.

Sylvia picked up the vase of rosebuds and held it above her head so everyone in the room had a good view of it. "As you can see, I already have the roses. American Beauty. By Saturday, they should be in full and glorious bloom. Many thanks to Fowler's Flowers for their generous donation. Well now, that takes care of the daytime festivities. As you know, this year we have added something new. The grand finale of the day will be a Champagne and Caviar Mystery Dinner right here at the castle. The Whispering Pines Summer Theatre has graciously provided its professional services for this gala evening, including the writing of an original mystery, which will have its premiere performance right here in Lickin Creek.

"I am indeed proud that the director of the Whispering Pines Summer Theatre is none other than the youngest member of my family, Michael Thorne." She paused and pointed dramatically at me. No, it wasn't me, but the dreamboat sitting next to me.

He got up and went over to hug and kiss Sylvia. His silver hair was exactly the same color as hers.

He didn't begin to speak until the polite applause subsided. A typical actor, I thought.

"I really don't want to tell you much about the exciting, wonderful Mystery Dinner we have planned for you. I'll only say that it will be a fun-filled evening of interaction— you, the members of the audience, will all be involved. You'll look for clues, interview suspects, and find the murderer. And I promise you that the dinner will be a true Lucullan banquet, catered by a famous New York restaurateur. The members of the winning team will all win season passes to the Whispering Pines Summer Theatre. I hope all of you here will purchase your tickets tonight, as we plan to limit attendance to one hundred people."

He sat down to more applause. "Tickets, as you know, are fifty dollars," Sylvia announced. "The profits will go to the Thorne Cultural Fund, which my sister, Rose, and I have established in order to bring a cultural event to the people of Lickin Creek every year. I expect each of you to support this worthwhile endeavor. The meeting is now adjourned. You may purchase your tickets at the table in the back of this room and then move into the dining room for refreshments." She whacked the poor table one last time with her gavel.

Michael Thorne turned to me. "I really did like your book," he said. "I went out and bought it after I saw you on 'Wake Up, New York.' That show was an absolute riot. I don't know who was funnier, the big-bosomed bimbo with the double-digit IQ, or you trying to correct all the asinine things she was saying."

"I'm glad to hear you say that. I thought the whole interview was such a disaster that no one would ever want to read the book."

"You sounded intelligent and interesting. And when you did get a chance to say something about the book, it

sounded a lot better than that ridiculous title would lead
one to believe."

"Picked by someone else. As a first-time author, I wasn't
in any position to argue."

He took my hand, and my heart did a little somersault.

"I'd like you to meet my mother," he said.

"I had that pleasure when I first came in," I told him, my
hand still in his.

"That was my aunt Sylvia," he said with a grin. "My
mother has been over there by the fireplace all evening."

He pointed to an old woman who sat on a Victorian love
seat, her knees covered with a pink crocheted lap rug. She
was wearing a long, pink silk dress, and despite the July
heat, she had a pink shawl draped over her shoulders. After
the Thornes I had already met, I expected another silver
head, but this Thorne had red hair that made Lucille Ball's
curls look drab.

Michael Thorne obviously enjoyed my surprise. "She used
to be a real redhead. That's why my grandfather named her
Rose. I'm sure everyone was relieved when her sister was
born with the family's famous white hair so they could use
the name Sylvia again." As he spoke, he led me through the
crowd until we were standing before the vision in pink.

"Mother, I'd like you to meet a new friend, Tori Miracle.
Tori, my mother, Rose Thorne."

I liked the fact that he remembered from the TV interview
to call me Tori.

I took her dried-up hand and used my best party voice to
say, "I'm pleased to meet you, Mrs. Thorne." Richard would
have been proud of me.

She squeezed my hand with surprising strength and
chuckled. Her voice was deep, and although she spoke
softly, it carried like an actor's to the far corners of the
room. "It's not Mrs. Thorne. It's Miss, or Ms., as you people say today. Like my sister, I never found a man who could
put up with me." She grinned at Michael. "It's just been me

and my little bastard, together against the world. Right, my dear?" She chuckled again.

"I really prefer not to be called a bastard, Mother," Michael replied curtly. This was obviously a subject that had been a point of contention for a long time.

"Nothing to be ashamed of. There's lots of people who have the bar sinister across their shields. Let's go get some goodies." Rose tossed aside her lap rug and stood up, and I found myself looking up—way up at her. She was as tall as her sister, although not quite as stocky. She led the way across the room, and we followed obediently, like two new recruits behind a Parris Island drill instructor.

Chapter

5

Sylvia was expertly herding her guests in different directions. Some, after having bought their Mystery Dinner tickets, were sent across the hall into the dining room where they received a paper cup full of punch before being ushered efficiently toward the front door. Others were discreetly directed to go into a small sitting room next to the drawing room. Nobody escaped without buying a ticket.

Michael and I followed his still-chuckling mother into that room. She must have thought she'd said something very funny. I told Michael that the joke escaped me.

"Just your typical small-town family scandal," he said in an offhand manner. "If you stick around longer than twenty-four hours, someone will be bound to tell you all about it." He smiled, but I could tell he wasn't pleased.

Richard was standing on a rickety wooden ladder in front of the fireplace, hammer in hand, attempting to hang the painting Alice-Ann and I had carried over. The nurse stood on a chair next to him, peering behind the picture at the hooks on the wall and giving him directions.

"A little higher—over to the left a little—no, no, too much—it needs straightening."

Sylvia stood in the doorway putting in her two cents. "It's too low—twist the wire a little—that will raise it. It's listing to the left. Don't drop it!" This last sentence was a shout as the ladder tilted dangerously and almost fell over backward.

Richard's upper lip was covered with beads of sweat, and his face was turning that ugly purple with which I was rapidly becoming familiar. Hypertension would kill him yet!

Others in the room stood around the ladder offering such advice as, "Don't you think it would look better over the couch?" "Move it over at least six inches to the right," "It should be lower, you have to lean way back to see her face."

At last it was hung to almost everyone's satisfaction, and we were all free to admire the portrait of a breathtakingly lovely young woman, and of course, the carved silver frame that Alice-Ann had recently repaired.

Sylvia gushed, "Ladies and gentlemen—my great-grandmother, the original Sylvia Thorne."

There was some scattered applause.

She had been a beautiful woman, if the painting was at all accurate. She appeared to be no older than twenty and stood in a garden, holding a pink rose in one hand and a large picture hat in the other. Her gown of white organdy, or some similar sheer material, flowed softly over her slender figure. She had eyes of brilliant blue and hair so startlingly white that I would have thought it a wig if I hadn't already met her descendants.

For me, though, the most interesting feature of the painting was the necklace she was wearing, because it was so ornate in contrast to the simplicity of her gown. It appeared to be a chain of flowers created from hundreds of diamonds. Hanging from the chain was a sapphire pendant as big as an egg, set in a circle of more diamonds.

"She's beautiful," I murmured to Michael. "And so is that diamond and sapphire necklace."

"When I was a kid, I used to daydream about her," he told

me. "I kept hoping that I'd meet someone that beautiful someday." He gave a wry little laugh. "I finally did—Elizabeth Taylor. I like to think they would have had a lot in common—both famous beauties and both the owners of some fabulous jewels. By the way, that isn't a sapphire in the necklace. It's a rare blue diamond, believed to be cut from the same Tavernier diamond as the famous Hope diamond that's in the Smithsonian museum. Family legend says that the original stone belonged to poor Marie Antoinette and was stolen during the French Revolution. The diamond was cut into two smaller stones, and both were found in London in the 1830s. This one was eventually named Sylvia's Star, in honor of its lovely owner."

"Is it in a museum now?" I asked.

"I wish. Unfortunately, it seems to have carried the same curse as its sister stone, the Hope diamond. During the Civil War, about a year after the Battle of Gettysburg, the Confederate army came through Lickin Creek and occupied it for a while. They threatened to burn the town down unless the local citizens turned over all their money and livestock.

"The townsfolk abandoned Lickin Creek to the rebs, and many of them sought shelter here at Silverthorne, which was far enough off the main roads to have escaped notice by the enemy. A few weeks later, the Army of the Potomac chased the rebs out of the area and the villagers were able to go home. The day they left, Sylvia was discovered dead in her bedroom. Her head had been crushed, and the necklace was gone. No one ever saw it again, or at least admitted to having seen it. It was assumed that Confederate soldiers broke in to steal the necklace and killed her when she surprised them in her bedroom."

"Wouldn't it be more logical to have suspected somebody from Lickin Creek? After all, the castle was full of them for weeks, and they probably all knew about the necklace."

"Bite your tongue, Ms. Miracle. Do you really think anyone would have pointed an accusing finger at one of their neighbors when there was a whole, wicked Confederate army out there to blame?" His eyes twinkled as he looked down at me. They were so blue I felt as though I could swim in them.

"Silly me! What could I have been thinking of?" What I *was* thinking was: married or gay?

"Is your wife here tonight?" I asked, trying to sound casual.

"No. Briana's appearing in *The Belle of Amherst* at the theatre this week. But you'll get to meet her this weekend."

That explained why the big TV star Briana Evans was doing summer stock in the mountains of Pennsylvania. It was definitely time to change the subject.

"You know, Michael, I keep thinking we've met somewhere before. Have we ever crossed paths in New York?"

"We couldn't have, because I know I'd remember you. But you might have seen me in some of my more memorable TV performances. Most recently I was the dancing tomato in a Burger King ad. Last year I wowed the critics with a brilliant toothbrushing sequence, and I have had a long run in a magazine commercial where I offer free telephones to each new subscriber. It still runs on late-night TV during the old-movie reruns; I think it has the potential to become a real cult classic, sort of *The Rocky Horror Picture Show* of commercials."

"That's it," I exclaimed. "I knew I'd seen you somewhere. I'm an old-movie fan—I stay up just about every night to watch the late-late shows. I've suffered through that magazine commercial many a time."

"At least you don't do what most people do and use the time to go to the bathroom or get a snack."

"Well, maybe sometimes . . ."

We laughed together. "I love the oldies, too," he said. "My very favorite of all time is *The Day the Earth Stood Still.*"

"That one was great. Do you remember what Patricia

Neal had to say to the robot to stop him from destroying the world?"

"Let's see . . . I think it was, 'Gort, Klaatu bara . . .' " He was interrupted by the nurse, who was clumping over to us in her Nikes, carrying drinks on a silver tray.

Michael kissed her on the cheek. "LaVonna," he said. "You look younger every time I come home."

She blushed with pleasure.

"Tori, this is LaVonna Hockenberry. She's been the housekeeper here at Silverthorne for over thirty years."

"Housekeeper? Aren't you a nurse?"

They both burst out laughing. "What did I say?" I asked.

"You'uns must of thought my prayer bonnet was a nurse's cap," LaVonna told me. "Lot of outsiders do. It's worn by all the adult women in my church to show our respect for God."

"I'm sorry," I began, but she stopped me with a warm smile.

"No need to feel bad. You'll see lots of us'ns around here—and Amish and Mennonites, too. This dress is special—made for my church. But the running shoes is my own idea. Lots of ground to cover in a place this big. Specially now I'm the only one left. Used ta be different—servants everywhere, and gardeners, lots of them."

She turned her attention to Michael. "I'm glad you'uns is home. There's things going on here that . . ." Her voice faded away as Sylvia Thorne approached us.

"LaVonna, I think the judge needs a drink." Thus was the hired hand dismissed.

"Victoria, my dear, I just learned from Alice-Ann that you are an expert on ghosts and haunted houses."

I cringed at the "Victoria, my dear" and started to protest, but I was silenced by an imperious wave of her hand.

"You must come back tomorrow evening, my dear. We are going to hold a small séance—just a few people, including, of course, your friends the MacKinstries. It should be interesting, and I would love to have a real ghost expert here. Perhaps you would share some of your experiences with us. Make it about seven."

She sailed regally into the crowd, leaving me with my mouth open.

Michael frowned. "I'll bet that damn Praxythea is back in town," he muttered angrily.

"Who's Praxythea? What a tongue twister of a name!"

"Praxythea Evangelista, if you really want to twist your tongue. Can you believe that name? She claims to be a medium or a psychic, or something. I'm not sure what the hell she calls herself, but I think a good, old-fashioned word for her would be charlatan. She's shown up in town a couple of times offering to help the police solve crimes. I think she actually did luck out a few years ago and tell them where to find the body of a missing girl; then she spent months appearing on TV talk shows bragging about it. I wouldn't give her the time of day, but my aunt thinks she's fabulous and is always begging her to come and visit. I wonder what she's up to this time?"

"Should I come to the séance?" I asked him.

"I wish you would. I'm sure she'll expect me to attend, so it would be nice to have an ally here."

A bear in a plaid macho-man shirt, his face hidden behind a bushlike red beard, threw his arms around Michael. They pounded each other on the back for a couple of minutes, then began to reminisce about their shared childhood experiences, mostly having to do with fish, so I excused myself and moved away, pretending to have an interest in antique furniture.

There actually was a piece that interested me, an old-fashioned record player in an oak cabinet. I was leaning over it to examine it more closely when I felt a hand on my shoulder. I stared up at Sylvia Thorne.

"I hope I'm not disturbing anything. I'm fascinated by

your Victrola. It must be one of the very earliest ones."

She smiled smugly. "It's not a Victrola, my dear. It's an Edison. Much rarer and more valuable. Here, I'll wind it up so you can hear it."

She cranked it up, and some tinny music came through the horn. She adjusted a knob and it played a little louder but sounded just as tinny.

"Isn't that wonderful? It's absolutely remarkable that Edison had the brilliance to create a machine which could record sounds and reproduce them. Did you know he never had any formal schooling?"

"No, I'm afraid I don't know much about him at all, other than that he was a great inventor."

"A fabulous inventor—the greatest genius our country has ever produced."

The music scratched to an end, and she flipped the machine off. Richard appeared at her side and casually draped an arm around her shoulders. It tickled me to see that he practically had to stand on his toes to do it. He had a drink in one hand—obviously not his first.

"What are you two girls up to?" he asked with a smirk.

Girls! I thought I'd retch, but Sylvia giggled like one.

"I was just telling Victoria something about Thomas Edison. It always amazes me how little young people know about our country's greatest figures."

"Damn shame," he said, directing a wink to me. He changed the subject abruptly. "Are you girls game for another motorcycle riding lesson this Sunday?"

Sylvia shuddered. "The last time, Rose and I both fell off twice, and LaVonna's left leg is still bruised from when she ran into the apple tree. At our age, it's a wonder we don't all have broken bones."

"Now, now, young lady, you're only as old as you feel. We'll concentrate on stopping lessons next time." He gave her broad shoulders another squeeze and turned his attention to me.

"Victoria. I'm being a terrible host. Let me introduce you to some of our friends."

With a domineering hand in the middle of my back, he steered me across the room, laughing as we walked. "Can you imagine that bunch of old bats trying to learn how to ride cycles? I just suggested it as a joke—never thought they'd take me up on it. I can just picture them in a few months—black leather jackets, helmets, 'Born to Be Wild' tattoos. God, what a riot!"

"It's not very nice of you to make fun of them like that, when it was your idea in the first place."

"The old babes needed some excitement; I gave it to them. Look, there's the judge. He's president of the Lickin Creek Historical Society. Judge Parker—Judge Parker, I'd like you to meet my houseguest."

I shook hands with the long-winded gentleman who had requested the artificial sweetener and just had time to mutter something polite before Richard steered me away.

"Hey! I was behaving," I complained.

"Just making sure you don't accidentally embarrass me in front of my friends with a fox pass," he said.

I checked to make sure nobody was listening to me, then said ever so softly, "Listen, Richard. Let's get something straight. I grew up in a world so formally polite that people still use calling cards—and know what it means when the corners are turned down." I could tell from the blank look on Richard's face that he didn't. "A world that's a hell of a lot bigger than your precious Lickin Creek—where courtesy is routine, and people know how to pronounce *faux pas*. Let me assure you that if I ever do something to embarrass you, it won't be an accident; it will be intentionally done. Which is something you don't need to worry about because my ingrained good manners wouldn't allow me to do that to you as long as I am your houseguest."

His response to my scathing remarks was to completely

ignore them. "Hey, Doc, Doc Jones. I want you to meet someone."

The object of his attention flashed a cold, hard look at Richard. "Sorry. Busy." And pointedly turned his back on us.

It was the first time I'd ever seen Richard look disconcerted. He seemed much relieved when we were approached by Rose Thorne.

"Stop monopolizing your guest, Richard. I want to hear about her book."

"She's all yours, Rose. But be careful, she bites." He laughed a little to show it was a joke. What an asshole!

I began to tell her about the terrible history of the haunted town house in Greenwich Village, but soon found out what she really wanted was to talk to me about *her* house.

"It has always figured prominently in the history of our town," she told me. "Did you know it was a stop on the Underground Railroad before the Civil War?"

"Fascinating," I said, wondering if there was a book plot there. "I'd like to know more about it."

She brightened. "I have an old book about the history of Lickin Creek I can lend you. Unfortunately, it was written before the Civil War, but there's still a lot in it about the castle. Let's go get it."

She led me out of the sitting room, down the hall, and into a musty, paneled library. Ashes from a long-dead fire lay stinking in the massive stone fireplace. The tarnished brass fireplace tools had stood unused so long that cobwebs stretched between them.

While she searched the shelves, I glanced about. Some of the furniture, though covered with dust, was beautiful and obviously antique. The one piece that was not dusty was a burled walnut desk in the Louis XIV style. Arranged on the top were an old-fashioned crystal pen and ink set, a red leather appointment book, and a matching leather-bound blotter.

"You like my desk?" Rose asked, noticing where I was standing. "It was a gift from my father on my sixteenth birthday. It came all the way from France."

"It's exquisite," I said enthusiastically.

"I found the book, but you'll have to climb the ladder to get it down from the top shelf."

I looked up at the top shelf, which had to be at least fifteen feet from the floor. I hate ladders, having just a touch of acrophobia, but I managed to get up and down without incident.

She grabbed the small book from my hand and blew off some of the dust. "Good," she said as she flipped through the yellowed pages. The smell of mildew was overpowering. "Here's a drawing of Silverthorne Castle. Wasn't it beautiful?"

The detailed pen and ink drawing showed the castle before the porches were added. The gardens around it were elaborate and formal, and several small rowboats were floating on the pond.

"You read it this week," she ordered. "Especially the parts about the castle. It has a very interesting history. Maybe you'll want to write about it someday."

I promised her I would read the book right away and tucked it into my handbag, which was big enough to hold a dozen books of that size.

By nine-thirty, only a few of us were left in the sitting room drinking coffee. I recognized some of the people, including Judge Parker, who sat slouched in a leather wing chair by the fireplace, hands folded across his belly. He seemed to doze off every few minutes, then would wake up with a loud hiccup and rejoin the conversation without missing a beat.

Dr. Jones sat in a corner talking quietly with an Asian man I hadn't met. Mrs. Seligman, of the doughnut committee, was still there with her husband, who had been introduced to me as a building contractor and developer. The priest had also stayed, probably to make sure nobody volunteered him to do anything else.

Michael made room for me next to him on a green velvet Empire-style sofa that desperately needed new springs. Alice-Ann joined us and sat on my left. In front of us was a coffee table about the size of a king-size bed, and on the other side of it, sitting unnecessarily close together on another green sofa, were Richard and a stunning blonde, who couldn't have been a day over twenty. Alice-Ann's face was flushed, and she fidgeted a lot with her cup as she tried not to look at them. It was trouble, not coffee, I smelled brewing in small-town paradise.

The conversation moved from Rose Rent to the high cost of real estate, a subject that seemed to be of as much interest here as it was in New York. Mr. Seligman was proudly describing his latest project, a strip shopping mall, which contained a pharmacy, a state liquor store, and a hardware store. "It cost plenty," he bragged.

"I think it's a disgrace, Hy," Rose chided. "That was perfectly good farmland you went and covered with concrete. And it's still half-empty."

"It takes time to attract tenants, Rose. That's why I built the subdivision outside town. As it attracts buyers, we'll need more businesses."

"So you can build more tacky houses, I suppose," Rose countered. "Why did you have to make them all look alike?"

"They don't. I used three different colors for the shutters. When are you people going to understand that there just aren't enough cutesy Victorian houses to go around for an exploding population?"

"Exploding population! Who? Where are they coming from, Hy? What are they going to do when they get here?"

"They're coming, Rose. From the cities. They want to bring their children up in safe, clean towns like Lickin Creek. Some of them are already here—they commute to work in places like Harrisburg and towns in Maryland.

Someday we'll have rapid transit, and you'll have them living here and working in Washington. You have to face the fact that we're almost in the twenty-first century."

"And we won't have anything to eat in that century if people like you keep using up the farmland."

Mr. Seligman didn't seem to mind her comments. "Lots of people would call it progress, Rose. Your sister for one. She doesn't mind talking about what your property would be worth if it were subdivided and sold. Right, Sylvia?"

Rose covered her mouth with her hands in shock. "How could you even think of such a thing?" she stammered at her sister.

The silver-haired woman looked annoyed. "It is hardly relevant what I think anymore, is it?" she snapped, glaring at Rose.

To everyone's astonishment, the redheaded woman burst into tears and ran from the room. Sylvia acted as though nothing out of the ordinary had happened. "Let's change the subject. Talking about money bores me."

"You could have fooled me," Richard said rudely. "I thought it was one of your favorite subjects." His words were slurred by drink.

"You're a damned fool, Richard," Sylvia said indignantly, then clamped her mouth tightly shut.

The blonde piped in: "Richard is not a fool, Mrs. Thorne. He's a darn good Realtor, you know. Like, just ask anybody." She placed her well-manicured hand possessively on Richard's arm.

"Who is *she?*" I whispered to Alice-Ann.

"Twanya Tweedy," she answered disdainfully.

"Twanya? Did I hear right?"

"You heard right. I think it was supposed to be Tanya, but her parents couldn't spell any better than she can. She's Richard's secretary."

Mr. Seligman snorted derisively. "Is the word *ethical* in your limited vocabulary, Miss Tweedy? If it were, I doubt very much that you would refer to your boss as a 'darn good Realtor.' "

Richard sat straight up. "Just what the hell is that supposed to mean, Seligman?"

"I'm talking about the screwing you gave Farmer Fenstermacher, when he came to you to list his property for sale. You convinced him it would be hard to sell, but you'd buy it from him as a 'special' favor. You knew damn well it was worth four times what you paid him."

"Come off it, Hy," Richard said. "Everyone here knows you wanted to buy that land from Fenstermacher yourself. You're still angry because I beat you to it."

"I was willing to pay him a fair price and you knew it, but you never took my offer to him."

"Listen here, Seligman—" Richard started, but was interrupted by Sylvia.

"I'm tired of all this arguing. Doesn't anyone want to talk about something interesting?"

Evidently not. Even the priest joined in. "Along those same lines, Richard. How about that vacant property next to the church school that I wanted for a parking lot? I was negotiating with the owner privately, until you stepped in and convinced him to ask twice as much for it as I could pay. Now there's a convenience store there, where my kids hang out after school. I've even heard stories about drugs being sold there. I hope you enjoyed spending that commission, Richard."

Judge Parker harrumphed and, seeing he had everyone's attention, gave Richard the kind of look that had probably struck terror in the heart of many a criminal. "Mexican oil," was all he said.

I was astounded by Richard's violent reaction to those two words. He leaped to his feet, his face contorted with rage. If Twanya hadn't caught him by the back of his shirt, I think he would have struck the old judge.

I sat cross-legged on the grass, under moon-dappled trees, and watched Fred and Noel hunt some invisible prey through the marigolds. The night sky was dotted with flashes of icy green fire from thousands of fireflies; a scene from my childhood's dream of fairyland.

But behind me the dream had become a nightmare. Through the door that opened from the porch to the kitchen, I could hear Richard and Alice-Ann continuing the argument that had started as soon as we left the castle.

Sylvia had put an end to the evening by announcing bluntly that it was time for everyone to go home. She pried Richard away from Twanya and walked with him to the front door. Alice-Ann and I trailed a little behind as we said our good-nights to the others.

I reached the door just in time to see Sylvia bend down to whisper something privately in Richard's ear. It was obvious she had a hearing problem because her whisper was so loud I could clearly hear every word. "Be sure you get it here early. I want it set up before the others see it."

"I don't like the idea of the séance, Sylvia," Richard said. "It's too soon."

"Just do what I say," she commanded. "You're in no position to argue with me." With her final word, she shoved him out the door.

She saw me and realized I had overheard her. "We're going to record the séance tomorrow," she explained. "I understand it's the scientific thing to do."

"Of course. And thank you for having me over."

"My pleasure, Victoria," she said with a tight smile that belied her words.

During the walk back to the cottage, the angry words began. Once inside, Richard went directly to the bar setup in the living room, where he poured a tumbler full of Scotch and downed it in several gulps.

"You've had too much already," Alice-Ann said, slamming her purse down on the hall stand.

"You ought to try drinking more, Alice-Ann. Maybe it would loosen you up. Make you fun for a change."

"Then you wouldn't have an excuse to find your 'fun' in Twanya's bed, you bastard!"

"Leave her out of this!"

"I most certainly will not. How could you have asked her to come to Silverthorne tonight? How could you have humiliated me like that in front of all our friends?"

He shrugged infuriatingly. "If you hadn't invited yourself and your pesty friend to the meeting, you wouldn't have been there to be humiliated."

Alice-Ann picked up a canning jar full of dried beans that served as a lamp base and heaved it at him. It was pure dumb, drunken luck that saved him from having his skull smashed. He staggered and almost fell just as the jar flew past him. Beans exploded into every corner of the room when the jar hit the stone fireplace.

I backed tactfully out of the room, leaving them to fight in privacy. The baby-sitter passed me in the hall, smiled, and put her finger to her lips. Apparently she was no stranger to these scenes. By the time I reached the kitchen I heard her car kicking up gravel as it headed down the driveway.

I tucked a cat under each arm and carried them outside. I left the door between the kitchen and porch open on purpose, so I could hear what was going on, just in case the fight got too violent and Alice-Ann needed my help in subduing the beast. It wasn't hard to hear them, since both participants had moved into the kitchen and were screaming at each other at top volume. Something crashed against the wall; it sounded like a dish breaking. Then another and another. Alice-Ann would have to shop for a new set tomorrow if this kept up. Finally, the front door slammed, and there was a blessed silence in the house.

I moved quickly around to the side of the house to see who had come out. It was Richard, furiously lashing a black suitcase onto the back of his motorcycle. When it seemed secure enough to suit him, he jammed his helmet on his head, climbed on the monster-machine, stomped down on the pedal, and took off with a roar down the hill. I wondered . . . did this happen so often he kept a prepacked suitcase ready for a quick departure?

When I saw a light come on upstairs, I picked up the cats and climbed the back steps into the house. The kitchen was a mess—a real shambles. Jagged shards of Blue Willow china littered the floor, and all the chairs were overturned. The round oak pedestal table had been shoved against the china cupboard, and both had fresh battle scars to serve as permanent reminders of the evening.

Since Richard was gone, I figured it was safe to bring the cats up to my room. I turned off the downstairs lights and climbed up through the painted clouds to the second floor.

Loud sobbing came from the master bedroom. At least I knew she was alive. I tapped on the door. After a few seconds, I heard her blow her nose. I opened the door and stuck my head in. "You all right?"

A nod. Her eyes were red and puffy, and her nose looked

like one of those pale, misshapen strawberries you see in the supermarket in the early spring.

Fred immediately saw he was needed and jumped out of my arms onto her lap, where he curled up and allowed her to pat him. I could see her beginning to calm down as she stroked his soft orange and white fur. I've read that they use cats in nursing homes and mental institutions to reduce stress and lower blood pressure (wonder if my mother ever had a cat to pet?). Noel, more reserved, jumped up on the dresser and began to wash her face.

"I'm all right. Guess you can probably tell this wasn't the first fight."

She rubbed Fred's chin. He closed his eyes and smiled. "But, I've got things worked out in my head now. Remember what we used to say in school when we were dumped on by somebody? Don't get mad . . . Go on to bed, Tori. Everything's okay." She sensed my reluctance to leave. "Really, it is. You'll see. And take this silly beast out of here." Fred was now on his back, with his front paws curled up under his chin, while Alice-Ann rubbed his belly. He looked as if he'd fallen in love.

"You'll call if you need anything?" I scooped up Fred and draped Noel over one shoulder. She nodded, so I left, closing the door behind me.

The cats were delighted with the new bedroom. Noel selected a perch on the window ledge while Fred claimed his favorite spot at the foot of the bed. Later, I knew, he would stretch his full fifteen pounds over my legs causing me to wake up with a cramp.

I slipped into my favorite nightwear, a very old, very soft Wizard of Oz T-shirt, and got into bed. It didn't take long to realize that sleep wasn't going to come easily that night.

I turned on the lamp and looked around for something to read, but there wasn't anything in the room. I made a mental note that if I was ever flush enough to afford a guest room, it would be kept well stocked with reading material. Even better would be a TV, VCR, and several classic movies. And a thermos of hot cocoa! That was such a good idea I decided I'd suggest it to Alice-Ann in the morning.

Then I remembered the book that Rose Thorne had insisted I borrow. I got it out of my purse, which would probably reek of mildew forever. I flipped through the pages of *The Illustrated History of Lickin Creek* until I came to the drawing of Silverthorne Castle. It must have been something when the owners had been able to afford the many servants and gardeners this kind of place required.

Leafing through the first chapter, I found basically the same story Richard had told me about how his ancestor had accidentally founded the village of Lickin Creek. I skimmed several more chapters and found the background history of Rose Rent Day. This, too, was exactly as told to me by Richard. Almost word for word, as if he had read and memorized the description.

At last, I began to feel drowsy. I flipped through some more pages and found an appendix titled "Lickin Creek Caves." Caves fascinate me. They always seem to be the setting for fabulous adventures, such as *Journey to the Center of the Earth,* which had also been a great movie, and *Tom Sawyer,* and a book I loved when I was a kid, *Five Boys in a Cave.* However, all my involvement with caves had been in books and movies. From what I knew, cave exploring usually involved climbing up and down some pretty spectacular heights, which was something I didn't ever want to do.

I read the appendix. *About two miles east of Lickin Creek is a very considerable cave, among the many which abound in this portion of the county. One entrance, at the base of a high ridge, which runs north and south, is only large enough for one person to walk in at once, by stooping a little. After passing through the entrance, one reaches an apparent vestibule, about thirty feet in diameter and twenty feet high. A tunnel, opposite the entrance, extends downward about one hundred yards, to*

*a huge underground lake of clear, calm water, the cavern roof
overhead being ornamented with innumerable crystal formations—stalactites—which sparkle profusely when illuminated
by torchlight. A number of passageways open from this cavern
and connect to other caves in the area. Several entrances to this
cave are found on the estate known as Silverthorne.*

*There is also a very remarkable series of underground pas-
sages under certain areas of the town of Lickin Creek. The entrances are through arches in the foundation walls of many
houses. These arched entrances are used in summer as refrigerators, being made very cool by a constant current of air coming up from the caves. Oddly enough, these passages represent
the streets of the town, leading in numerous directions, and often crossing each other at right angles, thus enabling visitors to
start, at a given point, and proceed around to return to the
place of starting.*

My eyes were burning by the time I finished reading. Already in the back of my mind was the idea that I might hunt
for one of the entrances that were supposed to exist here at
Silverthorne. From the description, it didn't sound as if
much climbing would be required to explore it. Perhaps this
would be the inspiration I needed for my new novel.

I fell asleep with the light on and dreamed of crystal stalactites sparkling in torchlight and a dark, mysterious underground lake.

Probably because I was in a strange bed, I slept fitfully,
and that's why the sound of the front door opening woke me
up. I turned off my light and went to the window. Alice-
Ann, in her nightgown and bathrobe, climbed into the same
ancient Volkswagen she had driven in college. The engine
coughed a couple of times before starting up, just as it always had. I watched the car until it disappeared around the
bend.

Automatically, I glanced at my right wrist to see what
time it was. Of course there was no watch there; I'd been
meaning to get my Timex repaired for months.

Later, I woke up again, thinking I heard a motorcycle in the distance. And once more, when I heard a car drive up, followed by the dull thud of the front door shutting.

Finally, all was quiet, and just before I fell asleep for the last time, I remembered what it was Alice-Ann had been referring to: our slogan in college, "Don't get mad—get even!"

Wednesday

Chapter

7

The sun was high in the sky when I woke up. I cautioned the cats to be quiet and tiptoed down the stairs with them. Good. No sign of Richard. I hurriedly put them in the laundry room and refilled their bowls with fresh Tasty Tabby Treats and water.

The kitchen had been cleaned up and most of the evidence of last night's battle was gone. Only someone who'd seen the room last night would notice that the china cabinet was almost empty, and that one oak chair had a cracked leg.

There was a fresh pot of coffee on the stove, so I got down one of the few remaining cups and poured myself some. Since there were no bowls left intact, I ate Sugar-frosted flakes dry from the box. On the table, weighted down by a set of car keys, was a note:

"Tori: My friends, the McFerrens, have taken Mark to spend the day and night at their house. Didn't want him to be home when I have it out with Richard tonight. Got a lot of work to do downstairs, so please take my car and have fun exploring the town. Love, AA."

It was pretty easy to read between the lines. I knew she wanted to be alone for a while. Since it appeared I had a free day ahead of me, I thought perhaps I'd visit the public library and see if I could find additional information about the Lickin Creek caves. The more I thought about them, the more eager I was to learn more about them, maybe even do some exploring. After all, if Jules Verne and Mark Twain could write about caves, why not Tori Miracle?

I dressed in my favorite yellow slacks and matching silk blouse and decided even if the outfit didn't make me look thin, it did complement my dark hair and eyes. I told the cats where I was going, and after a few minutes of trying to master the complexities of the VW's gearshift, I was heading down the shady drive toward the highway.

What a contrast the highway was to the peaceful seclusion of the old estate. Behind me were a forest, stream, stone bridge, and historical homes. Before me, a kaleidoscope of eighteen-wheeled trucks, cars from every state, motorcycles, bicycles, and even a few pedestrians who were crazy enough to risk their lives by walking on this road.

It took me almost thirty minutes to drive the mile and a half through that traffic. In town, I reached a confusing maze of one-way streets that didn't take me anywhere near the library. A series of left turns got me past the same appliance store—twice. I had just begun to feel I had been doomed to travel forever in one of Dante's circles of hell when I spotted the dome of the courthouse. I pulled into the municipal parking lot behind it and was pleasantly surprised to find an hour of metered parking cost only a nickel. I cut through a brick-paved alley to the front of the courthouse and found myself in the square. The library was across the street, just as I remembered.

There is something reassuring about a public library, like seeing a familiar face in a strange town. This one was no exception. Carved into the marble above the large double doors were the words POST OFFICE. A hand-lettered sign taped onto the door said LIBRARY OPEN. The exterior facade was grand, garnished by a row of Ionic columns. The interior was jammed with too many bookshelves, chairs, tables, and card catalogs. I loved it immediately.

A smiling gray-haired woman stepped out from behind the circulation desk. She knew I wasn't a regular patron and was determined to show me every square inch of the library.

"It's no trouble at all," she assured me when I tried to stop her. "I really enjoy showing people around."

On top of the card catalog was a display of novels about the supernatural by women authors: Shirley Jackson's wonderful *Haunting of Hill House*, Ann Rice's *Interview with the Vampire, The Mirror* by Marlys Millhiser, and to my great delight, my very own book. I managed to interrupt the librarian's explanation of a subject card long enough to tell her I was the author of that book, and the next thing I knew I was sitting in the small back room having a cup of bitter black coffee with the head librarian and several of the staff.

The head librarian, Maggie Roy, was a bubbly young woman, probably in her late twenties, who was well on her way to having a serious weight problem (I decided I was definitely going to start my diet tomorrow), but she was such a pleasant person that her looks were not a handicap. She wore a large diamond on her left hand, so obviously some man agreed with me.

The others finished their coffee and drifted back out front, but Maggie put a hand on my arm to detain me. "How is Alice-Ann doing? Is she working things out with her husband?"

I was surprised. "How did you know I was staying with Alice-Ann? And what makes you think she has marital problems?"

"Praxythea Evangelista isn't the only psychic in town," she said. Then laughed. "Honey, this is a small town and everybody knows everything that's going on. That was my second cousin, Janet, who works at the bus station. Naturally, she was on the phone the minute she got home."

"Naturally." I grinned.

"I was the assistant librarian here when Alice-Ann was head librarian. We became good friends. It really used to hurt me to see her come in with her eyes red and swollen from crying all night. Couple of times I suspect he even hit her, but she always had an excuse about having tripped in the garage or bumped her head on an open kitchen cabinet.

"I'd hoped when she had Mark, things would settle down, but Richard got worse than ever. Now he's absolutely blatant about running around with that so-called secretary of his. I'd be surprised if she can even type."

"There's one thing I don't understand, Maggie. Richard seems very ambitious, almost ruthlessly so, and social status is important to him. Wouldn't having an affair like this be a detriment, socially?"

Maggie hooted. "Richard MacKinstrie is so wrapped up in himself and his self-glorified position as a member of the 'first family' that he thinks he's above reproach. He actually believes he's an aristocrat because some idiot ancestor, who couldn't even fix a wagon wheel, got here before anyone else. He has one of those super-egos that says, 'If I want it, it must be right.'

"Enough about him. Was there anything particular you were looking for in the library?"

I told her of my interest in the Lickin Creek caves.

"I've heard about them. Before and during the Civil War they were used as part of the Underground Railroad. I'll dig around in the historical section and see if I can find something for you."

"Please don't go to any trouble."

"No trouble at all. I like doing research work. Makes me feel like a 'real' librarian. Just had a call this morning from Silverthorne asking me if I had any biographies about Thomas Alva Edison."

I groaned. "I'll bet that's for my benefit."

"What do you mean?"

"I was over there last night and admired Sylvia Thorne's

antique Edison phonograph. I was soundly berated for not knowing anything about the inventor. She's probably going to sit me down tonight and teach me what she thinks is lacking in my education."

"And you'll listen, I'm sure. She does have a way of getting one's attention." She looked at her watch and grinned. "Hey, this is great! I've successfully managed to stretch my morning coffee break right into my lunch hour. This is the kind of workday I dearly love. How about joining me at the drugstore? It's the local equivalent of the 'smoke-filled back room.' One of the regulars there is our chief of police, who's sort of a local-history buff. Been a hobby with him ever since he was a kid. If there's anybody who can tell you about those caves, he's the one. And the food's not too bad, either."

"Sounds great," I said with enthusiasm.

The drugstore probably hadn't changed at all since it was built. The wood-plank floors looked as if they hadn't been washed since then either. High overhead, squares of tin pressed into a star design covered the ceiling. Greasy black cobwebs filled in the corners, and a ceiling fan slowly stirred the soupy air. The place reeked of cigarette smoke.

The restaurant was in the rear. A long counter curved around a central area where one sweaty waitress was trying to serve at least ten men, all wearing plaid shirts. Last night, I'd noticed half the men at the castle wore plaid shirts, almost like an unofficial male uniform.

Through the blue smoke-haze, I saw four small booths on our right; the seats were covered with a vile yellow plastic and had black, hairy stuffing protruding from several large holes.

It was to the first of these booths that Maggie led me. The man sitting there, wearing the standard police uniform of light blue, short-sleeved shirt and navy trousers, jumped up and gave her a friendly kiss on the cheek. He wasn't too tall, about five ten maybe, with a well-muscled body that the form-fitting uniform covered but didn't hide. He had straight, sandy-brown hair, a little too long, that kept falling in his eyes. I liked what I saw.

"Maggie, love. You're looking wonderful, as usual. Is Bill meeting you here?"

"Not today. I really came to see you. I want you to meet a new friend of mine, Tori Miracle. Tori, this is Garnet Gochenauer, our local police chief."

"Garnet Go—Gok—?" I felt as if I were going to strangle over his name. Whoever heard of a man named Garnet?

"Go-ken-our," he pronounced slowly, as if talking to a very dull child. "I hear you're visiting the MacKinstries."

"Amazing grapevine system you've got here."

"Very useful when you're the chief of police," he said with a crooked grin. "Have a seat, please." He stepped aside to let me into the booth.

I ignored his gesture and squeezed in the opposite side. Maggie sat down across from me, and he slid in next to her. That crooked grin was damned attractive! The two front teeth on top that overlapped a bit didn't detract from his looks at all. I couldn't help but notice he had beautiful blue eyes.

"Maggie's been trying to find a girl for me ever since I came back to town. You are a definite improvement over the last dozen she introduced me to."

It was an egotistical, chauvinistic thing to say, and I despised myself for grinning like a ninny at him. Only one day out of New York, and I'd discovered my hard-earned layer of sophistication could be shattered as easily as an eggshell. I let the subject drop by asking Maggie what she recommended for lunch.

"Either the tuna-salad plate or the chicken. They both taste the same."

I thought that over for a moment and decided on the tuna. When the waitress came over, Garnet ordered for all of us, three tuna salads and cherry colas. "The real thing," he warned her. "Not that canned crap. Better make those diet colas."

After our order arrived, Maggie told Garnet that I was interested in learning about the Lickin Creek caves.

"Odd interest for a woman, isn't it?" he asked me.

"I don't see what being a woman has to do with it," I retorted. The feminist side of my personality was sending up furious warning signals: MCP alert! Male chauvinist pig! MCP alert! The other side of me, the less controllable female side, was admiring those bulging biceps.

"Hey, don't get so huffy. I didn't mean anything. Some of my best friends are women." He chuckled, then saw by the look on my face that he'd better shut up. He concentrated on his tuna salad, but I could see by the twitching dimples in his tanned cheeks that he was still amused by his cleverness.

"Stop teasing her, Garnet," Maggie reprimanded him. To me, she said, "Tori, he's really a very nice person. Just don't pay any attention to half of what he says. He likes to playact the role of a country-bumpkin policeman for strangers. Garnet has a law degree and is chairman of the county's Equal Opportunity Board."

"I'm surprised you're not in practice," I said. "Seems to me it would be a lot more profitable than being a police chief in a small town."

His blue eyes turned to ice cubes. "Maybe I was just a little kid who always wanted to be a policeman and never outgrew it."

"Truce time," Maggie broke in. "Garnet, Tori's a novelist. I've got her new book about a haunted house in the library right now, and it's good. She thinks our caves might make an interesting subject for a book. I told her you were our local history expert, so why don't you show her I was right."

"Sure, Maggie. Sorry, Tori." He smiled. "It would be my pleasure."

I accepted his apology, but couldn't help wondering why my remarks had upset him so.

"When I was a kid, one rainy day I was poking around in our basement trying to find something to do and noticed a place where some rotten wood had fallen away from the back wall. I pulled some more of it away and found it concealed an archway. Just beyond the archway was a small room with a trapdoor in the floor. The trap covered a hole about three feet wide, with a wooden ladder going down into it, so I grabbed a flashlight and climbed down. At the bottom I came upon a narrow, descending, limestone tunnel, which I followed for a while until I came to a large cave.

"I decided not to do any more exploring that day because there were at least four openings leading out of the cave, and I was afraid of getting lost.

"I asked my dad if he knew anything about the cave and the tunnels. He told me that the town was crisscrossed by tunnels. When the earliest houses were built, the owners intentionally left openings into the tunnels so they could use them as natural refrigerators. Dad said when he was a boy, he and his friends used to play down there, but after one of them drowned in an underground lake, most of the townspeople boarded up their entrances and gradually forgot about them. By then they had electricity anyway and didn't need to use the tunnels for food storage. I'll bet most of the new owners of the houses don't even know they're there. I used to go exploring with a friend, Michael."

"Michael Thorne?" I asked.

"Yeah, we were best friends back then. We took our duties as explorers very seriously. We started with some of the natural tunnels and caves that run under the town and made maps as we went along. I think we both felt a little like Columbus discovering a new world. Anyway, we eventually found a tunnel that would take us from the town straight out to Silverthorne Castle. To get there, you had to pass a beautiful underground lake, probably the one where the kid drowned years ago. You can read a description of it in a book called *The Illustrated History of Lickin Creek.*"

"I already have," I told him. "That's what got me interested in the caves in the first place."

"We found all kinds of stuff down there, things that told us what had happened in the past. There was clothing, remains of old fires, old tin cooking utensils, and once we found a diary that belonged to an escaped slave. He and others hid down there waiting for a chance to escape further north by the Underground Railroad. Worst of all, although we thought it was real exciting at the time, we found a skeleton in a Union Army uniform. We thought he must have been a deserter who hid down there and got lost."

"What did you do with him?" I asked.

"Left him. He'd already been there a hundred years. What would be the point of disturbing him?"

"Well, to give him a proper burial, I suppose."

"He wouldn't be any deader in a grave than he already was. Somehow he seemed to belong there. To be perfectly honest, neither of us wanted to touch him."

"You could have told someone."

"Then they wouldn't have been *our* caves anymore."

I could understand that. "Did you keep the maps you made?"

"Sure did. For a long time I had the idea that someday I might write a book about the tunnels, with the maps in it, but then I started thinking that might not be a good idea. People would start exploring on their own and make a mess down there, or get lost and need to be rescued, or go down there to do drugs, or . . . Oh, hell, there's lots of reasons not to."

Besides, I thought, then they wouldn't be *your* caves anymore.

He finished the last of his tuna salad, put down his fork, and said to me, "I just had an idea. There's a tunnel entrance under the building that the Historical Society uses as its headquarters. I had to go into their basement a few months ago when Miss Effie thought she heard a prowler down there. Turned out to be a rabid raccoon, but I saw that the archway was still open. There's a small room that used to be open to the public, but the steps down to the basement began to rot, so the Society closed that part of the house some years ago. If you'd like, I could show it to you."

I jumped up. "I'm ready to go."

He looked critically at my yellow outfit.

"You look awfully nice. It's kinda dirty down there."

"A little dirt never hurt anything," I said gamely. "Maggie, thanks for everything."

"My pleasure," she said with a smile that showed she really meant it. "Say, if you wouldn't mind, could you do me a little favor?"

"Sure, anything."

"Stop by the library when you're through and pick up the Edison biography that Miss Thorne wanted. Maybe you could drop it off at Silverthorne Castle on your way home, if it isn't too much trouble."

"No trouble at all. I've been invited over there tonight, so I'll just take it to her then."

We each paid for our lunch and said good-bye on the street. Garnet and I walked down the pleasant, tree-shaded sidewalk. He moved with the grace of a wild animal, his eyes constantly sweeping the area, searching for signs that things weren't quite right.

"It's hard to believe you and Michael Thorne were best friends. You seem so different," I commented. "I met him at the Thornes last night."

"People change as they get older. We went off to different colleges, and by the time we graduated we just didn't seem to have much in common anymore. After I became police chief, I moved into the little house I'd lived in as a kid, and I've been very happy with my rural lifestyle. Michael chose a much more exciting life—always on the move—New

York, Los Angeles, even toured Europe in a play. Married a TV star. Looking back, it wasn't unexpected . . . he was always the creative one . . . lead in class plays . . . editor of the yearbook . . . all that artsy stuff, while I was just your typical small-town jock.

"But don't get me wrong. We're still friends. I was real happy for him when he bought the Whispering Pines Summer Theatre. It brings him back to town every summer, so we've had a chance to get to know each other again. Old friendships seem to become of more importance as you grow older."

I thought of Alice-Ann and agreed.

We stopped in front of a white frame town house, with forest green shutters. I noticed the ground-floor shutters were solid wood, while the upstairs ones were louvered.

Garnet looked down at me with a small frown.

"Speaking of old friendships, you've known Alice-Ann for a long time, haven't you?"

"Yes, we met in college and were roommates for four years."

"Then you know about her and Richard?"

"I've just learned they're having problems." I didn't want to discuss Alice-Ann with a stranger.

"I thought you might know why he didn't come home last night."

I was astounded. My jaw probably dropped six inches. "How did you know that?"

"His secretary called my office just before lunch. He didn't show up at the office this morning, and when she called his house, Alice-Ann hung up on her. Rather natural, under the circumstances, I'd say.

"Anyway, I called Alice-Ann, and she told me that Richard had gone out last night, and she'd gone straight to bed and didn't realize until this morning that he hadn't come home."

I thought about Alice-Ann driving off after him in the VW.

"Did you hear anything unusual last night?" he asked me.

"I saw him go off on his bike. I thought I heard it again, later, but I don't remember hearing him come home."

"Did he and Alice-Ann have a fight last night?"

"You'd better ask Alice-Ann," I told him stiffly, beginning to resent his questions. "What do you think you're doing—interrogating a murder suspect?"

"Sorry, Tori. Just trying to keep on top of things. He probably just decided to take a break from both of them."

"What do you mean . . . both of them?"

"Alice-Ann *and* his typing tootsie, Twanya Tweedy. I'm not telling you anything that isn't common knowledge all over town. I can't understand why Alice-Ann doesn't boot his ass out the door."

"If you were married and had a son, you might understand why she doesn't want to give up on the marriage. You're not married, are you?" I asked innocently.

"No. Are you?"

I shook my head. "Not even engaged." Now, why did I think I had to say that? Guess I was just overwhelmed by meeting two good-looking, blue-eyed men in less than twenty-four hours! And one of them available!

He gestured at the green-shuttered building. "This is the Historical Society headquarters. Let's go in."

We entered the building through a small foyer. To our right, a cantilevered staircase curved gracefully up to the second floor. On the left, in what must originally have been the parlor, was the office-library-storage room of the Lickin Creek Historical Society. Gray file cabinets lined two of the walls, even stood in front of the windows and on both sides of the lovely Adams-style fireplace. Floor-to-ceiling bookshelves covered the other two walls, filled with leatherbound volumes of some antiquity. Oak library tables, in the center of the room, were littered with bundles of old newspapers and stacks of books. It looked a little like my apartment. On the floor lay a gorgeous Persian rug, glowing like a jewel.

A wisp of a woman sat at a desk in the far corner, almost hidden behind the pile of books in front of her. At first glance it appeared she had daisies sprouting from her head, but then I realized she was wearing a hat that must have been in her family since World War II. I'd seen pictures of my grandmother in something just like it. Little tufts of yellowish white hair stuck out from under the hat like dried straw.

She peered up at us through the top of her trifocals. "Why, it's the chief. What a lovely surprise." The daisies nodded their approval.

Garnet stepped across the room in three long strides, leaned over the desk, and kissed her cheek. "How's my favorite girl?"

They spent a couple of minutes asking each other about the health of various relatives before Garnet introduced me and told her the reason for our visit.

She looked worried. "Oh, please do be careful on those steps. I'm so afraid they're going to collapse someday and someone will get hurt."

"Don't worry about us, Miss Effie. We'll be very careful, I promise," Garnet told her.

She led the way through the old dining room and kitchen and opened the basement door. "Don't let the ghosts get you," she said with a pixielike smile.

I perked up. "Ghosts? Is this building haunted?"

"I was saving that for a surprise, but now the cat's out of the bag," Garnet said, directing a smile toward Miss Effie that said he really didn't care. He picked up the flashlight from a shelf next to the door and aimed its beam down the stairs. "Follow me and be sure you only step where I've stepped."

The stairs creaked alarmingly but held together under our

combined weight. At the foot of the stairs was another door. Garnet swung it open and we entered the basement. It would be more appropriate to call it a cellar than a basement. The walls were of thick, rough gray stone, and the floor was simply packed earth. The whole place had a damp, moldy odor that surprisingly wasn't unpleasant. Stacks and stacks of old newspapers were piled up against the walls; a real fire hazard, I thought.

Garnet moved the flashlight slowly, giving me time to see every part of the large room. Above us, ancient wooden beams supported the floors of the house. Several had split and were propped up by huge wooden pillars. Would the house collapse if one were knocked over? An enormous coal furnace stood in the center, its pipes stretching in every direction like the arms of a giant octopus. Built into one wall was a deep fireplace, big enough for Garnet to stand in.

"The fireplace was for cooking. This would have been the summer kitchen," Garnet told me.

"You mean women were actually expected to come down here to cook? That's horrible."

"In the days before air-conditioning, it was most likely a lot more comfortable down here than it was upstairs. And while you're feeling sorry for the poor housewife, don't forget her husband was outside in the heat, working the fields. Life wasn't easy for anyone a hundred years ago."

He moved the beam of light to the back of the room, and I saw a dark opening, framed by a brick archway.

"That's it," he said. "Follow me and be careful where you put your feet."

"Don't worry about me," I told him. So of course, the very next thing I did was stub my toe on a piece of rock sticking out of the dirt floor. I bent over to grab my toe and fell down.

"Shit," I muttered.

Garnet knelt down beside me. "What happened?"

"Stubbed my damn toe," I said between clenched teeth.

"Shouldn't have worn sandals," he said unsympathetically.

"I didn't exactly know I was going to be tramping around in a cellar when I got dressed this morning."

He took my foot in his big hands and examined it gently. "Looks okay. You'll have a bruise, but nothing's broken."

He stood, grabbed me under the armpits, and hoisted me to a standing position. "You'd better take my arm. I promised Miss Effie you wouldn't get hurt."

He made an elaborate production out of escorting me across the cellar. Each time we came to an overhead pipe or a low beam, he would hold his hand over my head and make sure I bent over low enough to avoid getting clobbered. Then, before we took another step, he would shine the light directly in front of me so I could see if there were any obstacles in my way. I went along with the game, clinging like a Victorian heroine to his muscular biceps, and enjoying the cinnamony smell of his aftershave. It suited his country-style masculinity.

We finally reached the archway, and he shone the light inside. I saw a small room, carved out of solid rock.

"See any ghosts?" he asked.

"Should I?"

"If there really are such things as ghosts, this is where they'd be. During the Civil War, this place was a stop on the Underground Railroad. Escaped slaves were hidden in this room until it was safe to move them. In the meantime, the entrance to the room would be boarded up and hidden by putting heavy shelves full of canned goods in front of it. To a casual observer, there was no sign of a room at all."

"Where do the ghosts come in?"

"In the summer of 1864, fifteen people were hiding in there, mostly women and children. As usual, they had been given food and water for a few days, and the entrance was sealed from the outside. Unfortunately, General Early's Confederate cavalry chose that day to appear. They surrounded the town and demanded five hundred thousand dollars in greenbacks or one hundred thousand dollars in gold, or they would burn the town down. The poor people of Lickin Creek did what they could to scrape up the ransom. They knew that the town of Chambersburg, across the mountains to the east, had been burned to the ground just a few weeks earlier when the residents refused to pay up.

"The rebs took what money the people had, then began to break into the homes looking for anything of value to steal. Frightened for their lives, most of the villagers fled to the country. Some hid in the hills, while others barricaded themselves in Silverthorne Castle.

"Sadly, for the unfortunates in this basement, the owner of this home was one of those who left town. It was several weeks before the occupying army left and the villagers returned home. All fifteen of the escaped slaves were found dead, starved to death in this little room."

I felt a cold whisper of air on my neck and shuddered. "What a horrible story!"

"It always seems to be the innocent who suffer the most during war. The real tragedy was that they could have escaped easily, if they'd known about the tunnels."

He stepped into the room and knelt on the floor. "Hidden a couple of inches under the dirt on the floor was the trapdoor that leads down into the caves. Those poor people died just inches away from freedom."

He brushed away some dirt and exposed the wood planks of the trapdoor. He lifted it and laid it to one side. "Ready to explore?" he asked with that endearing, crooked grin on his face.

I leaned forward and peered down into the black hole. All I could see was the top of a wooden ladder, which disappeared into the darkness below. There seemed to be no bottom.

"Is that ladder safe?" I asked.

"It was the last time I used it—about fifteen years ago.

Probably been chewed on a bit by termites since then."

I wasn't about to let him scare me. "I'm ready," I told him.

He handed me the flashlight, then started down, tentatively testing each rung with a foot before putting his whole weight on one. I pointed the flashlight at him, but he finally descended so far that I couldn't see him anymore.

"Come on," he yelled. "It's safe."

I stuck the flashlight in the waistband of my pants, which left me in total blackness. I was completely disoriented, but I managed to climb down, one rung at a time.

It was unbearably still. I felt alone, terribly alone. I didn't even know if I was anywhere near the bottom.

"Garnet?" I called out.

No answer.

"Garnet! Where the hell are you?"

Silence.

"Garnet. Please answer me," I begged, almost in tears.

His voice, almost in my ear, said cheerfully, "Okay, you've made it," and his strong arms lifted me off the ladder and set me down on the blessed firmness of the cave floor.

"Why didn't you say something?" I demanded angrily.

"Wouldn't have dreamed of it. You seem to like your independence so," he teased.

"There's a time and a place for—"

"Give me the flashlight," he cut me off, grinning!

I thrust it at him, and he immediately headed down the tunnel. I followed close behind, looking around at what I could see in the dim glow of the flashlight. Near the foot of the ladder were some wooden shelves—someone's old foodstorage area. The tunnel was so narrow that two people couldn't walk side by side, and so low that Garnet had to bend over to keep from bumping his head. Water trickled over the rough stone walls to land in puddles beneath our feet. As we walked, we were continually moving downward into the earth.

"I love it down here," Garnet said. "Always reminds me of one of my favorite books when I was a kid, *Five Boys in a Cave.*"

"Why, that was one of my favorites, too. I've never even met anyone else who's heard of it."

"Town librarian recommended it to me, right after I read *Tom Sawyer.*"

"The same thing happened to me. Those two books are one reason why I'm so fascinated by caves. I read everything I can find—" I was so busy talking that I didn't realize Garnet had stopped walking, and I bumped smack into his broad back.

"Watch it, kid," he said, not unpleasantly. "Remember the fat kid in *Five Boys in a Cave?*"

"The one who got killed. I always wished that hadn't happened."

"It happens a lot to inexperienced spelunkers. Look here. There's been a cave-in." He took a step to one side and held my arm to keep me from moving forward. Just ahead of us was a gaping hole in the ground.

He pitched a pebble, and after a dozen or more seconds we heard it hit bottom. If he hadn't been proceeding cautiously, we could both have plunged to our deaths.

There was just enough room to skirt the hole if we pressed our backs up tight against the tunnel wall. I felt a wave of vertigo as I looked into the pit and would have lost my balance if Garnet hadn't held my hand tightly, giving me the support I needed to move safely.

We proceeded without further adventure until we reached a sort of intersection, where tunnels branched off to our left and right as well as continuing straight ahead. Garnet pointed with the light to the right.

"That tunnel leads to Silverthorne. There's the secret mark Michael and I made to help us find our way."

The mark was an arrow scratched on the rock with an *S* under it. A grayish green mold had grown in the crevices, and I would never have noticed it if Garnet hadn't pointed it out.

"How long does it take to walk from here to Silverthorne?" I asked as I tried to see into the dark passageway.

"About ten minutes, if you know where you're going. Faster than you can drive through that damn traffic mess above us."

"Amazing," I said. "Where's the body you told me about?"

"It's in a large cave near the castle. I'm not sure I could find it anymore. At least, not without my maps."

The flashlight flickered; batteries were getting low.

"We'd better get back while we can," he told me.

I didn't need convincing.

The way back was tedious, in part because it was all uphill, and because it was over familiar ground. Thankfully, transversing the pit wasn't as frightening as it had been the first time, and we made it safely back to that tragic basement room before the flashlight died.

Outside, in the sunlight, it was hard to believe that less than an hour had passed since we went into the building. The narrow town house looked cheerfully normal in the light of day, but I knew I would never be able to look at it without thinking of those poor people starving to death in the darkness below. Garnet was right. This house met all the prerequisites for being haunted.

"Can I walk you back to your car?" he asked pleasantly as he glanced at his watch.

"No thanks. I'm going to stop in at the library and pick up a book for Miss Thorne. Thanks for the tour. I really appreciate it."

I reached out to shake his hand, but after he took my hand in his, he wouldn't let go.

"I'd like to show you my maps, sometime," he said.

At least it wasn't etchings. "I'd like to see them."

"How about over dinner, tomorrow?"

"Fine."

"I'll pick you up around six. Dinner's served early around here."

He let go of my hand, reluctantly I thought, grinned crookedly, and left.

I watched him until he turned down a side street. Tomorrow's dinner date just might be interesting!

Back at the library, Maggie was bursting with curiosity. Had we gone into the caves? Did I think the house was haunted? Would I write a book about it? Could she have an autographed copy? Didn't I think the police chief was sexy?

"Yes," I answered to all her many questions.

I took the book for Miss Thorne and was just getting ready to leave when Maggie stopped me.

"Tori, remember when you asked Garnet why he chose to be a policeman, instead of making more money in private law practice?"

"Yes. What about it?"

"His father was the police chief here for more than thirty years. He was shot by a kid on drugs, during a 7-Eleven holdup. Garnet had finished law school and was working for a big Philadelphia firm. When his father was killed, he quit his job and came back home. He was appointed to replace his father and has done a damn good job ever since. Just thought you ought to know, before you go asking him any more embarrassing questions."

Chapter

8

Alice-Ann was bent over a picture frame with a gold crayon in her hand when I entered her basement workshop. When she saw me, she laughed at my filthy hair and clothes.

"Good grief, Tori. You look like something that just crawled out from under a rock."

"That's pretty close to what did happen," I said, and proceeded to tell her of my underground adventures with the handsome policeman.

"You are absolutely amazing," she said admiringly. "One day in town and you've already hooked up with our town's most eligible bachelor."

"It wasn't a big deal, Alice-Ann. He just showed me a section of the caves."

"When are you going to see him again?"

"Tomorrow. We're having dinner."

Her lips twitched into a mischievous grin. I adroitly changed the subject. "Whatever made you switch from library work to repairing picture frames?"

"Okay, Tori. No more questions about your policeman. Richard insisted I quit my job at the library after Mark was born. I got bored and decided to look for appropriate frames for all his old family pictures. Found plenty at yard sales and flea markets, but they were almost always damaged. So like any sensible librarian, I got a book and taught myself how to repair them. When friends saw what I had done, they started bringing me their frames to fix. Before I knew what had happened, I was in business."

"So, why are you holding a kid's crayon in your hand?"

"I'm using this gold crayon to make some quick, inexpensive repairs on this antique frame. Here, let me show you."

A beautiful gold frame lay on the workbench. Several small chips had broken off, leaving ugly white gaps in the gold leaf.

"After I clean the frame with this soft camel-hair brush, I just melt a little of the crayon wax onto the part where the gold has broken off. As the wax cools, I press a design into it to match the rest of the frame. The gold crayons are exactly the shade of burnished gold you find on old frames."

She worked swiftly and expertly as she spoke, and in only a few minutes the frame looked as good as new. The touchup job was only noticeable if you looked hard for it.

"Now I'll wash it gently, using a soft brush and soapy water, and it will be a perfectly usable frame again. The worst thing people do to an old frame like this is paint it with gold paint, which is flat and brassy looking and covers all the lovely patina that the frame has acquired over the years. When they're finished, they have a frame that could have come from K Mart."

She showed me an example, and I saw what she meant.

"I'm going to strip off all this glitzy paint and refinish this one with real gold leaf. It'll be expensive, but the owner wanted the very best for her granny's portrait. I'm never going to get rich doing this, but I do get tons of pleasure out of restoring things to their original beauty."

She studied the frame she had just finished with a critical eye and discovered another small chip. She melted the rest of the crayon, dropped some wax onto the frame, and deftly worked the design with a tool that looked like something my dentist would use. Without looking up, she asked me to fetch her another crayon. "They're in a green box on the metal shelves back there," she said, jerking her head toward the back wall of the basement.

I hobbled over, my foot still sore from the fall I took earlier in the day, and found the box. Just as I picked it up, I saw something that got me so excited I dropped the box, spilling crayons every which way.

"Oh, no! I'm sorry. I'll pick them up. Really I will. But look! Behind the shelves. You can see the outline of an archway. It's been boarded over, but I'll bet you a nickel it's an entrance to the big cave I read about."

I gave the shelves a little jerk and was able to move the structure several inches away from the wall. Alice-Ann ran over to help me, and together we pulled it out several feet.

"I'm right. It's definitely a boarded-up doorway. See how it's set into the brick arch—just like the one I saw earlier today." I gave the wood a sharp kick with my good foot and made a small hole in it. It was crumbly with dry rot. "Okay to open it up?"

"Sure. I wonder where I left my hammer?" Alice-Ann studied the Peg-Board where her tools hung. "Oh, well, we can use these."

We attacked the rotten wood with a crowbar and a heavy-duty screwdriver. It took only a few minutes to pull it all out, and we entered a tiny room, not much bigger than a closet, where we stared down into a very deep, very dark pit. A wooden ladder leaned against the edge of the hole.

I was tempted to climb right down into it, but remembering the rotten condition of the door made me reluctant to test the ladder.

"Leave it for now," Alice-Ann suggested. "We'll need to borrow a sturdy metal ladder and find a good flashlight."

I was eager to start exploring but had to agree that what she said made sense. We picked up the crayons, then went upstairs.

Alice-Ann disappeared into the kitchen, and I went to my room, where I stripped off my filthy clothes and soaked my aching body for an hour in the tub.

I floated peacefully, almost asleep, and was startled when Alice-Ann knocked on the door. "Wine's poured," she called to me. "Come on down."

I reluctantly hoisted myself out of the tub and returned to my room where I dressed in white linen slacks and a white silk blouse. Appropriate attire, I hoped, for a séance.

I made sure the cats were okay and replenished their Tasty Tabby Treats and water, then went to the living room, where Alice-Ann was sitting in the wing chair, sipping from a glass of white wine. A glass for me sat on top of the washstand. She didn't seem to notice me come in, so I carried my wine over to where she sat, knelt on the floor in front of her, and placed my hand on her knee.

"Wanna talk?" Many times over the years one of us had asked this of the other. Sometimes, it brought no response. That was okay. More often it led to a soul-searching discussion. Most important, it was a reminder that there was someone nearby who really cared.

"You first," she said. "Tell me why you and Steve broke up."

I hadn't expected this. I tried to explain briefly how successful he was, how I had felt the need to see myself as his equal before we got married, and how he hadn't been willing to wait any longer.

"What are you afraid of, Tori?" she asked when I ran down.

"I don't know what you mean."

"Yes, you do. It's been the same pattern ever since I met you. You claim to be looking for that 'special someone,' but every time a man begins to get interested, you run like a wounded weasel."

"Wounded weasel! What kind of simile is that?"

"An alliterative one—not bad, hmm? But you're stalling. After all these years, I still don't know why you avoid commitment the way you do."

I took a delaying sip of wine and thought of all the people who had passed through my life and then drifted off into an uncharted sea of memories. I said nothing.

Alice-Ann sighed. "You're not going to talk, are you? Well, I don't believe in holding back—here comes the sordid synopsis of the Alice-Ann and Richard soap opera. I know you heard us fighting last night, so there's no point in my trying to hide anything from you. Our marriage was never ideal, but I always thought we could work things out. Twanya is only the last straw on the haystack of old girlfriends. I found out he's had a whole procession of them, even back when we were first married."

"Slimeball," I murmured sympathetically.

"That's not the worst thing, though. I've discovered he's just as morally dissolute in his professional life as he is in our marriage. Even though I'm still officially an 'outsider,' I've made some pretty good friends here, and I've been told that he lies, cheats, and has even been suspected of stealing. Nobody wants to do business with him anymore."

"Pond scum!"

"Last week, I was getting some of his suits ready to send to the cleaner, and I found a letter in one of his pockets. It was from a lawyer who said he'd looked over Richard's financial situation and recommended that we file for bankruptcy.

"I called our bank and learned that Richard had taken out several large loans, using this house—the family home he had inherited from his father—as collateral. He hasn't made any payments on the loans in more than a year, and the bank is getting ready to foreclose on the property. When I confronted Richard, he admitted he'd borrowed the money and invested it all in an oil discovery firm in Mexico that turned out to be a scam. Even worse, he'd talked a lot of local people into giving him money to invest for them. Now some of them are saying there never was an oil firm—that Richard stole the money. A lot of people lost everything, just like we have."

"So that's what the judge was referring to last night when he mentioned 'Mexican oil.' "

"Right. He lost a bundle, but not as much as some others."

We drained our wineglasses. I got to my feet, refilled our glasses, and sat down again, this time on a chair. "Surely you can keep the house?" I said. "Isn't there other property you can sell? How about that mill his great-great-something-or-other started up?"

"The land that used to belong to the family has been sold in bits and pieces by several generations of lousy MacKinstrie businessmen. This house and about three acres is all that's left. And the mill closed years ago.

"The thing that really gets me, Tori, is that his ego won't allow him to realize he's become the town clown. He still thinks this town owes him something because he's a descendant of the 'founding father.' He runs around bragging about this big deal and that big deal, just like this nonsense he told you of joining the Historical Society and becoming famous."

She snorted. "He doesn't have enough brains to read and understand a historical novel, much less do historical research. But, I guess I'm really the stupid one, to have fallen in love with him in the first place. Why couldn't I see how shallow and superficial he was?"

"I wondered that at the time," I muttered. But she didn't seem to hear me.

"I suppose that's why he's had so many girlfriends. At first women are charmed by him, as I was. Then as they get to know him, they learn what he's really like and dump him. Because he can't admit to himself that he can't hold a woman, he has deluded himself into believing he's the Warren Beatty of Lickin Creek—love 'em and leave 'em."

"Why haven't *you* left him?"

"I wanted so badly to make a success of our marriage—I really did love him, you know. And then Mark came along, and I kept hoping things would improve. They didn't, but I felt Mark needed his father. Now I realize I've been wrong. He's a bright little boy, and he knows what's going on. Oh, I don't mean about the sex and other women, but the kids at school tease him about his father being a real jerk. I guess they hear their parents talking about Richard at home. I finally decided if I was going to keep one ounce of self-respect, I'd have to leave him. That's why I'm going to ask him for a divorce, just as soon as he . . ."

"As soon as he comes home?" I finished for her.

She nodded.

"Where do you think he is?" I asked.

"Probably with Twanya, the Twat," she said bitterly.

"I don't think so. Garnet told me he'd had a call from her this morning. She was worried because Richard hadn't shown up at the office this morning."

"She's lying."

"Why are you so sure? Did you follow him to her place last night?"

"Don't be ridiculous," she snapped, then got to her feet. "I'm going to see what we can have for dinner."

I didn't tell her I'd seen her leave in the VW last night. Perhaps, after all the humiliation she had already suffered, she just didn't want to admit to one more indignity like following her husband. It didn't seem important, and I couldn't see any reason for causing her additional grief.

We drifted into the kitchen, where Alice-Ann started to prepare tuna fish sandwiches. I'd had tuna fish for every meal since I'd been here. Happily, it's low in calories.

"How about fixing us some vegetable soup?" she suggested. "We can have it in mugs."

I got a can of Campbell's down from the cupboard. Canned soup was my specialty! Life support for the live-aloner. By the time it was heated and poured, Alice-Ann had the sandwiches ready.

"What do you think of Garnet?" she asked with a sly smile.

"Don't shake the dust out of your bridesmaid's dress, yet. He's way too macho for me."

"Always looking for a reason to run. I hope you find a great guy someday."

"I will. We both will."

We finished our meal in companionable silence and washed up; by then it was time to leave for the séance at Silverthorne. Alice-Ann dithered about going for a while, but finally decided it would be better than sitting at home, wondering when or if Richard would show up.

"Besides, he's supposed to be there. Sylvia Thorne said she expects him, and I don't think he'd dare ignore a royal summons from her," I reminded her.

We had the front door open before I remembered something. "Hold on a second, Alice-Ann. I promised the librarian I'd deliver a book to Sylvia."

It lay on the hall table where I had placed it earlier. I picked it up, and we stepped into the warm summer twilight.

"What have you got?" Alice-Ann asked as we strolled down the hill.

"A biography of Thomas Edison. The librarian said Sylvia called and asked for it."

"Thomas Edison. That's funny. Richard's mentioned his name several times lately. Wonder what this sudden surge of interest in him means."

"I figured Sylvia wants to educate me about the great man. I demonstrated abysmal ignorance of his accomplishments last night when I admired her very early, and apparently very rare, Edison phonograph machine."

"She has an Edison phonograph? Are you sure it was an Edison?" She sounded agitated.

"It was in the parlor. She even demonstrated it for me. Why? What's wrong?"

"It's probably nothing, but several months ago, Richard brought an Edison phonograph home from a house he was selling to settle an estate. He told me the deceased homeowner was a distant relative of Edison's and that there were several mementos of the inventor in the house. He *said* he brought the phonograph home because he thought Mark would be interested in seeing it. Then he took it back, so it could be sold at the estate auction. Now, I can't help wondering if . . ."

"If Richard gave it or sold it to Sylvia?"

"Yes. After seven years of marriage to a congenital liar, suspicions pop easily to mind. Come to think of it, it was right after that that he started dropping Edison's name into conversations."

"How so?"

"Oh, he'd make little comments about what a genius the man was. Hinting that Edison had invented things no one knew about. Stuff like that. Tori, I'll bet Edison's the subject of the research he's doing to get into the Historical Society."

"Jeez, Alice-Ann, you don't think he's dumb enough to think no one else knows that Edison invented the phonograph?" That made us both laugh.

As we continued down the footpath, Alice-Ann said, "I'll bet he found something valuable in that house and kept it."

"Then I wonder why Sylvia wanted this information from the library?"

"Maybe she and Richard are hatching up something together. That could be why she's got the Edison phonograph. She's as bad as he is about thinking she's better than anyone else. I don't know how her poor sister could stand living with her all these years. Rose is so quiet and modest and always content to remain in the background, while Sylvia is just the opposite. I think she'd rather be dead than not be the high-society leader of Lickin Creek."

We arrived at the castle. A few cars were parked in the circular driveway but no other people were outside. Alice-Ann rang the bell, and we waited for several minutes before LaVonna opened the door. She was dressed even more strangely than before, in a light purple dress covered with chartreuse roses. Her skirt, unfashionable and unflattering, stopped at midknee, revealing black stockings, held up by old-fashioned rolled garters, and high-top sneakers. Strands of gray hair were escaping from her white net prayer bonnet.

"Come on," she ordered curtly. Her mouth was pursed like a prune. "Never seen such goings-on in all my days. And on top of it, me with this whole house to redd up before that mystery thingamajig."

"I'll be glad to help you, if you like," I told her, ignoring Alice-Ann's exaggerated gasp of amazement. I admit housecleaning is not one of my strong points, but it would give me a great opportunity to explore the castle.

"Well, that's right nice. I sure need helped." She stared pointedly at Alice-Ann as she spoke.

"I'll help, too," Alice-Ann said with little enthusiasm.

LaVonna accepted her offer with a nod of her head. Then she turned to me and spoke in a low voice as if she were afraid she'd be overheard. "When you'uns come over in the morning to clean, I have something I need to talk about. I don't got no one to talk to anymore, now that my family's all. Don't say nothing to nobody."

She spun around and started walking down the long, dark hall to the library, leaving us to follow or not, as we chose.

"What did she mean, her 'family's all'?" I asked Alice-Ann.

"Just another colloquialism. It means 'all gone.' "

I jumped a little, startled by a soft, rustling sound coming from behind the heavy draperies that closed off one of the parlors. Mice, I shuddered. I hate mice. That's one reason I love cats.

Only a few lamps were lit in the library, and the bulbs were so dim that the corners of the room were in darkness. Heavy wine-colored velvet drapes were drawn to keep out any light from outside. A small fire in the stone fireplace cast dancing shadows on the antique Persian carpet. The fire had obviously been lit to create a certain ambience, since the temperature outside was in the high eighties. With no air coming through the closed windows, and the fire blasting its heat into the room, it was, in teen jargon, "the room from hell."

9

In the center of the library stood a large, round mahogany pedestal table, with lion's-paw feet. Thirteen oak chairs, carved to resemble thrones, were placed around it. Some were already occupied by some very serious-looking individuals, most of whom I recognized from the previous night. The judge was there, as were the Seligmans. And Michael, naturally. I was stunned to see Twanya Tweedy.

Alice-Ann caught her breath sharply at the sight of the secretary, but gamely kept a smile on her face as she sat down at the table.

Sylvia Thorne entered the room, took a look at the book I handed her, and thrust it back at me. "I've already read it," she said curtly. "You can take it back."

"You're quite welcome," I muttered under my breath as I dropped the book into my pocketbook. Michael's eyes were twinkling with amusement as he motioned to me to sit next to him.

"She has her good qualities, but politeness is not one of them," he whispered with a chuckle.

On my right side sat an Asian man, who appeared to be

around fifty years old. I had seen him here last night but hadn't actually spoken with him.

Sylvia said, "Victoria, allow me to introduce you. This is our mayor, Prince Somping."

To cover my surprise, I extended my hand. "How do you do?"

"*Sabaydi bo,*" he said with a mischievous smile, shaking my hand enthusiastically.

Judge Parker, who as usual appeared to be asleep, opened his eyes and said, "Speak English, Mayor. We all know you can."

I ignored the judge. "*Kopchai sabaydi.*"

All heads turned to stare at me in astonishment. The mayor, still holding my hand, seemed to have an asthma attack.

I continued, enjoying myself. "*Khoy pak phasa lao day laknoy.*"

"I'll be damned," said the judge. "What the hell is all this about?"

"I simply told him I spoke a little Lao. Learned it when I was a kid," I explained.

The mayor pulled himself together. "What a great pleasure it is to meet to an American who speaks my language. And such a wonderful writer, too. I just read your book, Miss Miracle, and found it fascinating."

"I find you fascinating, too. Are you really a prince?"

"I was a prince in Laos. When the Communists seized control of the government in 1975, they deposed the royal family. After several years of near starvation, I escaped across the Mekong River, where I spent a number of unpleasant years in a refugee camp in northern Thailand. Eventually, I was sponsored by a missionary group to come to this beautiful country. They found a kind family here in Lickin Creek willing to take me in until I was able to support myself."

Judge Parker snorted. "The guy was absolutely useless. He'd never had anything to do back in Laos. Then Mayor Buchanan died, and it occurred to us that there was a good job for him. All he has to do is cut ribbons at supermarket openings and go to parties. With his background, he's perfect for the job."

"Only in America," sighed the mayor-prince with a smile.

"Perhaps I knew some of your relatives. When did you leave Laos?" I asked.

"It is too painful for me to talk about," he said with a long, sad face.

"I'm sorry. *Kho thot.*"

"*Bo pen yang,*" he said, using that wonderful Lao phrase that means everything from "you're welcome" to "it doesn't matter."

A stern-faced man in his early forties stretched his arm across the mayor and shook my hand. "I'm Dr. Jones. Call me Meredith."

There were still two empty seats at the table.

"Where's Richard?" Sylvia asked Alice-Ann.

Before she could reply, the judge mumbled, "Probably busy conning somebody out of their life savings."

While we waited, I had time to notice that both Sylvia and Rose were dressed in black, Victorian mourning dresses, with long, full skirts and high-necked, long-sleeved blouses that must have been suffocating in the heat of the room. At their throats they each wore one of those disgusting gold pins that contain braided hair from dead people. They also wore black kid gloves. They might have raided the attic looking for their idea of proper garb for a séance, but I had a nagging suspicion that they dressed like this on a regular basis. If it got any hotter in the room, I could picture them melting away like the witch in *The Wizard of Oz,* when Dorothy threw the water on her, leaving little heaps of black clothing on their chairs.

Sylvia rapped on the table for attention. "Before

Praxythea arrives," she said, "I'd just like to remind you all that she is a well-respected psychic who has worked with many police departments on numerous cases. I have asked her here to help us solve a very old mystery."

She paused for dramatic effect. "Tonight, we hope to learn who murdered the first Sylvia Thorne and to discover the whereabouts of her fabulous diamond, Sylvia's Star."

Alice-Ann caught my eye and made a face as if she were smelling a crock of shit, which was just what I thought of this whole séance idea. Sitting in a stifling, almost airless room, trying to solve a murder that had happened about a hundred and thirty years ago, was not my idea of a fun evening.

I sensed a slight movement of air behind me, and I smelled the spicy scent of carnations. The twelfth member of our group gracefully moved into view and sat in the empty chair between Sylvia and Rose Thorne.

"My friends, allow me to present Praxythea Evangelista." Sylvia was trying much too hard to sound grandly dramatic. She then introduced each of us.

Praxythea looked at me, and I felt as though I might drown in the emerald green sea of her eyes. She was absolutely the most stunning woman I had ever seen, on or off a movie screen. Her dark red hair was piled high on her head and surrounded her perfect face like a soft cloud, while several curling tendrils escaped to lie softly on her white, unblemished shoulders.

I think she was tall, but she was so ethereal that she made me feel like a giant klutz. She wore something long and black and so sheer that it was obvious she wasn't wearing a bra. This woman had probably never even heard of control-top panty hose. Her only jewelry was an enormous emerald and diamond ring she wore on the index finger of her right hand.

She spoke to me softly—intimately. "Tori Miracle. I've looked forward to meeting you. Your book about the Mark

Twain house was outstanding. It shows that you have remarkable understanding of the occult and the powers of darkness. You must be very proud."

Actually, I was, but modesty kept me from saying so. I shyly murmured my thanks, hating myself for sounding more like a schoolgirl than a published author.

The emerald green eyes turned to Alice-Ann, and a tiny frown line appeared on the perfect forehead.

"You have great sadness in your heart. Perhaps I shall be able to help you."

Sylvia was smirking with pleasure, but I didn't think it took much psychic ability to tell that Alice-Ann was miserable. Bags under her red, swollen eyes were a pretty sure giveaway.

"It is getting late," Praxythea said. "Let us begin."

There was still one empty chair.

"Shouldn't we wait for Richard?" Sylvia asked.

Praxythea shook her head. "We don't have to have thirteen people. Besides, I detest tardiness. Will someone please take the extra chair away?"

Michael moved one of the thrones, and the rest of us scooted around a little to fill in the gap.

Praxythea placed both hands on the table, palms down. For the first time, I noticed a Polaroid photograph lying on the table. The subject was out of focus, but I recognized it as the painting of the first Sylvia, the one Richard had hung in the parlor the evening before.

"First let me explain how I work," Praxythea said softly. "When I concentrate on something, I get a clear mental picture in my mind of the subject. I see people and locations in color, just as you would see a picture on a TV set. I see dead people and communicate with them in some way, although they don't actually talk to me. Now, I want you all to help me by concentrating on the photograph."

We all stared intently at the Polaroid.

"Please clear your minds. You must be open and receptive to any attempts at communication."

The more I tried to clear my mind, the more my attention wandered. By now, my eyes had grown accustomed to the dim light, and I noticed a black box, about two feet long by a foot wide, sitting on the floor in the farthest corner of the room, looking terribly out of place. It hadn't been there yesterday when I'd visited the library with Rose. A tiny ruby-red dot, like the tip of a lit cigarette, glowed on the top. I wondered if it was a tape recorder.

My thoughts were interrupted when Praxythea whispered, "Hold hands. Don't let go under any circumstances."

She closed her eyes, and we sat for a long time, holding hands, watching Praxythea's sexy breasts rise and fall rhythmically.

My hands were starting to sweat, and I was wondering if I could pull away for just a moment to blot them on my lap when Praxythea startled us all by inhaling sharply.

Her face suddenly contorted as if she were in great pain, and her long, bloodred fingernails were digging hard into the gloved hands of the Thorne sisters on either side of her. Although her eyes were still closed, I got the distinct impression that she was staring at something far away.

Then we heard her voice, coming as if from a great distance: "Ask your questions. But do it quickly for I cannot stay here long."

She was good. This was most impressive. She'd probably gotten started with one of those ads that used to be in the back of comic books: learn ventriloquism and astound your friends.

The room was growing cold; the ridiculous fire must have finally died down. I shivered and wished I'd brought a sweater with me.

Then a crackling sound from the fireplace caught my attention, and I saw that the fire was actually burning more furiously than before. Still, the room temperature continued to drop.

I felt as though I were trapped in a tangle of cobwebs. The room became so dark, I might as well have been trying to see through deep, murky water. The others seemed to be moving away from me, although I could still feel their hands holding on to mine.

My heart almost stopped beating; this was it—the fear, total and absolute—that I'd felt once before, the day I stood alone in the Mark Twain house in Greenwich Village, where unspeakable horrors had gone unchecked for generations. That was when I learned that there was an evil so strong it could become a physical presence.

Praxythea laughed, an unpleasant sound. "Ask your questions. Your time is flying faster than you know."

Although a cold wind blew through the room, nothing moved.

I clung tightly to Michael's hand, feeling I would lose my sanity or my life. Nobody could survive this terror twice in one lifetime. The air currents wrapped around my body, touching my breasts, caressing my face, pushing up between my legs. For a moment I surrendered to the pleasure, then gagged with disgust as I realized what was going on.

"Please don't touch me," I whispered softly. "I can't bear it again." To my surprise, it stopped.

From far away, I heard Sylvia's voice. "Do you know where Sylvia's Star is?"

"It is with her murderer."

"Who murdered her?"

"A friend."

"Who?"

"The dead have no names."

"Can you see the diamond? Where is it?"

"In the darkness by the edge of running water."

"Can you communicate with the murderer? Ask him where the diamond is?"

"It is not possible. There are no ghosts here."

Sylvia's voice became shrill. "There have to be ghosts here. Aren't there always ghosts when there are violent deaths? What about Sylvia? And my father? Maybe others who died here during the Civil War? Where are their entities? Edison said entities live forever."

"There are no ghosts here," Praxythea repeated, and opened her eyes. The wind stopped immediately, and the room began to warm up. The gray, gauzelike web that had covered me was gone.

She smiled prettily. "It was so dark. I'll have to try again."

Sylvia jerked her hand away and rubbed the spots where Praxythea's sharp red fingernails had almost dug through her glove.

"She said there are no ghosts here." Sylvia sounded indignant. "You'd think with all the violent deaths we've had here, we'd have a whole damn gaggle of ghosts." She seemed more upset about finding out her home wasn't haunted than she was about not learning where the diamond was.

I looked around. There was nothing in the room to cause the fright I'd felt. It was just your average castle library: books on shelves where they belonged, dusty knickknacks on marble-top tables, and the dying embers of a fire.

"Quite a show she puts on," Michael said to me.

"Are you sure it's just a show?"

"What else could it be? You'll notice she didn't give out any information we didn't already know. It's hardly a surprise that Sylvia's murderer stole the diamond. Even Inspector Clouseau could figure that one out."

"But the cold . . . and the wind?"

He had a puzzled expression on his face. "I didn't notice," he said, and my blood turned icy in my veins. Could I have been the only one to experience the horror that had just occurred in this room? I looked at the others. None of them seemed particularly upset, except perhaps for Sylvia, who was still grumbling about the absence of ghosts.

I was about to ask the princely mayor what he thought of it all when we were startled by the sound of the doorbell.

"I'll bet it's Richard, coming late," Rose said as we waited for LaVonna to answer the door.

We all stood up and stretched, and most of the group clustered around Praxythea asking her questions about whether or not she was conscious when having a vision, and if there were no ghosts present, how did she know the murderer had the diamond? She explained that when she concentrated on a subject, she went into a sort of trance, where she was still aware of her surroundings, but could also see other places and people.

"I think I communicated with a spirit," she said. "A spirit is not the same thing as a ghost. A ghost is a part of the human soul, which is sometimes left on earth when a person dies, especially if the person died feeling he had left something undone. Spirits exist on a separate level. They are all around us and aren't necessarily human. Ancient cultures knew the spirits of water, air, fire, trees, and so on. Then, when more people believed in them, they actively participated in our world. Now, they get to visit only through a few chosen people like myself."

Bunch of bullshit in my opinion. Take away that beautiful face, fabulous body, and see-through blouse, and see how much attention she'd get.

LaVonna came into the room, accompanied by two filthy children, a boy and a girl. Their clothes were torn, and fresh blood had turned the dirt on their skin to mud.

"Someone call the police," La Vonna said shakily. "These children say they found a dead body down by the road."

Michael ran into the hall and used the phone there to make a quick call.

Mrs. Seligman sat the frightened children down on a small Victorian settee and murmured soothing words to them.

That's when I noticed that the black box I'd seen in the corner earlier was gone.

"Where's the box?" I blurted out.

"What box?" Michael asked as he came back into the room.

"The one that was right there, in the corner. Somebody took it."

Sylvia shook her head. "You have a very active imagination, Victoria. That must be what makes you a successful writer."

"There was something there. It looked like a tape recorder. Didn't anybody else see it?"

No—from everyone else in that room.

Chapter

10

We didn't talk while we waited for the police; each of us was alone with our own fears and unspoken questions. All the color had drained from Alice-Ann's face, and her hands trembled on her lap. Dr. Jones, with some help from Mrs. Seligman, wiped some of the blood off the children's arms and faces, exposing nasty cuts and scratches.

It was only about ten minutes before Garnet arrived with a younger policeman in tow, but it seemed as if hours had passed. He went directly to the children, knelt in front of them, and spoke to them gently. "Can you tell me exactly what happened?"

The boy choked back tears and shook his head, but the girl proved to be of stronger stuff and started to talk. "We was playing at the Martin farm and didn't notice it was getting dark. So we was riding our bikes home on the highway when a big eighteen-wheeler came by doing about a hundred miles an hour. He made so much wind I went straight into those thorn bushes on the side of the road. My clothes got all caught in the thorns and I was bleeding. And when Tyler tried to get me loose, he got all cut up, too.

"We'd just about got my bike pulled out when we saw

something shiny under some bushes. I thought maybe it was part of my bike got broken off, you know, but we pulled the branches apart and saw a big motorcycle. There was a man on the ground next to it. He was dead."

Alice-Ann uttered a strangled cry and buried her face in her hands. I stood behind her and put my hands on her shaking shoulders to comfort her. From where I stood, I could see Twanya Tweedy sobbing quietly into a pink tissue.

Garnet continued questioning the child. "How did you know the man was dead?"

"Because I did what you're supposed to. Like on the TV. I crawled through the bushes and took his pulse. There wasn't any, you know, and his head . . . his head was all bashed in." The little girl started to cry.

I really admired the gutsy little kid. Not many people, kids or adults, would have done what she did.

Garnet spoke to LaVonna. "Please call the Eby farm and tell them that Tyler and Tiffany are safe. They're probably getting concerned about them being out so late."

He asked Dr. Jones, "Do you think they need medical attention?"

Jones nodded. "Most definitely. Those firethorns can cause blood poisoning faster than a bee finds pollen. I'll take them down to the clinic, give them tetanus shots and antibiotics, then come right back."

"LaVonna," Garnet said, "tell the Ebys to pick the children up at the clinic. Kids, I'm sorry, but I'll have to ask you to do one more thing. I need you to go with me in the squad car and show me exactly where the body is."

"We can walk. It's not far," Tiffany told him.

Garnet explained gently that there was police equipment in the car that he might need to use.

I was surprised when he asked me to ride along. "I think it would be better for them if they had a woman along," he explained.

Mrs. Seligman uttered an irritated "humph."

"I don't know about leaving Alice-Ann," I protested.

Praxythea sat down beside her. "She'll be all right. I'll stay with her until you get back."

Garnet appeared to notice Praxythea for the first time and was staring at her with obvious pleasure. "I didn't know you were in town, Praxythea. It's good to see you."

"It's nice to see you, too, Garnet. Perhaps I can be of some assistance to you again."

"I just might take you up on that."

I was afraid I'd have to wipe the drool off his chin, so I broke the spell by grabbing both children by the hands and leading them toward the door. Garnet followed, reluctantly I thought, trailed by his young assistant and the doctor.

Once we were in the police car, I was introduced to the sergeant, whose name, believe it or not, was Luscious Miller. Not Lucius. Luscious. Only in his twenties, he already had a receding hairline; a greasy strand of blond hair combed from one ear to the other only emphasized it. He was so tall that his knees touched his chin as he sat in the backseat of the car next to Tyler, and I doubted that he weighed as much as I did.

"Stop," Tiffany yelled after a few minutes. "Right there." She pointed across Garnet's chest into the bushes on our left. "He's in there. Not too far from the driveway."

Garnet braked, and we all climbed out. Dr. Jones, who had followed in his Mercedes, took the children away immediately.

Garnet opened the trunk of his cruiser, handed a flashlight to me and a machete to Luscious, and then carefully examined the driveway. There was still enough light so we could easily see the motorcycle tracks that headed directly into the thorny hedge. Garnet got a camera out of the trunk and took a series of flash pictures of the tracks.

It turned out that Luscious didn't need his machete after all. Where the motorcycle tracks disappeared into the hedge, the branches simply fell away when he touched them. Almost as though the opening in the bushes had been deliberately filled in with broken branches after the motorcycle went through.

"Wait here," Garnet ordered, taking the flashlight from me. He and Luscious cautiously entered the firethorn hedge.

"Do you see anything?" I called out.

"I'm afraid so," Garnet answered.

"Who . . . ?" But I knew. Time passed slowly while I waited. Ten minutes? Twenty? Thirty? A car pulled up beside me and Dr. Jones got out. I was glad to see his professionally solemn face.

"How are the children?" I asked.

"They'll be okay. My nurse is cleaning them up and their parents are already there."

"Poor kids. It must have been a terrible shock for them."

"I'm sure it was, but they'll get over it quickly. City folk don't realize how much danger and death there is on a farm. The kids learn early to accept it as part of living. Where's Garnet?"

"In there." I pointed at the gap in the hedge.

"I'll just get my bag," Dr. Jones said, opening the trunk of his car. He pulled out a large brown suitcase.

"Why do you need that if the man's dead?" I asked.

"Besides being Lickin Creek's only full-time doctor, I'm also the Caven County coroner." He flicked the switch on his flashlight. "Damn battery's dead. Would you lead the way, please?"

"Garnet," I shouted into the bushes. "The doctor and I are coming through. Could you please shine some light for us?"

A small circle of light showed through the blackness.

I pushed my way through, getting a few small scratches. It was pretty damn apparent why Meredith Jones had asked me to lead the way. When we reached a small clearing, I recognized Richard's motorcycle immediately. It didn't even have a dent on its shiny body. Richard was less fortunate.

He lay sprawled in the knee-high grass, the right side of his face looking like a squashed tomato. It was covered with flies. His left eye stared at eternal blackness. On his chest lay a long-stemmed American-beauty rose. Garnet's camera flashed several times.

I turned away, hand over my mouth, and took several deep breaths—don't let me cry, don't let me cry. But I did. Tears for a man I didn't even like. Tears for the rotten finality of death.

Garnet handed me a clean, white cotton handkerchief. "Are you going to be all right?" he asked, gently touching my shoulder.

I nodded.

Luscious reached into his hip pocket and produced a flask of brandy. Noticing Garnet's disapproving stare, he said, "Purely medicinal, boss. You never know when you might need to revive someone."

I took a deep swallow. It burned all the way down, and I felt better almost at once. Luscious took a quick sip from it himself before shoving it back in his pocket.

Garnet was down on his hands and knees, crawling around the body. Then he took more pictures. He nodded to the doctor, who rolled Richard over. When I saw him take a thermometer out of his bag, I turned my back. This was not something I wanted to watch.

I turned around when I heard them stand up. Thankfully they had covered Richard with a plastic tarp. Garnet brushed the dirt off his trousers and absentmindedly reached into his pocket for his handkerchief. When he saw it hanging damply from my fingers, he wiped his hands on his shirt.

"One thing is obvious," the doctor said. "He didn't die here."

"You mean it wasn't an accident?" I was totally confused.

"No way. There's no blood here."

Garnet added, " There's not a mark on the motorcycle, either, and there's nothing around here that could have caused that kind of head injury. Even if he'd been thrown off his bike, he'd have had to hit a rock or a tree to get smashed up that badly. My guess is he died somewhere else, and someone brought him here on the motorcycle and hid him here in the bushes."

"But if that's what happened, wouldn't that mean he was murdered?" I asked.

Dr. Jones nodded. "That's exactly what I'm putting in my report. I estimate he was killed by one or more right lateral blows to the head sometime around midnight. I'll know better after the lab work is done."

I remembered something. "He was wearing a helmet when he left home. Where is it?"

"How do you know that?" Garnet asked.

I explained about the fight, and how I had watched Richard leave the house, strap his suitcase on the back of his cycle, and roar down the driveway.

"What time was that?"

"Around eleven, give or take ten or fifteen minutes. My watch—"

"Do you know where he was going?"

"No. I just saw him go down the hill. I did wake up once, later on. I heard a cycle and thought it was Richard coming home. I don't know what time it was."

"Could you tell what direction the motorcycle was coming from?"

"I don't know. It sounded close. That's why I assumed it was Richard. Hey! His suitcase—it's not here either."

To make sure, we searched the area again. I described it as best I could. It had looked just like a big, black, old-fashioned suitcase, probably leather.

"So, wherever he went, he left his suitcase there," Garnet commented. "That could be a big help, Tori."

Behind us, a volunteer fire-department ambulance crew entered the clearing, carrying a stretcher. A few minutes later, Richard MacKinstrie was in a body bag being carted off to the local morgue. So much for a man's dreams!

Garnet held up the rose. "Looks like death paid the Rose Rent this year," he said as he dropped it into an evidence bag.

"How did it get here?" I asked, realizing as I did just how stupid I sounded.

"When we find that out, we'll know who killed him."

"Ouch—watch it—stop shoving—damn thorns . . ." The group from the castle was pushing through the bushes to find out what had happened.

Garnet yelled at them to stay away, but no one paid the slightest bit of attention to him.

"Luscious, didn't you cordon off the area?"

"Sorry!"

"Damn it, man, do something. Keep them out of here," Garnet ordered.

"Yes, sir, chief," Luscious said. "I'll take care of them."

In a few seconds the clearing was full of people, and poor Luscious was trying to ignore Garnet's furious glare. Except for Praxythea, Sylvia, and Alice-Ann, everyone from the castle was there.

They all started asking questions at once. "Was it Mr. MacKinstrie?" LaVonna asked.

" 'Fraid so," Garnet replied. He spoke to the whole group. "You might as well hear it from me instead of through the grapevine: we've found Richard MacKinstrie. He's dead, from a severe head wound. I have good reason to believe he was murdered."

Was it a trick of the light from the flashlight she carried, or did I really see a tiny smile appear on LaVonna's lips?

"Hey, people," Garnet yelled. "Watch where you're stepping. There's not going to be a damn clue left by the time you'uns finish tramping around."

"Ouch! Oooh! Damn!" bellowed Sylvia Thorne. "My

hand just got cut to shreds by these damn thorns." She entered the clearing and held her hands out like a small child for the doctor to examine.

"Nasty scratches," he commented. "You'd better go to the clinic for treatment. Hopefully you won't get an infection. Anybody else get scratched?"

Rose and LaVonna both nodded, looking a little embarrassed. One by one, everyone but Michael and me stepped forward and displayed their wounds.

Garnet threw his hands up in the air. "Of all the dumb things—okay, everyone with scratches, go on down to the clinic. Judge, Hy—can you drive them?"

It was quickly settled who would ride with whom.

I did have a few scratches myself, but I didn't want to admit it. I figured a good scrubbing with soap and water and some peroxide would take care of them.

"What about Alice-Ann?" I asked. "Did anybody think she might need some medical attention? Some sleeping pills or something."

Meredith Jones looked irritated. "I've already thought of that. I'll stop by the castle and drive her home. I can give her a shot that'll put her to sleep for eight hours or so. And I'll leave some tranquilizers for you to give her tomorrow if she needs them."

Garnet said, "You can't put her to sleep until I've talked to her. I've got to ask her some questions about what happened last night."

"*You'll* have to wait till tomorrow, Garnet," Jones said. "She's just lost her husband. Show a little compassion, please."

Garnet's jawline turned white with anger, but he said nothing more to Meredith, choosing instead to yell at the others to get out of the clearing. "Maybe, miraculously, there'll be a clue you clowns haven't destroyed. I'll need to talk to each of you tomorrow, so don't go anywhere."

It was quite dark by then, and Michael asked if I wanted him to walk me back to Alice-Ann's. "That is, if you're not afraid I'm the murderer."

"I would feel better having someone walk me home. Besides, what possible motive could you have for murdering Richard?"

"A pretty good one, actually. About a year ago, he persuaded my mother to back him financially in a 'double-your-money-quick' Mexican oil-discovery company. Mother mortgaged the castle to give him the money. The whole thing turned out to be a scam. The money disappeared, and now the castle and property are scheduled to be sold at auction by the Old Lickin Creek National Bank."

"Oh, Michael, that's awful! It's a crime to think of your beautiful home going out of the family!"

"I'd say that by this time next year, you'll be able to buy your very own split-level, two-thousand-square-foot castle, right here in Silverthorne Meadows. So, you see, if someone hadn't already done it, I might have bashed his head in myself."

At the cottage, he waited until I'd opened the door and turned on the lights. That's when I noticed the scratches: "Your hands . . . You've got some nasty scratches there."

"I know. I wasn't about to line up with the other idiots. I'll put some stuff on them when I get home. You'd better take care of yours, too.

"Damn shame about Richard," he added. "Sad part is I don't think many people will miss him. I'll wager that Rose Rent Day won't even be canceled. I'd better get home—busy day tomorrow. We're going to be building some special scenery to use at the Mystery Dinner."

"I'll be over in the morning myself. LaVonna wanted to talk to me about something."

"Good. Look for me. I'd like you to meet my wife. See you tomorrow," he said, and disappeared into the dark purple shadows of the night.

Before I had time to close the door, Dr. Jones's Mercedes pulled up, and we concentrated on getting a wobbly Alice-Ann up the stairs to her bedroom. I helped her undress, put her nightgown on her, and watched Meredith give her an injection. We both sat with her until she fell asleep. He certainly seemed more solicitous about her than was necessary. I wondered if the good doctor was planning to make a move on the Widow MacKinstrie.

Thursday

11

🌹 🌹 🌹

When I woke up the next morning, I found Alice-Ann in the kitchen drinking coffee and looking a lot better than she had last night. We hugged.

"Do you want a tranquilizer? Dr. Jones left some."

"He's such a thoughtful person. No drugs; I need to get my head clear. Right now I'm kind of numb and strangely ambivalent about Richard's murder. It was such a horrible way to die, and I really am sorry it happened to him, but I can't help feeling relieved that I don't have to go through a divorce. That's awful of me, isn't it?"

She didn't wait for me to say anything. "The worst is going to be telling Mark about his father's death."

Her hand shook as she lifted her coffee cup. I wished I could help her feel better, but only time could do that. The sound of a car coming up the gravel drive brought me to my feet. I looked out the window and saw a light blue Chevrolet with a red flasher light on top. A magnetic sign that said LCPD was stuck on the driver's side front door. It was askew, as if it had been slapped on in haste this morning.

Garnet climbed out, saw me through the window, and waved.

"Gendarme," I told Alice-Ann. "Want me to tell him you're still asleep?"

She shook her head. "He'll find me sooner or later. Might as well get it over with."

I ushered Garnet into the kitchen, where he helped himself to coffee before settling down across the oak table from Alice-Ann. I sat down next to her and took her hand. Garnet shook his head: "I need to talk to her alone."

"I know that."

"I'm sure you do, Miss Prize-Winning Crime Reporter."

He'd been checking up on me! Before I had time to get out of the kitchen, another car pulled up in front of the house. It was getting to be a regular morning rush hour out there.

Again, I looked through the window. "It's a beige station wagon," I told Alice-Ann. "A couple of people are getting out. Mark is with them."

"Tori, could you take him up to his room? Play with him for a few minutes while Garnet and I talk?"

I gave her shoulder a reassuring squeeze. "No problem."

When I opened the front door, the long, solemn faces on the couple standing there told me they knew. The happy smile on Mark's face showed he didn't.

"We thought it best . . ."

"Didn't know how to . . ."

"It's okay. Thanks for bringing him home." I shut the door before they had a chance to say anything else. Upstairs, Mark and I raced his Matchbox cars until Alice-Ann entered the room.

"Your turn downstairs," Alice-Ann said softly with a jerk of her head. "Thanks."

"Tori," Garnet began as soon as I walked into the kitchen, "tell me everything you remember about Tuesday night."

He flipped open a stenographer's notebook. "Last night you said you saw Richard take off on his motorcycle somewhere near eleven o'clock on Tuesday. You said the sound of

a motorcycle woke you up much later, and you thought it
was Richard coming home. Is that all correct?"

"Yes."

"Can you tell me if Alice-Ann was home during that
time?"

Now what do I do? I wondered. What had Alice-Ann told
him? To lie or not to lie?

I remembered what Mark Twain had said, "When in
doubt tell the truth."

"She went out for a while . . . in the Volkswagen."

"After Richard left?"

I nodded, miserable.

"For how long?"

"An hour . . . maybe more. I heard her come in, but I'd
been asleep, so I don't know what time it was. My watch is
broken."

"Was it before or after you heard the motorcycle?"

"After."

"Earlier, when the three of you came home from the castle, what happened?"

Reluctantly, I told him how I had sat outside with the cats
and overheard the argument about Twanya, then the fight,
the smashing of dishes and furniture, and finally how I saw
Richard strap his suitcase on his motorcycle and leave.

"What did you think he was going to do?"

"I figured he was taking some of his clothes and going to
Twanya's."

"Where do you think Alice-Ann was going in the VW?"

"I thought she was going to go to Twanya's to see if he
was there."

"The next day . . . did she say where she had been?"

"She didn't mention it. Neither did I. It was her business,
not mine."

Garnet closed the notebook. "Alice-Ann told me she
never left the house that night."

"I'm not a liar."

"No, I don't think you are. I don't think you're stupid either. You must be aware that if Alice-Ann really left you alone in the house, neither one of you has an alibi for the time of the murder."

"This is preposterous! What reason would I have to murder Richard?" I spluttered.

"From what I've been told, it's no secret that you were against Alice-Ann's marriage to Richard from the beginning. You two were very close until he came along. Many murders have been committed because of jealousy."

"Jealousy! Are you insinuating that Alice-Ann and I were . . . lovers?" I spat the last word at him.

"I'm not insinuating anything, Tori. Police have to look at all the possibilities. It's routine."

I knew that, but when I was the one being questioned, it didn't seem like such a routine matter.

"Who stayed at the castle after the meeting, besides you and Richard and Alice-Ann?"

I thought back for a minute, trying to remember the unfamiliar names. "Dr. Meredith Jones, the cream-and-sugar priest, Judge Parker, Twanya Tweedy, the mayor, Mr. and Mrs. Seligman . . . and, of course, Michael and his mother and aunt."

"Was Praxythea Evangelista there?"

"No. Michael said something about her being in town, but I didn't see her on Tuesday."

"What about LaVonna?"

"The housekeeper? Of course she was there. I thought you just meant guests."

"Did you hear or see anything to make you think Richard was planning to meet one of them later on?"

"He and Twanya looked like someone had stuck them together with Krazy Glue. It's possible they might have made a date."

Garnet placed something on the table. "Ever seen this before?" I caught my breath in shock. It was a plastic bag containing a heavy-duty claw hammer. Even through the plastic, I could see dark stains that didn't look like paint.

"The murder weapon? Where did you find it?"

"Have you ever seen it before?" he countered.

"I don't know . . ."

"You have. Alice-Ann identified it as hers. It has an AA engraved on the handle. She used it at the castle Tuesday night to hang the first Sylvia's painting."

"She must have left it there. We couldn't find it yesterday afternoon when we were opening the cave entrance downstairs."

"You found a cave entrance here? Promise me you won't go exploring without me."

"Promise," I said. "Where'd you find the hammer?"

"You must have been a good reporter—or at least a persistent one. There's no point in not telling you. We found it in a flower bed just below the front terrace of the castle. We also found traces of blood on the terrace. Someone had tried to scrub it up, but . . ."

"But you never can get it all, I know."

He continued, "It looks like Richard went back to the castle after he left here—maybe to meet someone—and was killed there."

"You think he was killed by the person he went to meet?"

"Or by someone who followed him there."

"Is that all then?" I asked.

"For now. See you at six."

"What?" What was he talking about?

"Dinner. Did you forget?"

"Sorry. I guess I did. Will you have time? What with investigating me and Alice-Ann and all?"

"I'll make time," he said with an infuriating, engaging grin. "Besides, I've got those cave maps you wanted to see."

"Six it is!" I confirmed heartily.

After Garnet left, Alice-Ann appeared in the kitchen and slumped into a chair. "Mark's sound asleep, bless his heart.

He cried a little bit, but really took it like a little man. I don't know what I would do without him."

"He's adorable."

"Your friend, the police chief, certainly spared no punches with me, Tori. I seem to be suspect number one."

"That's because most murders are committed by spouses or close friends. That's where the police always start." I was trying to make her feel better, but it didn't work.

"*Et tu, Brute?* You almost sound as if you think I'm guilty, too."

"Nobody thinks you're guilty. It's just normal investigative procedure. He'll be interviewing everybody. And we'll all have to prove where we were when . . . when it happened."

"Well, I told Garnet we were both home in our beds, so that takes care of our alibis."

I breathed a deep sigh. "There's something I have to tell you."

"How could you have told him that?" she said angrily when I was finished.

I felt terrible. "Lying only delays things, Alice-Ann. Someone always finds the hole in a lie."

"I lied because I was scared. I knew at the time it was a stupid thing to do. Then I didn't know how to get out of it. At least you took care of that for me."

She sat up straight. "I need your help, Tori. I want you to find Richard's murderer for me."

"Me? Why?"

"Because Garnet thinks I did it, and he's so overworked and understaffed that I don't think he's going to waste much time looking any further than the end of his nose. Think of Mark, Tori. If I'm in jail, he won't have any parent left."

"What makes you think I can help?"

"You've been a crime reporter. You know what needs to be done."

"Look, Alice-Ann, reporting about a crime is a lot different from investigating one." But I was thinking—is it really so different? I knew the procedures and thanks to Garnet, I knew the how, when, and where—all I needed to do was find out who and why.

"I think I'll get dressed and head over to the castle. After all, I did promise LaVonna I'd come talk to her this morning. Maybe I can find out a thing or two."

Alice-Ann jumped up and hugged me. "I knew you'd do it," she squealed.

Chapter

12

No one was around when I climbed the steps to the terrace, so I walked the length of it, checking the flagstones for bloodstains. Not surprisingly, I didn't find any, but I did find an area to the right of the door that looked cleaner than the rest.

It was Rose, not LaVonna, who opened the castle door for me in answer to my ring. She looked flustered, certainly understandable under the circumstances.

She stared at my SURRENDER, DOROTHY T-shirt for a few seconds, then looked at my face. At first, I wasn't sure she knew who I was, but she finally said, "Oh, Victoria. Come in."

"Where's LaVonna?" I asked her, as she swung the front door closed.

Rose heaved a deep sigh of exasperation. "Can you believe she left last night? And me with this whole castle to clean up, and Michael and his crew making a mess with building scenery in the ballroom, and—"

"She left? Why?"

"Something about her sister being sick. I don't really know. She left a note on the kitchen table and just upped and left in the middle of the night. You can't depend on anyone these days."

Hardly a fair thing to say about someone who had been a faithful employee for more than thirty years.

"I thought she didn't have any family," I commented, remembering that yesterday she had said her family was "all."

"Oh, maybe it wasn't her sister . . . I don't know. Sylvia threw the note away. What difference does it make? She's not here. That's what matters."

The chiming of a bell filled the great center hall where we stood.

"There's that damn doorbell again. I could just wring her neck," Rose said between clenched false teeth. She threw open the front door. "Oh, hello, Luscious. All finished destroying my flower beds? You'll find your boss ensconced in the large drawing room, interrogating innocent bystanders as if we were a bunch of criminals or something."

The sergeant stepped inside and she banged the door shut behind him. I said to her, "I have something I promised to give to LaVonna. Do you mind if I just put it in her room?" I was counting on Rose's irritation distracting her from what I was really saying. It worked.

"Whatever, I don't really care. Her room is the first one down there." She flapped a hand in the general direction of a hall that led into a wing I hadn't been in before.

I ducked out before she decided she did care and quickly found LaVonna's room was the first door on the right facing the front of the building. More accurately, I should say rooms, since there was a small sitting room as well as a bedroom and bath. Everything looked in order in the sitting room. Comfortable chintz-covered chairs and a couch faced a marble fireplace, over which hung a hologram of a blond, blue-eyed Jesus. The only personal touch was a silver-framed, black-and-white photograph of a young man, wearing an old-fashioned black suit and a serious expression on his angular face.

The bedroom was also in order. Too much so, it seemed to me, for someone who'd had to rush out on a family emergency in the middle of the night. Even the bed was neatly made up. The only other furniture in the room was an ugly "waterfall" dresser, a small chair, and an enormous walnut wardrobe with mirrors on the fronts of the double doors.

What had prompted her flight? Had she murdered Richard MacKinstrie, then run off after his body was found? I remembered the little smile on her face when Garnet announced that Richard was dead. Though what her motive might have been was something I couldn't even imagine.

I pulled open one dresser drawer after another. All full of neatly folded clothes. What had she taken with her?

The wardrobe seemed to loom larger. Too many late-night horror movies, Tori. You're afraid you'll open it and a body will topple out. I took a deep breath, pulled the doors open, and jumped back. Nothing there but clothes. I breathed again.

Six cotton dresses hung from the rod. On a shelf above them was a soft-sided suitcase. On the floor was a row of shoes: three pairs of sneakers and one pair of sensible black dress shoes with two-inch heels. Next to the dress shoes, in the corner, was a black purse. It could have been a spare, but somehow LaVonna didn't strike me as someone who would have an extra pocketbook.

I took it out of the closet and emptied its contents on the neat white chenille bedspread. It held the typical mess found in most women's purses—crumpled tissues, loose coins, two toothpicks in paper wrapping from the Cross Keys Dinette, a package of artificial sweetener, breath mints, comb, mirror, paper clips, safety pins, a white button, a miniature sewing kit, colorless lip gloss, and a wallet.

The wallet contained about twenty dollars in bills and change, a Visa card, and LaVonna Hockenberry's driver's license. Wouldn't a person "on the lam" take that with her?

"What the hell do you think you're doing, young woman?" Rose stood in the door like an avenging fury.

I was so startled I dropped the wallet and watched the coins scatter on the rug. I tried to stammer out an excuse, but she wouldn't listen.

"Get out. Now. How dare you snoop around my house like this?"

She stood to one side as I scuttled past her. Before I left LaVonna's sitting room I looked back and saw Rose replacing the contents of the purse. From the back, with her red curls flouncing, she looked like an irate Raggedy Ann.

Since she was occupied for the present, I followed the sound of carpenters at work and found the ballroom, where Michael and six others were involved in a major construction project.

He saw me at once and waved me in. "Great, you did come. Briana, come meet Tori—she's the wonderful writer I told you about."

Briana Evans immediately put down her saw and came over to Michael's side. She was even lovelier in person than on TV. Her face was makeup free, and her blond hair was pulled back in a shiny, bouncy ponytail. She wore a fuchsia outfit, shorts and matching top, and her long, tanned legs didn't even have a single cellulite dimple. Who said life was fair? We chatted for a bit about her TV show, the play she was in at the Whispering Pines, and her role in the upcoming Mystery Dinner. Not a word about my book, but still, I couldn't help liking her, despite her self-centeredness.

Michael introduced me to the others, all Equity membership candidates, then explained, "We're building a screen to hide the doorway into the next room, since we have to use it as a combination pantry and dressing room."

One young man wiped the sweat from his forehead with a red bandanna and laughed. "And I chose acting because I thought it was a glamorous profession." He picked up something that looked like an oversize black gun and touched it to the half-built wooden structure.

Zing! Zing! Zing! In one second it shot three nails into the wood.

"What is that? It looks deadly," I remarked to Michael.

"It's a cordless, power framing nailer. Pretty safe to use—it has to be in contact with the wood when the trigger is pulled. Imagine how long it would take to put all these three-and-a-quarter-inch nails in by hand."

I decided to be open with him and tell him the real reason why I was there this morning. After I explained about Alice-Ann's fear that she was Garnet's only suspect, he told me he'd do anything he could to help.

"Did you hear Richard return Tuesday night? Or hear anything suspicious?" I asked.

"Sorry. I left as soon as everyone went home. Met Briana at the theatre and we spent the night at the former caretaker's cottage which we've converted to a rather cozy home."

"Were you here last night when the women got back from the clinic? Did you notice anything strange about LaVonna's behavior? Did you hear the phone ring anytime during the night?"

He laughed. "Yes. No. No."

Rose walked in and stopped dead when she saw me. "I thought I told you to get out."

"Come on, Mom. Tori's my friend. I know you're having a bad day. Let's go get a nice cup of tea. Then maybe you can have a nap. Briana will take care of things." Michael put his arm around her shoulder and led her out of the room.

I said my good-byes to the set-building crew and went down the hall to see whom else I could question. So far, I hadn't learned much.

I turned a corner and came upon Sylvia standing just outside the entrance to the large drawing room. She jumped when she saw me, so I figured she'd been eavesdropping. Since her hands were heavily bandaged, I inquired about her scratches.

She shrugged off my concern. "They're not nearly as bad as they look."

"I was surprised to see Michael's crew working in the ballroom. I thought for sure you'd cancel Rose Rent Day since the guest of honor is . . . deceased."

She clutched her throat in shock. "Cancel Rose Rent Day? Whatever gave you that idea? It's our town's most important celebration. People depend on tradition for stability. For continuity—one generation following another—all with the same values. Mark can take his father's place."

It was my turn to look shocked. "That's putting quite a burden on a child who just lost his father."

Sylvia again shrugged. All heart, this woman!

"Is anybody in there?" I asked, nodding toward the drawing room. I knew damn well there was, or she wouldn't have been lurking outside, listening.

"Twanya Tweedy is being interviewed by the chief," she told me.

"Twanya! What's she doing here?"

"I invited her to spend last night here. She was much too upset to go home. No matter what you think of her, she was very much in love with Richard."

"Speaking of last night, did you hear the phone ring for LaVonna?"

"No, my sister and I always take a sleeping pill before retiring. I wouldn't have heard the attack on Pearl Harbor."

"She didn't take her purse with her. Don't you think that's odd?"

Another shrug.

"How about Tuesday night? Did you notice anything strange about Richard? Maybe overhear him making plans to meet someone? Hear his motorcycle when he came back to the castle?"

She pursed her lips in annoyance. "Really, young lady, you are wearing out your welcome rapidly."

"Did you know what his research project was? Were you helping him with it?" I was trying to get as many questions in as possible. One thing I'd learned as a reporter was that an obnoxious barrage of questions sometimes got one or two unintended answers.

"Was it something to do with Edison?" I pressed on.

"Listen to me, Victoria. Yes, Richard was helping me with a research project, the subject of which is none of your damn business. I will continue to work on it, alone, until it is complete. You will learn what it is about when I present it at the annual meeting of the Lickin Creek Historical Society and not before. And that is quite all I intend to tell you. I'm going to go lie down. The past two days have been very distressing."

I was pretty sure that it was my question about Edison that triggered her response. And now I was more positive than ever that Alice-Ann's and my suspicions about Richard's stealing something of Edison's were right. Although I had no idea at all what a research project about Edison had to do with Richard's death or LaVonna's disappearance—if anything.

Twanya appeared in the doorway, tears streaming down swollen cheeks. If she hadn't been my best friend's worst enemy I would have felt real pity for her.

She grabbed Sylvia's arm, and the older woman grimaced with pain. "Oh, Mrs. Thorne, I'm sorry . . . like, I forgot your scratches. I'm going home now, you know. Like, thanks a lot for letting me stay last night."

Twanya turned to me. "I know you must hate me, but Richard and I were really in love, you know, and we were going to get married as soon as he could get a divorce. She was only interested in his money, not him, you know."

I couldn't help laughing. "He didn't have any money, Twanya. He was going to declare bankruptcy any day."

"That may be what *she* told you, but I worked for him. I'd certainly know if he was bankrupt, you know. Like, we spent every minute together that he could get away from Alice-Ann and her brat. He told me everything, you know."

"Did he visit you on the night he died?"

"I only wish he had. He'd still be alive." She started to cry again and ran down the hall, high heels clickety-clacking on the cold, stone floor.

As I watched her retreat, I became aware of the spicy scent of carnations. "Praxythea's coming," I said to Sylvia.

"How do you know?"

"Her perfume. It's very distinctive."

Praxythea seemed to materialize from the shadows. No clickety-clack here, just the soft rustle of her white silk dress as she glided toward us in Italian leather sandals.

"Good morning, Sylvia. Good morning, Tori. I understand the police chief wants to talk to me."

Garnet appeared in the doorway. "Praxythea. I was just going to ask someone to get you."

"I know," she said with a smile.

"Hi again, Tori," he said. "You can come in, too, if you want."

That was all the encouragement I needed. I followed Praxythea into the room, which gave me time to see that her back was bare to the waist, revealing flawless skin. She turned slowly before sitting on the couch, giving Garnet the opportunity to admire the view. I heard him catch his breath. She smiled and arched her back, just a little, just enough to allow her large, erect nipples to show through the soft, white material of her dress. She crossed her legs and dangled a dainty foot enticingly in front of him.

Garnet stared.

In comparison I felt like a chubby twelve-year-old in my jeans, sneakers, and silly Oz T-shirt. All that was lacking was a pimple on my chin.

Questioning Praxythea was an exercise in futility. She

was charming, beautiful, and gracious and imparted no useful information whatsoever. She had neither seen nor heard a thing and hadn't even had a hint from her friends in "the other world" that anything was amiss.

I noticed that she, too, had a few marks on her hands. "How did you get scratched?" I asked her. "I didn't see you there last night."

"How observant. I went there early this morning. I thought perhaps I might pick up some vibrations that would tell me what had happened. Unfortunately, I didn't receive any visions. May I go now?"

Garnet stood up and ushered her to the door. "You'll be around if I have any other questions?"

She touched his cheek with the finger that wore the enormous diamond and emerald ring. "I'll be here whenever you want me."

I'll bet, I thought.

At the door she turned to face me. "Bellodgia," she said cryptically.

"Huh?"

"You were wondering what kind of perfume I wear. It's called Bellodgia."

I had been wondering, but how did she know?

I stayed where I was until Garnet returned to his chair.

"I'm concerned about LaVonna's sudden disappearance," I told him. "I looked in her room a little while ago, and while I'm not familiar with her wardrobe, nothing looked disturbed. And she didn't take her purse with her."

Two parallel frown lines developed between his blue eyes. "I'll check it out. Thanks. But I wish you'd cut out the amateur detecting. This is murder we're dealing with, not a parlor game."

"Then, why did you let me sit in on the interview with Praxythea?"

He smiled, but his eyes were serious. "Maybe I was just

trying to keep you out of trouble. As long as I can see you, I know you're all right."

"That's very nice of you, Garnet. But I can't spend all day being baby-sat. I've got things to do. See you later."

As I left, I noticed that the crystal vase on the Jacobean table now held only two roses.

Chapter

13

Some supersleuth I was turning out to be. So far, this morning, my investigation had achieved the following results: (1) I'd learned that—maybe—Richard's research project dealt with Thomas Edison; (2) discovered no one there had seen or heard anything unusual—ever; (3) managed to seriously antagonize both of the Thorne sisters; (4) made Twanya cry; (5) learned the name of Praxythea's perfume; (6) found out Garnet was concerned about my safety. I decided to withdraw gracefully, before someone planted a boot on the well-filled seat of my jeans.

What next? Maybe while I was on a roll, I could go downtown and endear myself to others by accusing Father Burkholder and Judge Parker of murder. What the heck, why not include the doctor and the mayor? What I did decide to do was return to the library and see if I could learn something about Thomas Edison that your average eighth-grader didn't already know.

I thought I'd borrow Alice-Ann's VW, but as I left the castle, I spotted Twanya pulling out of the parking lot in an old green Oldsmobile. I flagged her down and asked for a ride. For a moment I thought she was going to say no, but she finally leaned across the seat and unlocked the passenger-side door.

As I got in, I suddenly wondered how LaVonna had left the castle last night. Did she have a car?

"Sorta," Twanya said in answer to my question. "She has her husband's old pickup, you know. Started keeping it here after he died."

"Where would she keep it?"

"In the carriage house."

"Would you mind . . . ?"

She jerked the wheel and made a U-turn on two wheels. Behind the castle, she slammed on the brakes in front of an elegant building with six wide, double doors.

"I'll just be a minute."

"Second one from the left."

I swung the door open and saw a black 1965 Ford pickup. Twanya was right behind me. "That's hers."

"Are you sure?"

Tiny lines appeared for a second in her smooth forehead. "Sure. Look at how the bumpers and trim is all painted black. Her church doesn't let people have shiny stuff on their cars, you know."

We got back into the car and drove to town. Since no one at the castle had heard the phone ring, and since LaVonna hadn't driven away in her truck, it was reasonable to assume someone had come to fetch her. That might explain why she had rushed out without her purse.

Twanya pulled into a metered parking spot on the square, in front of the library. Before I could thank her for the ride, she spoke. "I didn't kill him, you know. I loved him."

I realized then that she was the only person in Lickin Creek who was genuinely grieving for Richard.

"I know that, Twanya . . . and I'm sorry."

She smiled wanly and drove away.

I spun around when someone called, "Yoo-hoo, Tori. Come to see me?" Maggie was standing on the library steps, waving at me. "Come on in and have a cup of coffee. I haven't had a patron all morning."

It was heaven to be sitting in the peaceful library staff room, even if the coffee did taste as if it had been made a week ago. Instant does have its advantages—never very good—but never really bad, either.

"I've brought back that biography you sent out to Sylvia. She said she'd already read it."

Maggie sniffed. "If she'd come down out of that highfalutin castle of hers and pick out her own books, she wouldn't have that problem."

I pulled the book out of my purse and dropped it. "Whoops, sorry." It lay open on the floor. When I bent over to pick it up, I noticed that a paragraph had been highlighted with a yellow marker.

"Must be the sexy part," I joked as I scanned the paragraph.

Maggie giggled, but I wasn't laughing anymore. In fact, I was having trouble believing what I was reading. "Listen, Maggie, according to this book, Thomas Edison spent his later years building a machine to receive messages from the dead—he believed that people's bodies contained entities that lived forever—and could be contacted. It sounds like old Tom went loony-toony in his old age."

"I disagree, Tori," Maggie said with a small frown. "At one time the idea of an electric light or a phonograph or a talking moving picture would have seemed crazy—but he discovered them all."

I reread the paragraph, then flipped through the other pages. Nothing else was highlighted. *Entities.* Hadn't I heard that word just recently . . . somewhere?

Of course. At the séance. When Sylvia was so upset about not contacting a ghost. She'd used the word then—at the time it had sounded odd, not a term often used to refer to ghosts.

I recalled the black box with the glowing red light on top,

which had been in the corner and then wasn't. I'd thought it was a tape recorder. Now a crazy idea was coming to me. Really crazy. Maybe Edison had invented a machine to talk to the dead. Maybe Richard had found it in the same house where he'd found the antique Edison phonograph. Maybe I was going nuts.

"Maggie, you librarians know everything. Can you help me get more information about this idea of Edison's?"

She rubbed her hands together, and her eyes brightened. "Love to! Some 'real librarian' work, at last. I'll get on the phone and see what I can find for you. It may take a while. How about if I call you later today?"

I asked if Lickin Creek had a newspaper. It did, a weekly. Did the library have it on microfilm? Fat chance. But Maggie gave me directions to get to the office of the Lickin Creek *Chronicle*.

Outside, I saw Mrs. Seligman heading south, leaving a thin white trail of doughnut mix behind her. I caught up to her and relieved her of one of the heavy, leaking paper sacks. She arched her back and uttered an agonized groan.

"Damn that Sylvia," she complained. "As if I didn't have enough to do supervising the doughnut frying at three different locations, now she says she's not feeling well, and I've got to take over the Rose Rent rehearsal tomorrow. I don't know how I'm going to get everything done. She should have canceled the whole thing when Richard was found dead. It's absolutely tasteless to go ahead with a celebration under these circumstances. And to listen to our chief of police, you'd think I was personally responsible for losing that prisoner!"

"What prisoner?"

"One of the men from the county jail that they let out to cook doughnuts. We had beds set up for them at the synagogue, but Rabbi Weil lost count or something, and on Wednesday morning we noticed one was missing."

"Richard was murdered Tuesday night! Maybe he came

across the guy trying to escape and was killed by him."

"Impossible! Vernel Burkholtz wouldn't hurt a fly. He's a local boy. Known him all my life."

"Why was he in jail?"

"Assault and battery. He caught someone screwing around with his 1956 Jaguar."

She caught the look on my face. "I know what you're thinking, but beating up a punk you caught wrecking your car is a lot different from murdering somebody. Here's the Presbyterian church. If anybody else runs out of mix today, they'll just have to fetch it themselves."

I continued south for two more blocks, turned right, and found the Lickin Creek *Chronicle,* exactly where Maggie had said it would be. From the tarnished brass plaque on the front door, I learned that the narrow, brick building had been built in 1846. The waiting room stretched the entire width of the building, about twelve feet I guessed, and was furnished with a red vinyl couch with chrome arms and two matching chairs. An imitation-maple coffee table held an overflowing ashtray and a pink plastic vase full of dusty, plastic daisies.

From another room, somewhere, I heard Katharine Hepburn's raspy, clipped voice call out, "Come in, come in, whoever you are."

I followed the voice through the half-open door in the rear wall of the waiting room. Sitting at a rolltop oak desk was a woman of about fifty, with short, steel gray hair, and little half-glasses perched just below the crook of her nose. A cigarette dangled from a corner of her mouth.

"I'm P. J. Mullins, publisher, editor, reporter, photographer, advertising sales, circulation manager, and janitor of the Lickin Creek *Chronicle.* Nice to meet you, Tori Miracle. I've been trying to find time to read your book so I can call you for an interview. What's that white stuff all over your shirt?"

I explained about the doughnut mix as I tried, ineffectually, to brush it off.

"Forget it. Nobody's going to care. I'm assuming you dropped by to ask some questions about Richard MacKinstrie. Right?"

The grapevine never failed.

"Do you have your back issues on microfilm?"

She waved her right arm in an encompassing gesture. "See those shelves? I've got bound volumes going back to when my grandfather established this paper in 1899. The indexing is all up here." She tapped her forehead. "Ask and ye shall receive."

"I hate to take up your time."

"Don't worry about it."

I groaned inwardly. This was not going to be as easy as I had hoped. "First, there was a man who died sometime this year. Richard handled his estate sale—he was some kind of relative of Thomas Edison."

She leaped to her feet. I saw that she affected Hepburn's style of dress as well as her accent—pleated men's-style slacks, and a white cotton shirt, with a bandanna at the neck. She smashed out her cigarette butt, increasing the noxious effluvium rising from her overflowing ashtray, hauled down a book, and dropped it on a large table in the center of the room. With computerlike precision, she flipped through the pages and slammed her forefinger down on a photograph of a golf ball.

"Sorry about the quality of the picture. He was bald and kind of pale—no contrast there at all."

She wheeled a chair up to the table for me and returned to her work. I sat down and read the obituary of Marlin Kirkpatrick, Jr., Thomas Edison's second or third cousin by marriage on his mother's side. According to the article, one of Marlin's "most memorable memories" was of when he was just ten years old back in 1920, and his famous second or third cousin visited the family in Lickin Creek for several weeks. Burial was to be at . . . As he was the last of his immediate family, his estate would be sold at auction on March 15.

I looked through the next several issues of the paper and finally found the estate sale listed. It must have been a large sale because the auctioneer's list, in tiny print, covered half a page. I read it carefully, but there was no Edison phonograph listed—or anything else with Edison's name on it.

"Excuse me, P. J. Could I look at your 1920 volumes—I don't know what month."

"If it's that Edison visit you're interested in, it was in November. I'll get it for you."

She was amazing!

Famous Inventor Visits LC

November 3, 1920. Citizens of Lickin Creek are honored to have the well-known inventor Thomas Alva Edison in town this week. Mr. Edison is visiting the home of relatives, Mr. and Mrs. Marlin Kirkpatrick of Elm Street. Mr. Edison granted this reporter a brief interview while on a tour of the Lickin Creek Historical Society building. He stated his visit was a combination of business and pleasure.

Thomas Edison Ill

November 10, 1920. World-renowned inventor Thomas Alva Edison, who is visiting relatives, Mr. and Mrs. Marlin Kirkpatrick of Elm Street, has taken to bed with a serious illness. According to Dr. Jonas Burger, Mr. Edison is suffering from a severe form of brain fever. The citizens of Lickin Creek wish Mr. Edison a speedy recovery.

"I wonder what brain fever was?" I mused aloud.

"Could have been anything: meningitis, encephalitis, earache, sinus infection. In those days, though, it was often a euphemism for a nervous breakdown."

"He must have been in his seventies."

"Seventy-three. He died in 1931."

I recalled the highlighted passage in the Edison biography; Edison had spent his later years building a machine to contact the dead. What if . . . no, it was impossible . . . but, what if he had brought it to Lickin Creek to test it? What if. . . . he was looking for a genuinely haunted place to try it out, and his cousin had told him about the Underground Railway tragedy in the Historical Society building? What if . . . he had experimented with the machine there and, disappointed that it didn't work, had fallen into a depression—the "brain fever" mentioned in the article?

What if . . . he had experimented with the machine, and it *had* worked, and he'd developed the "brain fever" from fright, not depression?

The one what-if I was pretty sure of was that Edison had brought his machine to Lickin Creek and left it here. And Richard had found it in the Kirkpatrick house. The box I'd thought was a tape recorder was that same machine. And the séance was an effort to see if it worked.

But what did that have to do with Richard's death . . . or LaVonna Hockenberry's mysterious disappearance?

"LaVonna Hockenberry," I said. "The castle housekeeper. Would there be anything about her in your papers, other than her birth announcement?"

P. J. nodded and brought last year's book to me. She opened it near the center and walked away without saying a word.

The article was dated last August, and the headline was straightforward: "Local Farmer Hangs Self in Barn." The gist of the article was that LaVonna had returned home to the farm from her work at Silverthorne Castle to find her husband, Micah, had committed suicide by hanging. The farmer was reportedly despondent over a recent bad investment that had made it necessary for him to sell the farm, which had been in his family for generations. Mr. Hockenberry, the article said, worked part-time at Silverthorne as a gardener.

A recent bad investment! "P. J., what do you have about the Mexican oil-scheme that Richard was involved in?"

"Hmph! Too much. Start at the beginning of that volume."

She was right about there being too much. But some of it I was able to skim over. It had started last year with a meeting at the Holiday Inn Ballroom in January, where some "specially selected" people were offered an opportunity to make the investment of a lifetime. Richard had introduced a financial manager from New York who had presented a plan whereby the people there would form a co-op, all putting in an equal amount of money, which would then be invested in a "no-fail" Mexican oil discovery company. Apparently most of the guests had leaped at the chance to make a quick buck.

Several weeks passed before someone asked Richard why he hadn't received the company's promised prospectus. The following week, it was reported that the financial manager had left New York with no forwarding address. For several weeks, meetings of irate stockholders were held, the Borough Council met in emergency sessions, and Richard MacKinstrie spent a lot of time explaining that he had entered into business with the financial manager in "good faith" and had lost a lot of his own money, too.

At last I found what I was really interested in. The paper listed all the people who had been conned, including Rose Thorne and Micah Hockenberry. So, it turned out LaVonna did have a motive for murdering Richard after all—revenge for her husband's death.

I needed one more bit of information from the Lickin Creek *Chronicle*. At the séance, when Sylvia had been so upset about not finding a ghost, she'd said she thought there were always ghosts where there had been violent deaths. And then she mentioned the first Sylvia and her father. The first Sylvia's violent death I knew about. Her father's, I didn't.

"No problem," the efficacious P. J. said. "That would be thirty-three years ago. Quite a tragedy for the family."

The entire front page of the paper had been devoted to the accidental death of Michael Thorne. His many business accomplishments were listed, as well as his many civic and charitable works. He died of a broken neck suffered in a fall down the great stone stairway at Silverthorne Castle. He was survived by one daughter, Rose, and one grandson, Michael.

"One daughter! How could they have forgotten to put in Sylvia's name?"

"You won't find the answer to that question in the paper," P. J. said with a grin. "How about if I just tell you the gossipy stuff? All the news that wasn't fit to print."

She lit another cigarette, inhaled deeply, coughed three or four times, and began. "I was in my early twenties. Just started working for my father here at the *Chronicle*. We got a call from one of the maids at the castle that there'd been a terrible accident out there, and old Mr. Thorne was dead. I rushed right out and found it was true. The ambulance was just taking him away.

"I walked into total pandemonium. Sylvia was doing a mad scene from *Hamlet*. Rose had collapsed and was unable to speak, and poor little Michael was crying for his 'gramps' to come back. It took several volunteer firemen to wrestle Sylvia to the floor and hold her down long enough for the doctor to sedate her. It was quite a spectacle.

"By the time she was carted off to bed, more reporters had showed up, and a TV crew had arrived from Harrisburg. The family lawyer read a statement, written by Mr. Thorne the day before his death, in which he disowned Sylvia. She was never to be referred to as his daughter again. She was to leave the castle immediately, and she was completely disinherited.

"The attorney had come to the castle that day to get the documents signed, including the new will. After Mr. Thorne did so, he called Sylvia in and told her what he had done. That set her off according to the maids—screaming and breaking antiques. Rose told me later she had even pitched a vase through one of their priceless Tiffany windows.

"Mr. Thorne ordered her to go to her room and pack. She ran out of the library yelling, 'I could kill you for this.'

"Poor Mr. Thorne announced he was going to his room to rest. A few minutes later, he lay dead at the foot of the great staircase.

"Poor Sylvia blamed herself for his accident. Told everyone that it had been her fault because their terrible fight had upset him so much that he lost his balance and fell.

"Rose, of course, insisted that Sylvia stay. She's always treated her as though they had inherited equally from their father."

"Whew! That's some story. I wonder what she could have done to have angered her father that much?"

"We all wondered, but I don't suppose we'll ever know. It's particularly strange because just the year before she had made a brilliant presentation about the forgotten Rose Rent Festival and had been the leader of the movement to resurrect it. Her father was enormously proud of her. She was considered quite the heroine—even named Woman of the Year by the Chamber of Commerce.

"On the other hand, Rose disappeared for two years, then came home with an illegitimate baby. You'd think if anyone was going to get disowned, it would have been her."

P. J. stopped and squinted at her watch. "You'd better get moving, Tori. You don't want to be late for your date with Garnet."

"How did you know . . ." Oh, hell—why even bother to ask? Everyone knew everything in Lickin Creek.

P. J. turned back to her desk, crushed out her cigarette in the ashtray's detritus, and lit another. Tendrils of bluish smoke coiled around her head. Her cough followed me out the door.

After being in that dark, cool old building for so long, the heat rising from the brick sidewalk was scorching. I thought I might walk back to Alice-Ann's, but soon regretted that decision. I was a sorry, sweaty mess by the time a bearded man in black Mennonite clothing, driving a truck from "Aby's Abattoir," picked me up. He drove me directly to Alice-Ann's front door, where he left me with a tip of his flat, wide-brimmed straw hat. I didn't even ask how he knew where I was going.

The front door was unlocked, as usual. A habit of Alice-Ann's that really bothered me, especially now that there was a murderer running loose.

"Hi, I'm back," I called out. My voice echoed through the downstairs rooms. I knew immediately there was no one home.

I thought of my poor kitties. I'd ignored them all day. There was just time to take them outside for a short romp. As I approached the sunporch, I saw a note tacked to the door. Except it wasn't tacked but pinned there by a heavy-duty butcher knife.

I pulled it off and read:

CURIOSITY KILLS CATS

The letters were of different sizes, crudely cut from newspapers and glued on an ordinary sheet of white typing paper.

I threw open the door in a panic, afraid of what I might find. Both cats hoisted themselves to their feet, yawned, stretched, and came over to weave around my ankles. I fell on my knees and kissed them both. What kind of monster could threaten poor defenseless animals? But I already knew—the same kind of monster that could cold-bloodedly kill a man with a hammer!

I took them into the kitchen where I treated them to a saucer of milk. Alice-Ann and Mark came in the back door. They were talking, but stopped when they saw my solemn face.

"We went out to lunch, and then to the park. Mark, why don't you go upstairs and wash up?" Alice-Ann said.

As soon as he was gone, she grabbed my arm. "What's the matter? You look like you've seen a ghost."

I handed her the note.

"Unbelievable. Someone doesn't want you to find Richard's killer."

"Well, that 'someone' doesn't know me very well. I'll move heaven and earth, if I have to, to find out who threatened my little sweethearts. And you, Alice-Ann, you've got to start locking your doors."

"I'm not even sure I know where the keys are."

"Find them," I ordered. "I don't want to scare you, but this person is a murderer, and there are three people in this house, besides two cats, who could be in danger."

Alice-Ann slumped into a chair. "This is awful."

"I think it's going to get a whole lot awfuller," I told her.

Chapter

14

I took the cats up to my room, where they stretched out on the bed and watched me do some serious body work. Tonight, I was going to knock Garnet Gochenauer on his chauvinistic ass!

Thanks to Alice-Ann's offer to help myself to anything I needed, I bathed in jasmine-scented bubble bath, pumiced dead skin off my feet, removed ugly cuticles from around my nails, and polished all twenty of them with a delicate frosted-peach color. With a curling iron, I tortured my usual boyish cut into a fluffy pouf, and I accented my dark eyes with three shades of eye shadow, as recommended in the six-page instruction booklet that came with the makeup. Powder, blush, mascara, eyeliner, eyebrow pencil, control-top panty hose, my only pair of high heels . . . and there she was . . . tah dah . . . "Cosmo Girl"!

I had only one dress with me, pale blue rayon, slim skirted, sleeveless and cut low in front. Wearing only the panty hose, I put on the dress and took a critical look at myself in the full-length mirror. Better leave bralessness to Praxythea, I decided, taking off the dress. But just wait till I lose fifteen pounds, I thought, as I fastened the hooks on my good, sturdy underwire Bali and put the dress back on.

At exactly six, I heard something grind its way up the driveway, splattering gravel in every direction. I peeked out a side window and saw the biggest, reddest granddaddy of all monster pickup trucks parked outside. It had tires nearly five feet high and four big searchlights mounted on top of the cab. There were enough antennas sprouting to receive messages from Mars. Mounted on the rear end was a winch with a chain that could have anchored the *QE II*. All that was lacking was a huge German shepherd to stand snarling guard duty in the back.

I waited for the doorbell to ring, then opened the door to find Garnet standing on the top step, wearing jeans and a black-and-white version of the local plaid shirt.

My first date with Paul Bunyan.

His grin went from ear to ear. "You look wonderful! Really great!"

Just seeing that smile made all the hard work worthwhile. I picked up my purse and followed him out to his truck.

"Where's your German shepherd?" I asked innocently.

"At home," he said, not getting the joke. "How'd you know I had one?"

"Lucky guess."

My skirt was too tight for me to step up into the cab, so he put his two big paws on my rear end and gave me a shove that sprawled me head first on the seat. He had a good chuckle over that, while I struggled to regain my dignity.

It wasn't long before we were out of the town and driving along a country road through some of the loveliest scenery I had ever seen. Garnet acted as tour guide, pointing out the apple and peach orchards, the canyons of green corn, topped with waving golden tassels, and the harvested fields where the hay was left rolled in neat cylinders awaiting winter. Between farms were low walls built of piled-up gray stones, reminding me of Yorkshire, England. The barns were all much larger than the farmhouses and were decorated near their peaked roofs by open-work designs in the brick. Garnet explained that the openings were originally left for ventilation, and that it gradually became a source of pride for the craftsmen to come up with their own unique designs. Some of the barns were decorated with hourglass figures, several with stars, and one with a donkey.

In contrast to the large, whimsically decorated barns, the farmers' homes were mostly small, neat, two-story brick buildings, often with second-floor balconies, but definitely no-frills housing.

The road we were on rose steadily, and before long we were able to look down over the entire valley. Garnet pulled the truck over to the side of the road and stopped.

"We're on Rattlesnake Ridge Road," he told me. "It's one of my favorite drives. Want to get out and look at the view?"

"I can see it okay from inside the truck. Is it true that snakes can wrap themselves around a tire, slither through the engine, and get inside a vehicle that way?"

"Absolutely!"

I tucked my feet up under me, and he roared with laughter.

It really was a breathtaking view. From where we were, the houses and barns looked like the miniatures that hobbyists set out around their model railroads. We could even see the Borough of Lickin Creek, with its many church spires rising above the trees. And there were more shades of green down there in the farms and orchards than I ever dreamed existed.

"I've always had a dream," Garnet said, "of someday buying land up here and building a log home. The living room will have a two-story-high cathedral ceiling and a glass wall overlooking the valley. Can't you imagine how beautiful it would be to sit in front of a roaring fire, with a glass of wine, listening to *La Bohème* on the stereo, and looking down on a blanket of fresh, white snow? Or maybe you're not an opera lover?"

Garnet was deliberately showing me a side of his personality I hadn't seen before. One I liked a lot.

"Indeed I am an opera lover, and your dream home sounds heavenly. I hope it becomes reality for you soon."

From his smile, I could tell he liked my response.

We continued on to a tiny village, hardly more than a few buildings at a crossroads. According to the small white sign, with several rusty bullet holes in it, the village was named Rocky Mound Forge.

There were dozens of cars and trucks parked along the sides of both roads. Garnet pulled in behind a truck that could have been the twin of his, except it was blue instead of red.

After he amused himself by lifting me out of the front seat, he led me along a cracked sidewalk to the fire hall, where a plastic banner hung across the front announced: TONIGHT—SLIPPERY POT PIE AND HOG MAW—BENEFIT FIREMEN'S AUXILIARY.

"Garnet, is this where you're taking me for dinner?"

"Well, yeah. The fire halls always serve the best meals— real Pennsylvania Dutch home-cooking." My face must have shown the disappointment I felt because he added, "Remember where you are, Tori. Lickin Creek isn't exactly known for its gourmet restaurants."

As soon as we walked in, I knew I was seriously overdressed. Most of the women wore plain cotton dresses or polyester pants suits, and the men *all* had on jeans and plaid shirts. Whether they wore boots or high-topped sneakers seemed to be optional.

They sat on metal folding chairs at long tables covered with white paper. Every person in the room turned to stare at us as we entered.

After a moment of curious silence, there came a chorus of: "Hey, Garnet." "Yo, Chief. How's it hanging?" "Ten-four, good buddy."

Garnet returned the greetings: "Hey, Darnell." "Hi, Luke." "Yo, Marlin." "Got ya, Peck." "Prettier than ever, Roxy." "How's the baby, Myrna?"

It took about fifteen minutes to hail and yo our way to the food table.

A three-hundred-pound woman, with a disastrous permanent, lumbered around the counter to embrace Garnet. He almost disappeared in the rolls of blubber but didn't seem to mind at all.

"How's my favorite girl?" he asked.

She trilled that familiar girlish giggle that he so often managed to elicit from women. "Jest fine, Garnet. Gittin' married again, next month."

"Who's the lucky fellow this time, Velvet?"

"Phares McPherson. Know him?"

"Sure do. He's a good man. I wish you both all the best."

"At least he ain't a drinker like the last two." She smiled at me. "You the chief's girlfriend?"

Garnet broke in quickly, "This is a friend of mine, Tori Miracle. Tori's a writer, Velvet."

"No kidding? Do you write for them love-story magazines? I really like them . . . they're so true to life and all."

"No, I write books."

She was obviously disappointed, but patted me on the shoulder and said, "I've never been much for reading books. But that's okay, hon. You jest write what makes you happy."

"Thank you," I murmured weakly.

"Land sakes. Here I am a jawin' away and you'uns starvin' to death. I'll jest dish you'uns up the best dinner you ever et."

She proceeded to heap food upon two enormous white styrofoam platters. First there was a thick slab of some kind of mystery meat wrapped around stuffing. Over that she poured two huge ladles of gravy, the color of dandelions. That was joined by a heaping spoonful of sauerkraut and another spoonful of green beans, potatoes, and ham chunks. The whole thing was topped, like a sundae, with a bright red, peeled hard-boiled egg.

Garnet and I carted our overflowing plates to an empty

table in one corner. Velvet followed carrying two plastic bowls, which she plunked down in front of us.

"You'uns forgot your slippery pot pie," she said with a smile. "Now, when you'uns is ready for dessert, jest wave. I'll save yuh some shoofly pie."

Garnet had already cut his red egg in half, revealing the brilliant yellow yolk in the center.

"Why is it red?" I asked.

"Beet juice," he said as he stuffed half the egg in his mouth. "Try it. It's good."

I cut a small slice and took a bite. He was right. It was good. I decided to be brave and try the meat, after first scraping off the congealing yellow gravy. It was sort of grizzly and greasy, but I did like the stuffing in the middle.

The slippery pot pie was strange to my tastes. I think it had some chicken in it and some hunks of slimy boiled dough. "Are you going to tell me what I'm eating?" I asked, taking another mouthful of meat and stuffing.

"Hog maw."

"What's that?"

"Just your basic pig's stomach, stuffed and baked."

The food in my mouth refused to go down. I tried to chew it some more, but finally gave up and spit it, surreptitiously, into my napkin.

Garnet didn't notice. He was eating his with obvious enjoyment. "It's a local favorite. On the nights it's served at the Moose, you can't get in."

You can spare me the pleasure, I thought.

Velvet descended upon us bearing steaming mugs of black coffee and about a quarter of a pie for each of us.

I took a bite of the pie, found it much too sweet, and pushed the plate to one side. Garnet finished his and started on mine.

"Garnet," I asked, "how is the murder investigation going?"

"You mean Richard's murder?"

"Of course I mean Richard. Are there any others?"

He stuffed a forkful of pie into his mouth and shook his head. "About as well as can be expected, I guess."

"Meaning . . . you don't know who did it, right?"

He shrugged noncommittally.

"Something happened this afternoon that frightened me." I reached in my purse and pulled out the threatening note that had been left on the sunroom door. Something made me pause as I started to hand it to him.

"What's the matter?"

I sniffed the paper. "I was too upset to notice it earlier, but it smells like Praxythea's perfume."

Garnet held it up to his nose and inhaled deeply. "I don't smell anything."

"I have a very sensitive nose."

He read the note with a frown on his face. "How could anyone get in the house?"

"Alice-Ann doesn't lock her doors. She doesn't even know where the keys are."

"Of all the damn fool things . . . you bolt those doors from the inside tonight. I'll send Lucy Lockit out tomorrow to put new locks on."

"Lucy Lockit? Fowler's Flowers. Uriah's Heap. Did anyone every tell you this town suffers from terminal cuteness?"

He nodded. "My ex-wife. Just before she went back to Philadelphia."

"I didn't know you'd been married."

"Right out of law school. She promised to take me for better or for worse, but not for Lickin Creek. She's married to another lawyer now and lives on the Main Line. We're all a lot happier."

"Children?"

"One boy. He's eleven. Nice kid, I think. Don't get to see him as often as I'd like."

"Sorry. It seems I have a talent for asking you irritating questions."

"Don't worry about it," he said with a grin. "I'm beginning to enjoy it. But seriously, to get back to what's important, you have got to leave the detective work to me. It's obvious someone is worried by something you've done. I don't want you to get hurt."

"I have an idea. Let's list all the suspects and their motives, the way they always do in mystery novels."

"It's reassuring to know you listened to every word I just said."

"Oh, come on. Humor me. You know damn well you don't know who murdered Richard. What harm will it do to try and figure it out together?"

He shook his head as if I were a hopeless case, but I could see laugh wrinkles form around his eyes. In a few years, he might be all crinkly like Clint Eastwood—which wasn't bad. He pulled a pen out of his shirt pocket. A fountain pen! He was beginning to earn my respect.

"Here," he said, handing me the pen. "Make your list."

"Got any paper?"

"Use the tablecloth."

I wrote a large number one on the paper. "Who goes here?"

"The first and most logical suspect is always the spouse."

"Come on, Garnet. You know Alice-Ann's not a murderer."

"She's number one, until I'm proved wrong. She had a motive. He was running around on her, spent all their money, made her life a living hell. And she left the house that night and then lied about it. Motive plus no alibi equals murder."

I reluctantly wrote down Alice-Ann's name.

"Number two," I said as I wrote the number on the table. "Tori Miracle."

"What?"

"If you were alone in the house, you have no alibi either. And you've never made any secret of your dislike for Richard. You and Alice-Ann were pretty close until he came between you. And you were overheard, at the castle, threatening Richard—something about if it happened, it wouldn't be an accident."

"Me? Threaten Richard? I don't know what you mean. Oh, hell! Yes, I do. But I was threatening him with embarrassment, not murder. I didn't think anyone heard me. Damn grapevine! You mean you were serious earlier when you suspected me of being jealous . . . of having a . . . a relationship with Alice-Ann? I can't believe you'd be sitting here having dinner with me if you thought that."

"I told you earlier, if I can see you, I know you're not in trouble. Or causing it."

"This is ridiculous. If you knew either one of us, you'd know that numbers one and two should be scratched right off this list."

"Tori, this suspect list was your idea. Now stop being so huffy. Let's get to number three."

"Fine!" I wrote Garnet Gochenauer in big black letters.

"Do you want to explain that?"

"Sure. Maybe you used to be sweet on Alice-Ann before she got married. Maybe you wanted to get rid of Richard so you could have a chance with her."

"That's asinine!"

I smiled. "No more so than numbers one and two. Shall we go on to number four? How about that escaped convict? What's his name?"

"Vernel Burkholtz."

I wrote it down. "Maybe, while he was escaping, he encountered Richard on the road and killed him to keep from being sent back to jail."

"Wrong, Tori. Vernel Burkholtz walked out of the synagogue and across the street into the AMVETS, where he proceeded to get stinking drunk in front of about fifty people. He turned himself in this morning, with a hell of a hangover and a perfect alibi."

So much for Vernel.

"Let's get to my favorite suspect," I said. He watched as I wrote Praxythea's name next to number five.

"Mind telling me why?"

"Does the name Marlin Kirkpatrick, Jr., ring a bell?"

"Of course. He died earlier this year. What's he got to do with this?"

"I did a little research today, at the library and the newspaper. Marlin was a relative of Thomas Alva Edison, and he remembered Edison visiting his family back in 1920. I have good reason to believe that Edison came here to experiment with a strange invention, which he left here in Lickin Creek. And I think it's something that Praxythea would kill for . . . did kill to own."

"And just what was this strange invention no one's ever heard of before?"

"A machine to communicate with the dead."

His burst of laughter raised eyebrows all around the room.

I told him about the highlighted paragraph I'd seen in the book, mentioning Edison's attempts to talk with the dead. And Richard and Sylvia's sudden interest in Edison after Richard had been involved in selling Marlin Kirkpatrick, Jr.'s estate. And that I believed Edison had brought the machine to his cousin's house and left it there. And that Richard had found the machine there and stolen it to use as a research project to earn membership in the prestigious Historical Society.

"Richard told me, and I believe he was right, that he had discovered something that would make him famous. Now, Sylvia already is established as the local society leader and member of the Historical Society, not to mention her position as founder of the modern Rose Rent Day, so she really doesn't need any more glory. I think Richard enlisted her help because he realized he couldn't handle the research himself, and I think she agreed to help him because she enjoyed playing the part of the local history expert."

Garnet finished my pie. "I still don't see where Praxythea fits in, or why you think she murdered Richard."

"They brought Praxythea in to help them. She recognized an opportunity to become world famous. Think about it, Garnet. She's already got some national recognition as a psychic who helps police solve crimes. If she could produce a machine that can communicate with the dead—whether or not it works—it would make her career. She'd be right up there with—uh—Jeanne Dixon or Peter Herkos or—"

Garnet interrupted. "Why would someone in her position take a chance on ruining an already successful career by committing murder?"

I shrugged. "Why does anybody commit murder? Most people would never consider it to be an option, no matter how much they had to gain; others are willing to do anything to get what they want.

"Remember, I told you I saw a suitcase on Richard's motorcycle? At least I thought it was a suitcase then, now I'm not sure. I think I saw it again at the castle the night of the séance. It was stuck away in a dark corner of the library, and I thought it was a tape recorder. After the children came in and told us they'd found a body, there was a lot of confusion. Later, the case was gone. Nobody else admitted having seen it. I think Praxythea hid it because she knew it would be incriminating."

Garnet looked skeptical. I couldn't blame him. It had all seemed a lot more credible in my mind, unspoken. "How do you think she got the machine?" he asked.

"I overheard Sylvia tell Richard to 'get here with it early' because she wanted 'it' set up before the others arrived for the séance. She told me it was a tape recorder, but I believe 'it' was the Edison machine. After the fight with Alice-Ann, I think Richard decided to go ahead and take the machine over to the castle that night."

"And I suppose you think Praxythea met him at the

door, clobbered him with Alice-Ann's hammer, and stole his discovery."

"She's the only one with a motive."

"It's possible, I guess, but I have a hard time with it. I've worked with Praxythea. The first time she came to Lickin Creek was when she saw a picture of a missing girl in a New York paper. She said she'd had a vision of the girl lying in the dark near the edge of running water. She described the land-fill near Pig Run so accurately that we drove there immediately and started digging. Unfortunately, she was right. We found the girl with a bullet hole in her head, buried under a couple of tons of trash."

I groaned with exasperation. "Garnet, that stuff about 'lying in darkness at the edge of running water,' that's exactly how she described the location of the lost diamond, Sylvia's Star. It's probably a standard line she uses to impress suckers. For heaven's sake, there was even a novel written back in the thirties called *The Edge of Running Water*. It was about a man who was trying to prove immortality and invented a machine to communicate with the souls of the dead. She probably doesn't think anybody would remember it. And don't you find the subject matter of that book an odd coincidence, in light of what I've told you about Edison's invention?"

"Despite what you say, Tori, she did find that girl."

"Sure. And if we go back and dig in that trash dump for the next twenty years, maybe we'll turn up Sylvia's Star, too. She just made a lucky guess. If you hadn't found the body there, she'd have had you digging up every creek bed in the country before she threw up her pretty hands and said there was an 'error' in her information source. Look at all the free publicity she got!"

Garnet shook his head. "You're basing your whole theory on a completely implausible supposition—that Edison did build this machine and that he left it here. Even more implausibly—that Richard found it. What evidence do you have that this machine ever existed?"

"After I read about it in the book that Sylvia asked me to return to the library, I went to the newspaper. I found an article that said Edison had visited your haunted Historical Society building while he was in town—'combining business and pleasure.'" Even as I spoke, I knew I sounded like an idiot. It had all seemed so logical when I was at the newspaper office.

"I think we ought to go on to number six," Garnet said. "There were a lot of people at the castle that night. All of them claim to have gone to bed right after the party broke up, which means none of them really have alibis. Put down Michael Thorne."

I wrote Michael's name down. "Why?"

"Revenge. Thanks to Richard, Michael is no longer going to inherit a castle or the very valuable property around it."

"Michael told me about that. Naturally, he's upset about it, but I can't picture him murdering anyone . . . any more than I could picture his mother doing it."

"Put Rose down for seven."

"Rose! You're nuts."

"She was there. She had a motive. Put her down."

I did. "Then Sylvia has to be number eight for the same reasons."

Garnet shook his head. "Sylvia isn't in line to inherit the property. There's no motive there."

"So you think Rose did it?"

"No. I just wanted to show you how foolish this whole exercise is. Rose looks perfectly normal, but I happen to know she has cancer and has only a few months to live. She's very weak from chemotherapy—wouldn't have the strength to bash anyone's head in. And how would either she or Sylvia manage to ride the motorcycle down the driveway to where we found it?"

"At last, there's something I know that you don't. Richard was giving all the old ladies in the castle motorcycling lessons. He thought it was a hoot."

Garnet scratched his forehead. "Motorcycle lessons. Now I've heard everything! Anybody else you want to put on the list?"

I nodded. "Number nine: the missing LaVonna Hockenberry."

"What's her motive?"

"Same as Michael's—revenge. Her husband killed himself because of Richard and his oil scam. The night we went to the séance, she asked me to come back the next morning because she had something she wanted to talk to me about. Maybe she planned to confess, then lost her nerve after the body was found and took off instead."

Garnet stopped me. "Which reminds me, Tori. I checked out LaVonna's room. Her purse was not there, in the wardrobe or anyplace else."

"But I saw it. Someone must have taken it. Rose was putting stuff back into it the last time I saw it."

Velvet interrupted us. "Everything okay? You'uns ready for some more coffee?" She poured it without waiting for an answer. She noticed the writing on the tablecloth, but if she was curious about it, she didn't ask any questions.

Garnet took a sip, then added cream and sugar. "You did more than just a little research today. Seems to me you know almost as much about the people in this town as I do."

"There are others, too." I was on a roll. "Twanya Tweedy should definitely be on the list. Maybe they had made plans to meet later that night at the castle—they had a fight and she killed him."

"Come off it, Tori. You're talking about the only person in Lickin Creek who liked the bastard."

"I know that, but love can turn to hate very quickly. Especially if he told her he was dumping her for someone else. He wasn't exactly known for his fidelity."

"Okay. Who's next on your character-assassination list?"

I slowly wrote down the number eleven, but I was running out of ideas. "The Seligmans were there. He seemed to have some sort of gripe about being cheated out of some prime real estate."

"Tori, if that were a motive, we could include half the people in town. Why not put down Father Burkholder? He was furious with Richard when he lost the chance to buy the property next to his school."

"I think we're both getting squirrelly, Garnet."

Number eleven was still blank.

I thought for a moment, then wrote down Mayor Somping. Garnet abruptly sat up straight in his chair and stared at me sharply. "What made you put the mayor down?"

"Because he's no more a member of the Laotian royal family than I am. When I spoke to him in Lao, he answered in the vernacular of the commoners."

Garnet's jaw dropped as his eyes widened in surprise. "You speak Lao?"

"I just said I did, didn't I?"

Did I detect a faint glimmer of admiration in those blue eyes? "You're right, you know," he told me. "The whole bit about being an escaped prince was something Somping dreamed up to impress Americans. And it worked. Without that phony title, he'd be lucky to have a job as janitor. Somehow Richard found out and had been blackmailing him for several years."

"Blackmail! I knew Richard was a slimeball, but I never thought he was that low. Does the mayor have enough money to make blackmail worthwhile?"

"Richard didn't ask for money. He got special treatment when he was applying for zoning changes to make some property he was selling worth more. He also demanded that the mayor turn a blind eye to a lot of building-code violations."

"Maybe we should move the mayor up to number one," I said.

"Somping came to me and admitted this on his own. He's deeply ashamed of himself. I spoke to Richard several months ago and told him the blackmail would stop immediately—or else! That took care of the problem."

He drained his coffee cup and frowned. "We've certainly been successful at destroying the reputations of half the leading citizens of the town, but there's something else I bet you don't know."

"What's that?"

"You saw Richard's body. Did you get a good look?"

"I saw enough."

"Do you remember where his head wound was?"

I shuddered, remembering his one eye, his left eye, staring at the sky. "The whole right side of his face was smashed. I get it! He was most likely hit by someone left-handed. A right-handed person would naturally have hit him on the left side of his face."

"Good for you. This doesn't mean it couldn't have been done by a rightie, but it gives us somewhere to start. Now, how many of our suspects are left-handed?"

"I don't have any idea."

"I do. I checked everyone out while I was interviewing them. Everyone in the Thorne family is left-handed, talk about your genetic quirks. So is Praxythea. I don't know about LaVonna, and nobody could remember. Of course, that doesn't necessarily mean any of them did it. There are a lot of lefties in the world."

"Fifteen percent of the population."

"You should know," he said smiling as he stared at the pen in my left hand.

I tried to shift his attention away from me. "This just makes me more sure than ever that it was Praxythea."

"How about considering our '92 presidential candidates, Bush, Perot, and Clinton, if we're going to suspect all the lefties in the world?"

Something beeped and we both jumped. Garnet reached

into his pocket and pulled out one of those annoying little electronic devices that have become status symbols in so many professions.

"Excuse me, office calling." He disappeared into the kitchen in search of a phone, while I sat there doodling on the tablecloth, trying to ignore the curious stares of the other diners.

When he returned, his face was serious. "We have to go," he said as he pulled out my folding chair.

He took my arm and guided me from the building. No time was spent in saying good-byes.

As he was boosting me into the truck, Velvet came running out of the fire hall, waving what looked like a white flag of surrender. "You'uns forgot your tablecloth. I thought it might be important when I saw all them names on it."

I wondered if I'd be saying "you'uns" by the time I got back to New York.

"Thanks, Velvet," Garnet said, taking the greasy sheet of paper from her. "Love ya."

"Love ya, too. Hope the judge is all right."

Garnet clenched his eyes shut and rubbed them with his fists. "How'd you know about the judge?"

"Jest heard it on the scanner."

Garnet jerked the monster truck onto the road, made a wide U-turn that threw me up against the door, and headed back toward Lickin Creek.

"What happened?" I asked.

"Judge Parker. He's been killed."

"Oh my God. Was it . . . ?"

"I'm afraid so. Murder."

Chapter

15

Several cars and an ambulance were already parked in front of Judge Parker's large, turn-of-the-century house, and the inevitable crowd of curious onlookers stood in small groups in the street and on the brick sidewalk. This time Luscious had remembered to put up the yellow police-barrier tape.

We pushed our way through and were met by Luscious, reeking of brandy, who led us into an elegant, high-ceilinged, blue-and-gold living room. The judge had been sitting in a leather chair at his desk. He'd fallen facedown on his green blotter. The ugly black stain on the blotter was blood, not ink. His right hand clutched a long-stemmed American-beauty rose. Behind him an open door led into a hallway. A large, formal dining room adjoined the living room.

Meredith Jones was already there and had declared the man dead.

Garnet asked him, "Any possibility it's a suicide?"

Meredith slowly shook his head. He looked sad. "He's got three nails driven into the back of his neck, right through the medulla oblongata. At least he died instantly, thank God."

Garnet stared at Meredith in disbelief. "Nails? How on earth could someone just sit there and let someone hammer a nail into the base of their skull?"

"Battery-operated framing nailer," I told him. "I saw one in use at the castle this morning. They were building a set for the Mystery Dinner."

Garnet threw the doctor a questioning look.

Meredith nodded. "Quite likely, she's right. I've seen some nasty accidents caused by those things. They shoot nails with the power of bullets."

"Wouldn't he have heard someone come up behind him?" I asked.

"Not if he had his hearing aid turned off." Meredith checked the judge's ear. "Yup, it's off. It usually was. He always said people were too boring to listen to."

"Who found him?" Garnet asked.

Luscious answered, "Tammy Zook. The Plain woman does his laundry. She was bringing his shirts back and got worried when he didn't answer the doorbell. Said she always came at the same time, six-thirty on Thursday night, and he was always here to pay her. She tried the door, found it locked, and walked around on the porch to see if the kitchen door was open. It wasn't, so she peeked in some windows to see if maybe he'd fallen down, and that's when she saw him lying here. She went across the street to Mrs. O'Brien's house and called me."

"So all the doors were locked. How about the windows?"

"Everything was locked and bolted, Chief. I checked everything."

"Great—a locked-room murder! Just what we need," Garnet said sourly.

Nothing had been touched. Luscious had zealously guarded the house until his boss showed up, and now they set to work examining every inch of the room, carefully and methodically.

I had no desire to remain in that room of horror, so I went

into the dining room to wait. Time passed slowly, and I wandered around looking at the paintings on the walls and the Canton china in the large corner cabinet. I opened a door and found a small pantry with another door leading into the kitchen. The strong odor of mold drifted through the cellar door, which was opened just a crack. The basement was as black as a starless night and smelled of evil.

I didn't really want to go down there, but curiosity got the better of me. A string was dangling in front of me, and when I pulled it, the stairwell lit up. With light, it was less frightening, and I went down. I found just what I thought would be there, an old brick archway with a wooden door set in it, and a ladder that led down into a cave.

I went back upstairs and waited in the dining room. After a while, Luscious went outside to question the bystanders, and I heard Garnet snapping pictures. A half hour or so went by, then he opened the front door and gave a signal to the ambulance men, who came in with a stretcher and carried out the remains of Judge Parker.

Garnet, Luscious, and Meredith joined me in the dining room. I took Garnet by the hand and showed him the open basement door.

"There's an open cave entrance down there," I told him.

He told me to wait while he went downstairs. When he came back up, he cautioned me not to mention it to anyone else. We rejoined the others in the dining room.

"Anybody out there see or hear anything?" Garnet asked.

Luscious opened his notebook and flipped a few pages. "Mrs. O'Brien, who lives across the street, said when she went out on the porch about five o'clock to get her paper, she saw the judge get his and he waved to her. She went back outside to work in her garden at six. She likes to do yard work then, ' 'cause it's cooler.' Anyway, she said she saw Rose Thorne coming out of the house about then."

"Did she know it was Rose Thorne for sure?"

"Yes, sir, Chief. She even described her." He read from the notebook, " 'Rose came out of the house looking very upset. I think she was crying because she had a handkerchief out and was wiping her eyes. She was wearing one of those pink dresses she likes. I recognized her right away because of that awful red hair. I don't know why she doesn't get a hair-dresser who knows something about coloring hair.' "

"Sounds like a positive ID," Garnet acknowledged. "Did Mrs. O'Brien hear anything from the house? What the hell does a power nailer sound like, anyway?"

"Zing, zing, zing," I said, keeping a straight face.

Luscious went on, "Nobody heard nothing, Chief. But it seems the power company was out cutting the tops off trees, and there was so much noise no one could hear anything except them chain saws."

"Did you talk to the power company crew?"

"Yes, sir, Chief. They all saw an elderly red-haired woman coming out of the house. Uriah's Heap picked her up while she was walking down the street. They didn't see no-body else go in or come out."

I shook my head in disbelief. "Rose just can't be a murderess."

Garnet said, "We already agreed she had the motive and opportunity to kill Richard."

"Wrong. You suggested it. I didn't agree."

"And, she is left-handed."

"So are lots of people," I protested weakly.

"I think I'd better go talk to Rose."

Our little procession, Garnet and I in his red truck, Lus-cious in the baby blue patrol car, and Meredith in his black Mercedes, arrived at Silverthorne in about twenty minutes. Praxythea, wearing black silk pajamas and an emerald green robe, opened the castle door in response to our ring. She was obviously surprised to see the four of us standing there.

"What is it?" she asked.

Garnet spoke. "We need to see Rose, please."

"I think she's in bed, Garnet."

"Then you'll have to get her up, Praxythea. You know I wouldn't do this if it weren't important."

Sylvia joined us in the great hall. She had on a long-sleeved flannel nightgown and a tartan wool robe.

"What's the meaning of this, Garnet?" Sylvia asked imperiously.

"I'll tell you when Rose comes down. Is there anybody else here?"

Praxythea answered, "Just Michael and Briana. They decided to stay here instead of their cottage because Rose wasn't feeling well."

"Get them down here, too," Garnet ordered.

From his tone of voice, Praxythea seemed to realize it was best not to argue and ran up the stone stairway to the second floor, presumably where the bedrooms were located.

"Let's go into the library," Garnet said when they had all come down. Michael and Briana were in matching white cotton pajamas and robes, Rose in a pink satin negligee that had seen many better days.

As they followed him down the gloomy hallway, I ducked into the large drawing room and flipped on the lights. As I expected, there was only one rose left in the crystal vase!

I turned the lights off and left, reaching the library just as Sylvia turned on a lamp. Praxythea had gone a little heavy on the Bellodgia tonight. The spicy perfume was making my eyes water.

I whispered in Garnet's ear that another one of the roses was missing. He nodded slightly to show that he heard me but made no comment.

Garnet told them to sit down, and they did. Everyone looked sleepy and confused. According to the ormolu clock on the mantelpiece, it was well after midnight.

Garnet jumped right in with both feet. Looking at Rose,

he asked, "Miss Thorne, you visited Judge Parker this afternoon, did you not?"

She pressed both hands to her mouth in surprise. "How did you know?"

"You were seen coming out of his house. Can you tell me why you went there?"

"I'd rather not."

"Why?"

"It's personal, Garnet."

"What condition was the judge in when you left, Miss Thorne?"

"Why do you keep calling me Miss Thorne, Garnet? We've been on a first-name basis for years."

Garnet said patiently, "Please, just answer my question. What was his condition?"

"He was fine. My God, Garnet, are you telling me he's sick?"

"I wish he were, Miss Thorne. Judge Parker is dead. He's been murdered."

Gasps of shock and dismay came from everyone in the room.

"Poor old man," Michael said. "Other than boring us to tears for years, he never harmed anyone."

Rose whimpered.

Garnet continued, "Now Miss Thorne, please tell me why you went to the judge's house and what you talked about while you were there."

Rose burst into tears, opened her mouth as if to speak, took a deep breath, and slid off her chair, unconscious.

Meredith was at her side instantly, feeling for her pulse.

"Way to go, Garnet," he said angrily. "She's just fainted. I'm putting her to bed, and no one is going to talk to her until I say it's all right." Rose's eyes fluttered open, and she struggled to a sitting position. After a few minutes she was able to leave the room leaning on Meredith's arm.

Garnet looked miserable, and Sylvia took advantage of

his discomfort to assume charge. "We have a lot of work to do tomorrow, cleaning, rehearsing downtown. I think we should all go to bed."

I gasped in disbelief. "You mean you're going to go ahead with the Rose Rent celebration and the Mystery Dinner after all this?"

"Judge Parker would have wanted it that way. After all, he was the president of the Historical Society. Preserving local tradition was the most important thing in his life. More important than personal relationships or . . ." Sylvia began to cry.

"Oh, hell. You're going to find out sooner or later, so I might as well tell you now," she said. "Judge Parker was Michael's father!"

"I'll be damned," Garnet blurted out. "How did they keep that quiet all these years?"

"It was Rose's wish that no one ever know," Sylvia said.

"She never even told me," Michael said sadly. "I never had a chance to know my own father." He let his head drop and covered his eyes. Briana gently placed a hand on his knee.

"I have to ask everyone—where were you this afternoon from five until six-fifteen?" Garnet asked.

"I was rehearsing my cast," Michael said, not looking up.

Briana said she was at the theatre, appearing in a matinee.

Sylvia had gone to bed early in the afternoon with a headache and slight fever. "I still feel sick," she said.

Praxythea had been cooking and cleaning all afternoon. "I boiled a ham for tomorrow's rehearsal lunch and did some dusting."

Garnet spoke gently. "Michael, I hate to ask anything of you right now, but I need to see the framing nailer Tori said your people were using earlier today."

Michael, eyes moist, nodded and led the way to the ballroom. At Garnet's request, I went with them to identify the nailer. It wasn't there. We searched every inch of the room, even lifting every piece of wood. Nothing.

"I don't understand this," Michael said. "We wrapped up here around noon so we could rehearse, and I told the crew to leave everything right here. I can't imagine where it could be. Why do you need it?"

Garnet told him how the judge had been killed. It prompted another outburst of emotion from Michael. Briana, after a nod from Garnet, led her husband upstairs.

"That's it for tonight," Garnet announced to Praxythea and Sylvia, the only two left. "I'll be back tomorrow. Come on, Tori. I'll take you home."

When we pulled up in front of the cottage, Alice-Ann jerked the door open and waited for us to come in.

"You shouldn't open that door unless you know who's on the other side of it," Garnet told her.

"I know the sound of your truck. You two don't look very happy. Didn't you have a good time?"

We sat down in the living room and Garnet told her of the judge's murder.

"You were right," Alice-Ann said to me. "Things *are* getting a whole lot awfuller. I'll get us some herbal tea. It always makes me feel better."

Fred and Noel, no longer imprisoned in the laundry room, rubbed up against Garnet's legs. He absentmindedly scratched Fred under the chin. "I don't usually like cats, but these are kind of cute."

"The rose in the judge's hand—it came from the castle, didn't it?" I asked.

"Looks like it," he said. "Which means it was probably someone from the castle who killed him. Or someone who's been to the castle—which could be just about anybody. I can't figure out why the murderer left the roses with his victims."

"Or *her* victims," I interjected.

"Okay, or her victims. And I can't figure out why any one

of those people at the castle would want to kill the old man. He was the exact opposite of Richard. Didn't have an enemy in the world, that I know of."

"I'm beginning to think it was Rose, after all," I said. "Maybe she hated him for getting her pregnant."

"It's been thirty-five years. You'd think she'd have done something a lot earlier."

He stopped speaking when Alice-Ann entered bearing a tray with a teapot and three unmatched mugs. She poured and we all sipped the chamomile brew.

Alice-Ann stretched and yawned broadly, too broadly. "I think I'll leave you two to clean up. I'm really worn-out."

We heard her footsteps on the stairs, then the bedroom door closing.

"Before you ask," I said, "we were both here from about four-thirty until you picked me up at six. Now, back to Rose—you told me earlier she just found out she has only a short time to live. Maybe she's cleaning house, so to speak, taking revenge on people who have hurt her, like the father of her child who deserted her when she needed him. And Richard, who caused her to lose the property that meant so much to her."

"Perhaps, but it just doesn't feel right to me. Maybe I'm just tired. I spent all morning questioning half the people in town about Richard's murder. This afternoon I thought I'd be able to hole up in the office and get some paperwork done, but at two o'clock Mrs. Ferguson called to report someone stole a potted palm off her porch. At three o'clock, two fire trucks, one from Chickentown and the other from Sink Hole Township, took a shortcut through town on the way to a barn fire and collided in the square, and at four, there was a fight at Daisy's Bar and Laundromat. People expect me to be on duty twenty-four hours a day with only Luscious to help—and hell, if they gave Olympic medals for incompetence, he'd win a gold. Sometimes I wonder why I don't say the hell with it and go back to Philadelphia."

I touched his hand. "Because you love these people. And they love you. I could see that at the firehouse tonight. They need you. And, Garnet, being loved and needed by someone is the most important thing in the world."

He smiled and stood up. "That was an awfully nice thing to say. Somehow I didn't expect you to be so sensitive."

"There's a lot you don't know about me."

I walked with him to the door. "You forgot something," I said.

"What's that?"

"You were going to show me your cave maps."

He groaned. "Not now, Tori. I'm way too tired."

"Then leave them here, please, Garnet. I'll look at them tomorrow, and we can talk about them the next time we get together."

I tried to look sweet and appealing by gazing up at him and gently batting my eyelashes.

"Got something in your eye? Just kidding! Okay, I'll leave them with you. But you've got to promise me you won't go down into the caves without me. It can be very dangerous down there."

"I wouldn't dream of it."

I waited on the porch while he went out to his truck. In a few minutes he was back with a large folder.

"Please be careful. I don't want anything to happen to you," he said gently. He put his arms around me and bent down to kiss me. I turned my face up to his, closed my eyes, tilted my head to the left just as he tilted his to the right, and we suffered a painful nose collision.

"Damn trouble with being left-handed," I muttered, rubbing my nose. "I always zig when everybody else zags."

He smiled, took my face between his strong hands, held my head perfectly still, and planted a delightful kiss on my lips.

"Nothing we can't work out," he told me.

He kissed me again. His kiss was tender, but firm, and becoming increasingly passionate. His muscular body felt wonderful pressed tightly against mine, but I had to remind myself it had been a long time since I'd been kissed by anyone.

I finally pulled back. "Hey," I joked. "Don't think I'm the kind of girl you can seduce after one dinner of red eggs and pork bellies. It's going to take at least one more gourmet meal—maybe some kippered herring and pickled pig's feet."

"You're on for this weekend! Now, I want to see you safely inside. And Tori, stay out of the caves *and* leave the murder investigation to me."

Half an hour later, I was pinned between the two cats when the phone rang. I ran downstairs to answer it before it woke up Alice-Ann or Mark.

It was Garnet. "Did you bolt the doors? Make sure all the windows are locked?"

"Of course I did," I sighed.

I hung up, bolted the doors, checked the windows, and went back to bed.

I lay awake for a long time, staring at a hairline crack in the plaster ceiling and thinking about Garnet's kiss. How casual had he meant it to be? Was he looking for a relationship? Was I? I was beginning to like him a lot, but maybe I was so hungry for affection that anyone would look good. I thought I'd never get to sleep, but I did.

Friday

17

On Friday morning, I ate breakfast in the kitchen with Alice-Ann and Mark. Alice-Ann suggested that Mark feed the cats, which he eagerly agreed to do. Tails erect, they followed him to the sun porch.

After he left the room, she said, "I didn't have time to tell you yesterday, but Garnet called and said he'd had my hammer checked for prints. There weren't any at all."

"That doesn't surprise me. It doesn't take a great brain to know that prints should be wiped off a murder weapon."

"What are you going to do now?"

I was running out of ideas, but didn't want to admit it.

"I think I'll go back to the castle and see if I can't find that missing power nailer. If it turns out to be the one that killed the judge, it might have some prints on it, although I doubt it. Certainly some traces of blood. While I'm gone, there's something I want you to do here."

"Anything."

"Look through Richard's desk, files, drawers—wherever he might have kept papers. We need to find out what he was working on for the Historical Society. Even if he didn't have a finished paper, he certainly must have had some notes."

"I'll do it. But Mark and I need to be downtown at noon for the Rose Rent rehearsal. Did I tell you Sylvia called yesterday morning and asked Mark to take Richard's place?"

"Won't that be hard on him?"

"That's what I thought, but when she asked him, he got excited about being the 'star' of the day."

"He's a tough little guy."

I showered, dressed, kissed the cats on the little soft spots between their ears, and waved good-bye to Alice-Ann, who was already digging through the desk in the living room.

As I walked down the footpath, it was hard to believe that everything could look so normal. To the east, the sun was hovering above the treetops, birds sang, bumblebees buzzed about their business, flowers released sweet scents into the soft summer air, and water rippled calmly in the tiny lake; so peaceful, one could almost forget two murders had recently taken place.

Rose opened the door for me. She looked tired, but better than I expected.

"How are you feeling this morning?" I asked her.

"I'm all right. There's so much to do I haven't had time to think much about what happened. Would you mind helping me prepare lunch for Michael and his actors?"

"Be glad to," I fibbed.

At that moment, a shot rang out, and a man rolled slowly down the great stone staircase to land almost at our feet. I knocked Rose to the floor and threw my body across hers as protection.

"Get off of me, you damn fool!" came Rose's muffled voice.

Then, to my humiliation, the "body" stood up and helped me to my feet. He knelt on the flagstones and checked Rose for broken bones.

"I'm okay," she grumbled. "Just help me up."

"I'm so sorry," I murmured. "I thought we were having another murder."

"Perfectly understandable, my dear," Rose said with a tight smile. "This is Doug. He's part of our murder mystery cast."

Doug shook hands and excused himself quickly, saying he had to become another character in the next five minutes.

A tall, elegantly thin woman, wearing a tight red satin gown and a Miss America–type tiara, came down the steps, smoking gun in her hand. A young woman in a French maid's outfit—short black skirt, fishnet hose, and preposterously high heels—entered from a side door and let out a piercing scream. "There's a body in the front hall!" she screeched.

The detective—I could tell because he was wearing a trench coat and fedora—ran into the hallway from the front parlor and yelled, "I've got you now, Countess. You've been caught in the act, at last."

"But you don't understand," she said, using a reasonable facsimile of an Eastern European accent. "I heard a shot and found this gun on the landing."

"You're going to jail for murder, Countess. And this time they'll be throwing away the key," said Trench Coat.

He was interrupted by a shrill scream from the library. "The ambassador . . . he's been stabbed!"

Trench Coat and the countess fled down the hall and out of sight.

"It's been like this all morning," Rose said with a tired sigh. "Come on, I'll take you to the kitchen."

I followed her through a maze of hallways and down a flight of steps into a kitchen that was larger than most three-bedroom homes. As big as it was, though, it was dominated by what had to be the most enormous stove in the world.

"It's a restaurant stove," Rose told me, noticing my stare. "When Father was alive, we did a great deal of entertaining to large crowds of people, sometimes even a hundred at a time. I suppose we could get rid of it, but once you get used to having all those ovens and burners, it's hard to cook on anything else."

Since it was against my landlord's religion to repair anything, my cooking, during the past year, had been limited to what I could fix on two working burners, so I had trouble imagining what one would do with all those burners, ovens, wells, grills, and drawers. But I'm no dummy. I know life in a castle is a lot different from life in a Hell's Kitchen fourth-floor walk-up.

There was an unpleasant odor in the room I couldn't identify. I finally decided there must be some rotten potatoes in the mile-high pile in the sink.

"Darn," Rose said as a bell rang somewhere upstairs. "Now who? Victoria, can you finish up the potato salad?" She stomped out of the room, leaving me staring at the unpeeled potatoes.

Potato salad was something that came from the corner deli in little plastic containers. I groaned at the sight of all the spuds in the sink. The doorbell rang again. Poor Rose really had her hands full. It wouldn't kill me to peel a few potatoes.

I took a deep breath and attacked a potato furiously with the little knife. The level of potatoes in the pot of boiling water grew higher, as did the pile of peelings in the sink.

"You're throwing away enough food to feed half the starving people in Somalia," said an unfamiliar, deep voice from behind me.

Right then and there, I learned what the expression *leaped out of my skin* meant. I spun around, paring knife pointed, ready to protect myself from the possible murderer who had sneaked up behind me. My knife was practically embedded in the lean belly of a Michael Rennie look-alike. Remember *The Third Man?*

He was at least six four and had those same piercing eyes, high cheekbones, and swept-back black hair, brightened

with just the right amount of silver, so that he could be anywhere between thirty and fifty. He wore a light gray suit
with a barely perceptible pin stripe, which probably cost
more than I earned last year.

He raised his arms in surrender. "Watch that knife, lady.
Castration would put me in a real bad mood," he said
menacingly.

"Who are you?" I raised the knife a couple of inches to
just above his belt.

"George Lambroso. I just got in from New York to cater
the Mystery Dinner. Nobody answered the front door when
I rang, so I wandered around until I found the kitchen door.
It was open, and here I am."

I laid down my weapon, and he whistled with relief as he
lowered his arms.

"Sorry. Two people have been murdered this week—we
don't know by whom—so naturally we're all a little jumpy."

"Naturally. Here, I'll do the peeling and chopping. You
tell me about the murders."

He took off his jacket and rolled up immaculate white silk
sleeves, revealing amazingly muscular forearms, a part of
the male body I find particularly attractive. This was the
third good-looking man I'd met this week. Maybe I should
have left New York sooner.

While he expertly took care of the rest of the potatoes, I
sat on a wooden stool and told him about Richard's disappearance and eventual reappearance as a corpse and the
judge's gruesome death.

He wanted to know if the Mystery Dinner was canceled.

First things first, I thought. "No. They're going ahead
with everything. Michael's got his cast upstairs rehearsing
right now. Do you know Michael Thorne?"

"We're good friends. I'll look for him later."

The potatoes were already cubed and boiling away. In
practically no time at all, he rinsed them with cold water

and drained them. Somebody had already hard-boiled some eggs and left them in the refrigerator. George added chopped egg yolks to the potatoes.

"No whites. I think it spoils the texture." He added chopped scallions, pickles, sliced ripe olives, and a selection of herbs from a shelf of them. Then he stirred in French dressing and placed the large bowl in the refrigerator.

"No mayonnaise?" I asked, eager to show I wasn't completely hopeless in the kitchen.

"That goes in just before serving. I like to let the potatoes marinate in French dressing for an hour or two. That's the difference between plain old potato salad and *salade de pommes de terre,* and everyone knows if it has a French name it's better."

The ham Praxythea had cooked yesterday was in the refrigerator. George carved it into paper-thin slices. With a few deft twists of the wrist, he created a rose out of a tomato and centered it on the platter of ham. He arranged parsley and watercress around the edges of the platter, then popped it back into the refrigerator. "Good, there's fresh fruit. With some bread and a couple of gallons of iced tea, that should be enough lunch for anybody."

He looked at me speculatively. "Do you want to take care of the iced tea?"

"Sure. Where do you think they keep the jar of instant—"

"Never mind. I'll do the tea. By the way . . . what's your name?"

I told him and was thrilled to hear he'd read my book. I was dying to ask him how he liked it, but we were interrupted by Rose's return. After I introduced her to George, and Rose expressed her admiration of the wonderful lunch we'd prepared, George excused himself to go look for Michael.

"I'll go with you," I said before Rose had a chance to think of something else for me to do. I led the way upstairs, glad to escape the unpleasant odor that still lingered in the kitchen. We found Michael in the ballroom, dressed as an

Arab sheikh, pouring over some papers. The lovely Briana stood next to him in a white tennis outfit. I'd always thought those models in *Playboy, Sports Illustrated,* and the like were airbrushed to perfection. Now, before my very eyes, was the depressing, living proof that there really were women who didn't require airbrushing.

I was acutely aware of my faded jeans, the T-shirt that read THERE'S NO PLACE LIKE HOME, DUDE, and stained sneakers. And my hair! As a result of the potato-boiling misadventure, it had frizzed up; I looked a little worse than Elsa Lanchester in *The Bride of Frankenstein.* The longer I stayed in the room with Briana, the more unattractive I felt.

Michael greeted George warmly, then turned to me. "Tori, the strangest thing has happened. That power nailer we looked for last night?—it was here all the time. Can you believe it?"

"Quite frankly, no. Where'd you find it?"

"Under this table. It was covered by some of the set designer's sketches."

I knew damned well I'd looked under that table last night, and the power nailer had not been there.

"Did you touch it?"

"No way. I've been in enough cops-and-robbers TV shows to know better than that. I picked it up with a wooden dowel and dropped it into a plastic bag. I called Garnet to tell him, but he wasn't in the office."

"I'm going downtown later. I'll drop it off."

He looked doubtful, but I picked up the bag before he had a chance to object.

"I'll see you all later," I told them, and beat it out of there before someone realized I shouldn't be removing evidence.

I climbed the hill to Alice-Ann's and burst in on her.

"You don't have the door locked," I accused. "Didn't Lucy Lockup, or whatever her name is, get here yet?"

"She's been here and changed all the locks, but it's broad daylight. What could happen?"

"I'd tell you what could happen, but you don't want to hear it."

She locked the door.

Papers were strewn all over the living-room and dining-room floors.

"I couldn't find anything down here," she said. "I'll check upstairs after I get home. It's about time to leave for town."

I held up the plastic bag containing the nailer. "I think this is what killed the judge. I want to get it to Garnet right away." I dropped it into my purse. What was another eight or nine pounds?

After making sure every door was locked, the three of us got into the VW and left for town.

We parked behind the courthouse and walked to the square. All around us, preparations were going on for the festival. In the center of the square, just in front of the fountain, a small, wooden platform, not much larger than a picnic table, had been temporarily erected. On it was a single metal folding chair.

His highness, the mayor, waved at me and resumed drawing chalk marks down the center of the street. From the church on the opposite side of the square, came the greasy odor of doughnuts frying.

A few people, all holding notebooks, were standing in a semicircle around Mrs. Seligman, who was giving them instructions for their groups. "Skateboard competition will be in the bank parking lot, please. We don't need another spectator accident like last year. Mr. Hartzell is still using a walker.

"The Glockenspiel Gymnastic Marching Band will follow the Civil War reenactors, and I don't want to hear any complaints about the horses, Nedra. You'll just have to watch where you step. And be extracareful with those cartwheels.

"We'll space the youth bands out in the parade, so they won't all be playing different songs at once. I've prepared copies of a list that give the order you will appear in the parade. You'll gather at the corner of Second and Hemlock at nine A.M., sharp. Does everyone understand what's going on?"

Of course, at least half the people there didn't and asked questions about what they'd already been told.

Mrs. Seligman finally broke free and came over to where we stood. She looked about ten years older than the last time I had seen her.

"Thanks to Sylvia," she said, "I'm up to my neck in gymnasts, ladies' poetry societies, marching bands, magicians, jugglers, Civil War nuts, and even some weirdos in suits of armor, who showed up this morning and wanted to participate . . . although what that's got to do with the founding of Lickin Creek, I certainly don't know."

Some people passed us, pushing a brass bed on wheels. "Over there, by the bank," Mrs. Seligman said, gesturing across the square.

"Bed race," she explained to me. "Teams race down Main Street, pushing people on beds. The first group to make it to the fountain without a serious injury is the winner.

"Hey, watch it, Mr. Koontz, you can't set up the model railroad display there . . . that's where the food tables go. Excuse me," she said as she took off at a trot across the square.

While we waited for her to come back and tell Mark what to do, I heard Maggie's cheerful call from the library door. She came down the steps and over to us.

"Tori, that information you wanted, about Edison's invention to talk to the dead? I called the Penn State University Library, and the librarian found several references to it. If you have a car, I suggest driving over there. It would be a lot faster than waiting for interlibrary loan, and you'd be able to pick out what particularly interests you."

"Penn State University? Isn't that somewhere in the middle of Pennsylvania?"

"Sure, main campus is, but there are Penn State campuses

all over the state. The idea is to make higher education available to everybody, even Appalachians, like us."

"Funny, I never thought of Lickin Creek as being part of Appalachia."

"We're sitting smack-dab in the central Appalachians. You've read about the Pennsylvania coal mines. They're just to the west of us, what's left of them."

"How far is it to the nearest campus?" I asked, envisioning a two-hour drive.

"Merely a day's stagecoach drive away. Twelve miles. Just go out of town, past Silverthorne, and make the first left after the Windmill Fried Chicken House. It'll take you right onto the campus."

Alice-Ann handed me the VW keys. "Don't worry about us. We'll catch a ride home with someone."

"I need to find Garnet first," I told Maggie. "Do you know where his office is?"

She pointed. "Two blocks west, turn left after you cross the creek. It's on the right, behind Hoopengartner's Garage.

"Too bad about Judge Parker," she added. "What a way to go."

I was tempted to show her the actual weapon right there in my purse, but I liked her too much to scare her like that!

I parked in front of Hoopengartner's, and since I didn't see a police department sign, I went inside the garage. A teenager in red shorts and a blue tank top had her bare feet propped on a desk and was concentrating on polishing her toenails.

"Hi," I said.

"Shit. You scared me. Now I'll have to start all over again." She wiped a bloodred smear off her little toe.

"I'm looking for the police department."

"Back there." She aimed her right elbow at a door in the back of the room.

"Thanks for your help."

"Don't mention it."

I knocked on the door. No answer, so I pushed it open. Garnet was speaking to someone on the telephone and motioned for me to sit down.

While I waited, I studied the office of the Lickin Creek Police Department. The two chairs looked like rejects from the Goodwill store. Both desks were gray metal, army surplus, and the dusty curtains on the only window were an indeterminate color and didn't close all the way. On the wall were some framed diplomas, a citation from the mayor, and a school photograph of a young boy, all in cheap, black wood frames.

He hung up and groaned. "Shooting out on Four Horses Road. Mabel Stine's husband beat her up one too many times, so she blew him apart with his deer rifle."

"How horrible!"

"Real mess, according to Luscious. She's waiting at the trailer with her six kids for me to come and arrest her."

He stood up and strapped on his gun. "Is this a social visit, I hope?"

I handed him the plastic bag containing the power nailer.

"Where'd you get this?"

"At the castle. Exactly where it wasn't when we searched for it last night."

"You should have left it there and called me."

"Michael tried to call you. You weren't in. And I wasn't about to leave it there and have it disappear permanently like LaVonna's purse."

"I'll get it checked out. Thanks, Tori. Now, will you please, please, please stop trying to play detective?"

"Garnet, have you checked out Richard's office? Alice-Ann and I are trying to find his research notes for the Historical Society."

"It's been thoroughly searched. If the notes were there, I'd have found them. Why do you want them?"

"Idle curiosity," I said, trying to sound casual.

He walked me to the door and planted a light kiss on my lips. We seemed to have mastered zigzagging.

"I was going to call you later. Wondered if you'd be my date tomorrow at the Mystery Dinner?"

"I'd like that."

"Good. In the meantime, if anything happens, call me. Anytime. The advantage of renting this office from Hoopengartner is it's a twenty-four-hour garage so they answer my phone when I'm not here. The Borough Council decided that was cheaper than hiring a dispatcher."

He kissed me again. "Where are you off to?"

"I just thought I'd take a ride. See some of the valley. Maybe visit the university."

"Good. I don't think you can get into any trouble doing that."

As I left, the girl at the desk wiggled good-bye with her fingers. Or maybe she was just drying the polish.

The drive to the university was twelve miles all right. Straight up and down on a narrow, two-lane road. I clutched the wheel so tightly that I could barely pry my hands from it when I finally reached the campus.

The campus was perched on the side of a rocky, wooded mountain. A perfect location if you were a mountain goat. A flight of about a zillion concrete steps was built into the side of the incline. The buildings on the lowest level, nearest the parking lot, were of stone and brick. Above them were three or four Victorian buildings with all the requisite towers and gingerbread. At the very top of the steps, almost lost in the summer mists, were several of those ubiquitous creations of cement and glass that have sprung up on every campus over the last several decades. The library was one of these. I had to stop and rest three times on my way up to it.

A drinking fountain stood just inside the door. Sticky with perspiration, I sucked up a gallon or so of water to replace my lost body fluids.

The librarian had the girth of Pavarotti and the vocal volume to match. His booming voice filled every corner of the building as he introduced himself as Bob Johnson and pointed out that a parking lot was directly behind the building. When he laughed, it seemed the walls shook with him. The few summer students there must have been used to him because they didn't even look up.

"So you're the famous author." He smiled, holding up my book. "Would you mind autographing it?"

"Would I mind? Hand it over before you change your mind!"

That taken care of, he took me into the reference section where a stack of magazines, books, and papers lay on a table.

"I had main campus fax a few articles, since we don't have their periodical resources. I'll leave you to it. Holler if you need any help."

I started with the books, the most recent ones first. The dear man had even marked certain pages with slips of scratch paper, so I didn't have to waste time looking in the indexes. I was surprised to learn that Edison had been a follower of the notorious Madame Helena Blavatsky, who had founded the Theosophical Society, based on the belief in reincarnation. One book mentioned that Edison had made secret attempts to communicate with spirits, and that others had experimented with the same type of research as recently as 1974.

When Edison was in his eighties, he claimed that a life was made up of highly charged *entities* that lived in the cells of the body. When a person died, he believed the entities went into space and then entered another body and were therefore immortal.

Entities. There was that word again that Sylvia had used.

I moved on to the collection of articles that had been faxed from Main Campus. As early as 1920, Edison claimed to be working on an apparatus to communicate with the departed by scientific means. He concentrated on using certain sound waves, which he had discovered in 1875 and called Etheric Force. These waves were described as lying somewhere between the low acoustic frequencies heard by the human ear and higher frequencies associated with X rays and so on.

Although in 1887, Heinrich Hertz, the physicist, identified Etheric Force as electromagnetic waves, which became the basis for modern radio, Edison still believed Etheric

Force could also be used for contacting the entities he was sure existed.

Before he died, Edison told people it was logical to assume that if personality survived death, it would retain intellect and memory. The scientific part of it was way beyond my high school physics background, but I already had enough material to be sure that Edison had really been working on some sort of apparatus to communicate with the spirit world.

But all of the information, fascinating as it was, wasn't going to do me any good unless I could prove he had brought his invention to Lickin Creek. What I needed was a witness—someone who had seen it. But it had been more than seventy years since his visit. Impossible!

An image of a little old lady with daisies sprouting from her head floated before me. Miss Effie at the Historical Society building. How old was she? I wondered.

I found Bob Johnson behind the circulation desk and asked him if a call to the Lickin Creek Historical Society would be local or long distance.

"It's local, but if you're trying to reach Miss Effie, you'd better let me make the call. She thinks there're deadly X rays coming out of the telephone receiver, so she won't hold it close to her ear. I doubt she'd be able to hear you."

I explained that I wanted to visit her in about half an hour to ask a few questions. Bob dialed and bellowed at Miss Effie for about five minutes. It surprised me that he even needed the phone to be heard in Lickin Creek. He hung up.

"She's waiting for you."

I thanked him and descended Everest to where I had left the car.

Up and down, across the mountain, and twenty-five minutes later, I was standing in the Historical Society building speaking with Miss Effie, who was growing daffodils on her head today.

She was quite miffed when I asked her if she had been

working for the Historical Society in 1920.

"How old do you think I am, anyway? You young people think anyone with gray hair is at least a hundred. I most certainly am not old enough to have been working here in 1920!"

I sighed with disappointment. "Do you know anyone who might have been here when Thomas Edison visited the building with his cousin that year?"

"Well, certainly, dear. *I* was here."

"But you just said . . ."

"I said I wasn't old enough to be working here. But my mother did, and she brought me to work with her that day so I could meet the famous man."

"How old were you?" If she'd been two or three, I was probably out of luck.

She trilled a girlish giggle. "I'm telling my age, I guess, but I was eleven years old, and Mr. Edison was my hero."

"Miss Effie. This is very important. Do you remember him bringing anything with him? Like maybe a black box?"

"Why, yes. How did you know that? It looked a lot like a suitcase."

"And what did they do here? Do you remember?"

She sniffed. "I remember everything. They asked Mother some questions about the room where the slaves died. Then they requested permission to visit it. Mother took them down and came back alone a few minutes later. While we waited, we heard a strange humming noise coming from the basement. It grew so loud that we had to cover our ears. I was afraid, but Mother said they were trying out a new invention and Mr. Edison said we were not to worry if we heard anything odd.

"After about half an hour, the two men came back upstairs. Mr. Edison's face was as white as his hair. His cousin, Marlin, didn't look too good either. They said good-bye and left very quickly. That was it."

"And Mr. Edison was carrying his black suitcase with him when he left?"

"Of course."

I hugged her, gently so as not to break anything. Now I was sure the machine had been in Lickin Creek. "You're wonderful, Miss Effie. Thank you . . . thank you."

"My pleasure, I'm sure, even though I don't know what I did."

I left the building and practically pranced down the sidewalk to the drugstore since I hadn't had anything to eat since early morning. Over a diet cherry cola and a chicken-salad sandwich, I thought about what I had learned so far.

There was no doubt in my mind that Edison's machine was the spectacular discovery that was going to make Richard world famous and, even more importantly, get him into the Lickin Creek Historical Society. I couldn't figure Sylvia's interest in it, though. Since the séance had been planned before Richard's murder, it seemed reasonable that the two had planned to test the machine together. Even if it was a fascinating discovery, I could see no need for her to go through all the research and secrecy nonsense—her position as local society leader was uncontested. And the preparations going on outside for the Rose Rent Festival, which she had reestablished single-handedly, testified to the importance of her contributions to local historical research.

So, again it came back to who would benefit the most from the discovery? One person. Praxythea. It would make her the most famous of them all in the wacky world of psychic research. Even legitimate scientists would be excited by this . . . especially if it worked!

Good God, what was I thinking of? Of course it couldn't work!

The one part of the puzzle I couldn't figure out was who killed the judge? And why?

If I took the Edison factor out of my equation, Praxythea

really had no motive for killing Richard, and certainly no reason for doing in the judge. I was back to the one person who had the opportunity and motives for killing both victims: Rose Thorne.

I knew she had traveled to the judge's house by the local taxi. I wondered if there was anything I could learn from the driver. A public telephone was near the cash register, and on an impulse, I looked up the Uriah's Heap number in the attached directory and called.

I explained where I was and that I needed a ride to Silverthorne. He said he'd check his appointment calendar. Lucky for me, he had a half-hour opening. He'd be right there.

He meant it. In about two minutes, a 1977 Dodge station wagon, trimmed with phony wood, pulled to a stop before me.

I'd half-expected a tall, thin, hand-wringing Dickensian character. I was mistaken. The driver was a little younger than Miss Effie, powerfully built, with a Captain Grizzly beard and faded blue eyes. He wore a blue, Greek fisherman's cap in addition to the ever-present plaid shirt. We exchanged a few pleasantries like "Hot enough for ya?" and "It's not the heat, it's the humidity" before I got down to serious business.

"Did you drive Rose Thorne out to the judge's house yesterday afternoon?"

"Why ya want to know?"

"I'm helping the police with the investigation."

"I'll bet."

"Okay, I'm conducting a private investigation. Can't you just tell me, yes or no?"

"Yes."

"What time? Please?" I wheedled.

He pulled over to the curb and turned his whole body around so he could look at me. "Look, young lady. I saw you drive into town in Mrs. MacKinstrie's Volkswagen, which is parked right in front of the Historical Society, so I know you don't need a ride out to Silverthorne. I don't know what you're trying to pull, but it better be important."

"I wouldn't bother you like this if it weren't."

"Rose's an old friend of mine. I don't want to get her into trouble."

"It might help her."

He opened his glove compartment and extracted a black notebook, which he flipped open. "Let's see. Yup, here it is. Picked Rose up at Silverthorne at four-forty. Dropped her off at Judge Parker's house at five oh five. Came back to get her at six. She was about halfway down the block, by herself, crying. I took her home, arriving at six-thirty."

I complimented him on his careful record keeping. He beamed with pride as he patted his little book. "Better safe than sorry, I always say. No telling when some nosey parker might come along and want some information." His blue eyes twinkled as he spoke.

"One more question, then I promise I'll quit. Did you take anyone else to the judge's house, or anywhere nearby, either before or after Rose's visit?"

He shook his head and started his engine. "Nope. And in answer to your next 'one more question,' I didn't see anybody hanging around there, either."

"Would it mess up your schedule if we drove past the judge's house?"

"Is it supposed to help Miss Rose?"

"Of course."

"No problem."

It really wasn't, since the judge's home was only two blocks from downtown. Uriah stopped the cab in front of the property where the yellow police tape still fluttered.

Now what? I wondered.

I saw Mrs. O'Brien beheading roses in front of her house.

"Hold on a minute," I told Uriah as I jumped out of the car.

Mrs. O'Brien didn't recognize me, but when I explained I

was working for the police, she was so open and friendly that I almost felt ashamed of my deception.

When I got back into the car, I felt like an accomplished detective. After answering several questions, Mrs. O'Brien had casually mentioned that she saw Judge Parker standing in his doorway when Rose *left* his house. She couldn't remember if she'd mentioned it to the police chief because it hadn't seemed very important. After all, the poor man was dead. What difference did it make when it happened?

If he was alive when Rose left, and Uriah picked her up just a few moments later, it eliminated her as a suspect. Unless she had gone back to the castle, rushed back to town through the underground tunnels, killed him, and got out of there before his laundry showed up. But Uriah's meticulous records indicated they didn't get back to the castle until six-thirty, just the time the body was being found.

Uriah dropped me off in front of the Historical Society, charged me a dollar fifty, wished me a nice day, and drove off to his next appointment.

Alice-Ann had a glass of wine poured for me before I mastered the front door lock.

"Everything okay?" I asked.

"No problems. Mark's upstairs playing in his room, and your cats are making pests of themselves by following me everywhere."

We sat in the living room, each with a lap full of cat, and I told her where I'd been and what information I'd managed to ferret out.

When I was finished, I asked her if she had found anything in Richard's papers about his research project. She hadn't, not in his office nor in the house. She swore she had gone through everything, even trunks in the attic.

At least the search hadn't been a total waste of time; she'd found some Victorian dresses in the trunks that we could wear to the Mystery Dinner Saturday night.

Close to ten, the phone rang.

"There's Garnet," Alice-Ann said with a smile.

She was right.

"Just called to see if everything was all right at your place," he said.

"We're fine. How did things work out with the woman who shot her husband?"

"She's already out on bail. The women in her trailer park took up a collection. She'll probably end up getting a medal for killing that bastard. How was your drive in the country?"

"Nice." I shuddered thinking of the twisting, narrow mountain road. "I went to the Penn State campus library. Garnet, I found out a lot about Edison. He really was working on something to communicate with the dead. Then I visited Miss Effie at the Historical Society, and she told me that when she was a child, Edison actually brought a black box to the building to test it—downstairs, where the slaves died. I checked with the taxi driver, Uriah, and he said . . ."

I wasn't getting any response at all from Garnet. Not even an occasional *uh-huh* or a *hmmm*.

"Are you still there?"

Patient, pained, Garnet said, "Tori, I asked you to stay out of this. I'm taking care of it. Please stop!"

"It's just that you're so busy . . ."

"Tori, it's my job. Trust me to do it right."

"What'd he have to say?" Alice-Ann asked after I hung up.

"He said I'm a great help. And to keep up the good work."

We succumbed to a fit of giggles after that.

Saturday

Chapter

19

❧ ❧ ❧

Still wearing the Scarecrow of Oz T-shirt I'd slept in, I pulled on my jeans and went down to the kitchen where I fixed a mug of instant coffee and watched the sunrise. A real treat for a city dweller. Lickin Creek was going to have a beautiful day for its Rose Rent Festival.

I got Garnet's cave maps from the hall table and quickly found the one that showed Alice-Ann's house and the castle. Noel strolled into the kitchen and mewed with pleasure when she saw me. She rubbed against my legs and jumped on my lap as soon as I sat down. We both studied the map I had spread on the table. It was interesting to see that this house and the castle were connected by a straight stretch of tunnel. And, best of all, I saw the location of the underground lake, and drawn next to it, a little stick figure, with *body* written in childish print above it.

Noel was now sitting on the map, right on top of the lake, naturally. I picked her up and scratched behind her ears and was rewarded by loud purring. "Where's Fred?" I called. "Come on, sweetie. Mommy's up early."

After a few minutes, when he still hadn't shown up, I felt

a twinge of concern. Usually he was begging for food the minute he woke up.

That's when I noticed that the door to Alice-Ann's basement workshop was open. One of the cute tricks both cats had taught themselves was how to jump up and hang on a doorknob until the door opened. You'll never find a dog doing that!

I called down the stairs. "Fred? Are you down there?"

Some people might think that cats don't answer, but anyone owned by a cat knows they talk to you. Right then, Noel was uttering little squeaks and moans, showing she was worried, too.

I pulled the string that turned on the bare bulb at the top of the stairs and went down, with Noel following, still expressing her concern. In the workshop, Alice-Ann had installed fluorescent lights, and the room sprang into view when I turned them on. There was no sign of a large orange and white cat anywhere.

I peered under the worktables, calling him, to no avail, until I noticed Noel standing at the cave entrance that I had uncovered several days ago. She meowed several times, and I heard a faint echo in the dark below.

"Fred. Here, boy. Come on, baby."

Another faint meow came up the shaft.

I found a flashlight and pointed it into the hole. Two green spots glowed back at me.

"Stay right there," I ordered. "I'll come and get you."

Meow.

I put the flashlight on the floor, turned around, got on my knees, and placed one foot on the ladder. It seemed secure, so I put my other foot on the next rung and felt it snap under my weight. If I hadn't still been hanging on to the brick sides of the arch, I would have plunged straight down. Possibly it wouldn't have killed me, but breaking a leg or my back was not a pleasant prospect.

I almost split myself in half getting one leg on the floor while hanging on to the rough bricks for dear life. I wiggled and twisted and pulled myself up inch by frightening inch until I was lying facedown on the solid workshop floor. The muscles in my arms, unaccustomed to exercise, were trembling, my hands were shaking, and my legs quivering. When I had somewhat recovered, I looked down into the hole and surveyed the damage. The ladder was useless.

"Fred?"

No answer. He must have become frightened by the noise of the ladder's breaking and scampered deeper into the cave.

"Fred?"

I heard a meow so faint that I knew he must be going in the wrong direction.

Don't panic, I told myself. There must be a way to get down there. I looked frantically around the room. No ladders, no ropes, nothing I could use.

I grabbed Noel and beat it up the stairs into the kitchen, put her into the laundry room, grabbed Garnet's cave map, and ran out of the house, heading as fast as I could for the castle. According to the map, there was an entrance there, and I was betting it was below the kitchen, just like all the others I'd seen. I prayed their ladder was in better condition than Alice-Ann's.

I circled around the castle and went directly to the kitchen door. As I burst through the door, I suddenly realized what a sight I must be, barefoot, in my rumpled Oz T-shirt and no bra, and oldest jeans. So, could I get away with it, sneaking in and out unnoticed? Of course not, the room was full of people. Some of the actors were already there, as were several people wearing chef's aprons and others in blue jeans.

They seemed to be in a state of mass confusion, but I didn't have time to wonder why. "Excuse me," I said, pushing my way through to the basement door.

"What are you doing?" George yelled at me.

"Looking for Fred," I hollered over my shoulder as I ran down the stairs.

Sure enough, there was a familiar archway in the basement; this one with a real door. I opened it and saw with relief that there were stairs leading into the caves instead of a ladder. They looked pretty sturdy, so I took a chance and started down.

Above me, I heard George calling, "Come back. It's too dangerous. Something's happened."

I thought I heard him telling someone to get help, but I had already gone too far to hear him clearly.

I used one hand to shine the flashlight on the ground before me, being careful to watch for cave-ins. With my other hand I kept in touch with the wet, cold cave wall, both to keep my balance and to reassure myself that I was still in the tunnel between the castle and the cottage. Water dripped from above and quickly soaked my T-shirt. My teeth were chattering from the cold. Thank God the tunnel was fairly straight, just as Garnet's drawing showed it. However, the descent was quite steep, and my feet often slipped on the slimy floor.

"Here, kitty," I called in that silly falsetto voice people use when calling their pets. "Here, good boy. Come on, Fred."

No answer, but I figured I was still some distance from the cottage, and he probably hadn't gone terribly far from it.

The hand that had been groping its way along the wall was suddenly touching nothing. I stopped and used the flashlight to examine the map. It should be the tunnel that led to the underground lake. I could hear running water below me.

I listened carefully and was sure I heard something familiar.

"Kitty?" I called, stepping a foot or two into the new tunnel.

"Fred? Are you down there?"

There was no doubt about it this time. I heard a very definite *mrreow* coming from the darkness.

Keeping up a running patter of, "Here, boy, good kitty, come on, baby," I was reassured by little mewling sounds as I splashed through an ankle-deep stream of ice-cold water.

I emerged from the narrow, low tunnel into an immense fairyland of crystal. The light from my flashlight reflected and bounced from thousands of jewellike stalactites and stalagmites in the cavern. Before me was the underground lake, dark and still as black velvet.

Something touched my leg, and I jumped six inches into the air.

I swept Fred into my arms and hugged him. He smelled of damp and mold, but that didn't keep me from burying my face in his beautiful fur. I was glad there was no one there to see me cry.

"Come on, Fred. As long as we're here, we might as well take a look around."

Cat draped over one shoulder, I circled the lake and was constantly amazed at the magical formations that came into view. Deep in the glowing crystals, I saw unicorns and elves, ice princesses and buried treasures. This was the cave of Merlin, and the Hobbit, and all the other mysterious and wonderful dreams of childhood.

And then I came face-to-face with reality. Leaning against the cavern wall, legs casually crossed, was a human skeleton, its clothes still intact enough to be recognizable as a Union Army uniform. I knelt next to him, feeling no revulsion. Perhaps because his skeleton was so clean, and he looked so peaceful. Fred jumped down and sniffed at the bones. When he found nothing that interested him, he sat down and licked his bottom.

It was immediately apparent that the man's right leg had been broken in several places. Bone protruded from a tear in his trouser leg. I could imagine him coming down here to hide, falling and breaking his leg, then lying here in the dark until death released him from his pain.

A leather pouch, almost concealed by his shirt, hung from a strap around his neck. I knelt beside him and carefully lifted it over the skull. Perhaps it would contain letters that would tell me who he was. It felt lumpy in my hand and heavier than I thought it would be. Maybe he carried daguerreotypes of his loved ones with him, as so many Civil War soldiers did.

I emptied the contents onto my lap and touched, for the first time, the fabulous blue diamond that was Sylvia's Star. It actually seemed to glow from within, while the brilliant white diamonds surrounding it reflected points of light on every surface. Even Fred reached out one white paw and touched the cobalt blue gem with reverence, before I tucked it back into the pouch, which I slipped over my head.

I was extremely pleased with myself. I had solved the mystery of the first Sylvia's death. While the local citizens were hiding in the castle from the Confederate army, a Union soldier, someone whom they thought they could trust, plotted to steal the fabulous necklace. I wanted to believe he hadn't planned to kill Sylvia, but quite likely she surprised him in the act, and he seized something and struck her before she could call for help. Then he had hidden in the caves, probably planning to wait for night to make his escape, but had broken his leg and had to wait for death, knowing he had in his possession a treasure great enough to buy everything he had ever dreamed of. A treasure to die for!

I'd solved the mystery, found the diamond, and had the subject for my next book! What a great morning!

Praxythea had said the jewel would be found "by the edge of running water." For a moment I was almost a believer.

I stood up and was bending over to pick up Fred when I heard a tiny sound, off to my right. No more than a pebble rolling on the cavern floor, but something must have disturbed it. Something I couldn't see. I thought of snakes, bats, rats, and other things so horrible they had no names. There was the sound again, behind me now. I wanted to call out, yell, scare it away, but no sound would come out of my open mouth. I tried to will away the darkness, and that's when I noticed that one of the jewellike reflections in my flashlight beam was not a reflection at all, but a tiny, red light that resembled the tip of a lighted cigarette. I moved quietly in that direction and saw that the light was coming from the infamous black box, which I was sure was Edison's spirit communicator. But who was down here with it? Someone had to have turned it on. The noise . . . again . . . behind me. Before I could spin around to face it, something hit the middle of my back with such force that I crashed facedown on the wet floor.

It's possible I lost consciousness for a few minutes. I thought I heard footsteps moving away from me, but I was totally disoriented by the darkness. My flashlight was lost or broken, and I was lying in pitch blackness with Fred licking my ear. I groped for the flashlight, found it, and listened in horror to it rattle when I tried to turn it on.

Sylvia's Star! Where was it? I caught my breath as I clutched at my chest, then exhaled with relief when I felt the leather pouch, still hanging from my neck. I stuck a finger through the drawstrings and ran it across the faceted surfaces of the stone. It seemed intact. What an ironic twist it would have been to have found the gem after all the years it was missing, only to lose it again.

I felt a strong empathy with my dead companion. This is how it must have been for him as he waited to die. Sitting in the dark with a fabulous jewel hanging from his neck.

But there was a big difference. I had a headache from my fall, but I didn't have a broken leg, and I was not going to lie down and die. I was going to get out of here, but first I was going to get my hands on that elusive black box.

"Come on, kitty," I said, crawling on my hands and knees toward the place where the little red light still glowed. As I got closer, the light dimmed. By the time I bumped my head on the stone wall of the cavern, the light had gone out.

I cursed. Fred emitted a timid squeak, and as I reached out to pet him, I touched something hard, not hard like a rock, but hard like a leather suitcase. I collapsed with my back against the wall, hugging Fred for warmth.

My nose had become accustomed to the damp, earthy odor of the cave, but now I could smell something else. Very faint, but definitely the scent of carnations. It reinforced my earlier suspicions of Praxythea.

In frustration, I threw a rock and screamed, "Damn it!"

And from far away, I heard someone call my name.

"Here. By the lake. Help!"

Fred added his meows to my cries for help.

A dim glow lit up the tunnel on the other side of the lake. It grew brighter as the person carrying the light drew closer.

"Tori, where are you?" It was Michael's voice.

"Thank God it's you. I'm across the lake."

Michael entered the cavern, and the magnificent crystal formations began to glow again, reflecting light from the kerosene lantern he carried.

He swiftly circled the lake and knelt beside me. I hadn't even realized I was bleeding until he wiped my forehead with his handkerchief.

"You should have known better than to come down here alone," he scolded. "If George hadn't seen you head down here . . ."

"I had to do it," I explained weakly. "Fred got lost and . . ."

"I understand. I've got a cat of my own. We've got to get you to a doctor. What did you do? Slip and hit your head?"

"I was hit. Someone tried to kill me."

"Who? How? Why?"

I pointed to the leather-covered box. "It has something to do with this."

222

He held the lamp closer to the box, and I saw that it had gold initials stamped under the handle: TAE.

"I knew it!" I exclaimed. "Hold that lantern still. I want to open this thing."

The two brass snaps opened easily. The front lifted off, revealing an array of glass-covered dials, knobs, and a switch. I flipped the switch up and down a few times, and the little red light on top of the box began to glow again. When I turned one of the knobs, there was an unpleasant humming sound. I quickly turned it off.

Inside the lid was a pocket, which held several folded pieces of paper. I pulled them out and opened them with shaking fingers. Yellowed with age, folded in thirds, one was a hand-drawn diagram, similar to a blueprint. The other page was covered with the shaky handwriting one associates with the very old or the very sick. It took only a few seconds for me to realize that I was looking at Edison's own handwritten directions for building and using his strange invention.

"What do you suppose it is?" Michael asked.

"I'm not sure," I lied. "We'll let Garnet take a look."

As I refolded the pages, I pretended concern about Fred. "My cat! Do you see him anywhere?"

Michael looked around. Of course, Fred was right underfoot. "Here he is," Michael said, and bent over to pick him up. As he did, I slipped the papers into one of my jean pockets. I wanted to examine the plans more carefully before turning them over to someone else.

"Let's get out of here. This place is giving me the creeps." Michael regarded the box. "What are we going to do with this thing?"

"Take it with us. I think it's the key to Richard's murder. And maybe the judge's, too."

I led the way, carrying the lamp and Fred, while Michael carried the box. It was a relief when we finally climbed the stairway into the basement of Silverthorne Castle. Michael blew out the lantern and hung it on a hook at the head of the stairs.

"Is that always kept there?" I asked him.

"I suppose it is. I used to leave it there when I was a kid, so it would be handy for exploring. Why do you ask?"

"If it hasn't been used in years, wouldn't it have stopped working? I mean, you'd think all the kerosene would have evaporated or the wick would have rotted or something. Unless someone has used it lately for his own purposes." Like sneaking through the tunnels to enter Judge Parker's basement and murder him, I was thinking.

I also couldn't help wondering how Michael had found me so fast, unless he had been there when I was attacked. He looked so guileless, so genuinely worried about me—but I had to remember, he was an actor.

20

Having been so long in the dark, I was nearly blinded as we stepped into the brightly lit kitchen, so it was a moment or two before it registered that the room was full of people, and they were all staring at us in amazement.

I was acutely aware of the inadequacy of my flimsy, wet T-shirt. And then, from somewhere, Garnet appeared at my side and draped a red-checked tablecloth around my shoulders. Fred buried his head in its folds, like an ostrich seeking security.

"What are you doing here?" I asked in surprise.

"I should be asking you that," he growled. "I told you not to go down into those caves without me."

"I had to. Fred fell in, and I had to find him."

"That's some excuse," he said, eyes blazing. "That T-shirt you're wearing is really appropriate."

I looked down at my chest and read upside down IF I ONLY HAD A BRAIN!

He was scolding me as if I were a child, and the child within me responded by bursting into tears.

"Oh, shit! Tori, I'm so sorry. It's just that I was so worried about you." For the first time, he noticed the bloody wound on my forehead. He put his arms around me and held me close so my nose was mashed against his badge. "Someone get the damn doctor. Why isn't he here?"

"He's on his way," someone answered. "Should be here any minute."

George slid a kitchen chair under me, and I sat down. It seemed as though there were a dozen people staring at me. Even the lanky Luscious was standing by staring at me with curiosity. Something smelled dreadful. If that was the Mystery Dinner entreé, I'd skip it tonight.

"Why are all these people here?" I asked Garnet. "Surely not because of me?"

The people stepped back, parting like the Red Sea, giving me an unobstructed view of most of the kitchen, including the huge stove and . . . oh . . . no!

The door to one of the gigantic ovens hung open. Inside was stuffed a body in a lavender dress covered with chartreuse roses. The dress LaVonna had been wearing the last time I saw her. I suddenly realized what I had smelled cooking and gagged.

George handed me a roll of paper towels, but I shook my head. "I'm all right. Poor LaVonna."

"I came down early and turned on the ovens to preheat them," George said. "Then I went upstairs to shower and dress. When I came down about half an hour later, I knew that something was terribly wrong. While I was waiting for the police, you came galloping through here like a crazy woman, yelling about some guy named Fred. I thought New York was strange, but it's nothing like this place."

Then everyone started talking at once. Garnet held his hands up for quiet. From behind me came the scent of carnations, which signaled Praxythea's presence. I turned and saw Sylvia in a sensible blue chenille robe, Rose in her inevitable pink negligee, and Praxythea in some sort of shimmery gray satin that clung to every curve.

226

Sylvia's eyes grew huge when she saw the body in the oven. "LaVonna?"

Garnet nodded.

Rose started to sniffle. "I've been so worried about her. I knew she just wouldn't go off like that."

Praxythea ran her fingers through her tousled red hair. "I had a vision of her lying in darkness."

"Where have you three been?" Garnet snapped. "Didn't you hear all the commotion down here?"

"Have you forgotten that two people have already been murdered?" Praxythea asked. "I didn't care to be the next victim, so I stayed in my room until I heard your police siren. We all met in the hall and came down together."

I pounced. "You weren't in your room. You were down below, in the cavern where the lake is."

She regarded me with all the warmth of a guest discovering a cockroach on the birthday cake. "Why on earth would you say that?"

"I smelled you," I said, realizing and not caring how stupid that sounded.

"Don't be ridiculous." She lifted her chin, indicating she was helpless in dealing with a fool.

I pushed on. "Is there another way to get out of the basement . . . I mean, besides coming through the kitchen?"

Sylvia answered, "Of course there is, Victoria. This is a castle, you know. There are several stairways up: one from the wine cellar to the ballroom, another through the servants' quarters in the rear. There're probably more I've forgotten about."

"So Praxythea could have been down there and gone up to her room without anyone in the kitchen seeing her," I said triumphantly.

"Garnet," Praxythea said, turning the full power of her blazing green eyes on him, "I've been upstairs since I awoke. Why is your friend doing this to me?"

"Forget it," I grumbled. I knew when I was outclassed.

Dr. Jones came into the kitchen then, carrying his big doctor's bag. He poked my forehead, twisted my neck from side to side, pressed the small of my back when I told him where I'd been bit, shined a penlight into my eyes, and pronounced me fit.

My case dismissed, he turned to Garnet. "Are you ready to take her out of there?" he asked, referring to LaVonna.

"Yeah. Go ahead, Luscious."

Luscious had taken advantage of the excitement caused by my unexpected arrival in the kitchen to fortify himself with the contents of his flask.

"Yesh, shir, Chief," he responded.

Garnet winced. "Come on, Doc. I guess you and I will have to do it."

Together, they extracted LaVonna's body from the oven and laid it on the flagstone floor. While the doctor examined her, I turned my attention to the blue and white Staffordshire plates hanging on the kitchen walls. Fascinating things, blue and white plates.

"Might as well take her to the morgue. I'll finish up there," Dr. Jones said.

"Any idea of what the cause of death was?" Garnet asked.

"Offhand, I'd guess it was that carving knife stuck in her heart," he replied cynically. "Roasting her only added a bizarre twist."

"Can you tell how long she's been dead?"

"Establishing the time of death has been made complicated by the heating of the body. But certainly more than forty eight hours."

"But she left a note Wednesday night saying she had to leave because of a family emergency," I said.

"How do you know that?" Garnet asked.

"Because LaVonna asked me to come over Thursday morning. Said she had something she wanted to talk to me about, but when I got here, she was gone. Rose told me she'd left a note saying she was called away in the middle of the night."

"Did you see the note?"

"No, Rose said Sylvia threw it away. I said I thought it was odd, because LaVonna had told me she didn't have any family, then Rose got vague and said maybe it was some other kind of emergency."

Garnet turned to Sylvia. "Do you remember what the note said?"

"I never saw a note," Sylvia said.

Rose stared at her sister. "You told me—"

"I did not."

"Did too."

We listened helplessly to the juvenile squabblings of two siblings in their seventies. If they had been children, someone would have sent them to bed. As it was, we had no idea how to stop them.

"Oh, dear," Sylvia cried out. "I think I'm going to faint."

Dr. Jones ran to her side and caught her as she fell. As big as she was, he almost went down with her.

"She's burning up," he said, not realizing the irony of his comment when LaVonna's body lay, still smoking, a few feet away.

"Sylvia," he said. "I want to put you in the clinic. We need to find out what's wrong."

"No!" she yelled, quite loudly for a woman who had just almost passed out. "There's too much to do. I've got to be at the Rose Rent ceremony at noon, and there's the dinner tonight to get ready for."

The doctor threw up his hands in exasperation. "Okay, you're the boss, as usual. But if you won't go to the clinic, I insist you go upstairs and rest for a few hours. I'll give you some aspirin to see if we can't get that fever down. If you're not better by tonight, you'll go into the clinic, like it or not!"

She nodded and allowed the doctor and Praxythea to assist her out of the room.

Luscious managed to pull himself together long enough to help the ambulance driver place LaVonna's corpse onto a stretcher. As they carried her out the back door, I went over to Garnet. "The box over there by the basement door . . . it's the Edison machine I told you about . . . it's real."

Garnet opened it. Several people joined him to stare at the odd configuration of knobs, dials, and switches. He flipped the switch and the light came on. "I suppose you'll say it runs on magic," he said.

I sighed. "Haven't you ever heard of batteries?"

He grinned, and I realized he was rattling my chain.

"It doesn't look like anything special," he remarked, still staring at it.

"I'm positive it's the key to the whole thing. Richard's death . . . and LaVonna . . ."

He looked at it skeptically. "I'll just put it upstairs in the library for now. No one is to touch it, does everyone understand?"

Nods all around. Garnet placed his hand on my shoulder. "I'll have the ambulance driver drop you off. And when I'm finished here, I'll stop by to see you."

I nodded, then reached up to touch the little leather pouch I had taken from the body of the dead soldier.

"I'll bet when you guys were kids, you were afraid of dead bodies," I said, looking from Garnet to Michael and back to Garnet again.

They both squirmed self-consciously.

"What makes you say that?" Garnet asked.

"Because if you hadn't been, you would have examined the body in the cave, and if you'd done that, you would have found what I found today."

I pulled the pouch over my head.

"Come here, Michael. I don't think you need to worry anymore about a developer building split-levels at Silverthorne Meadows." I handed him the pouch.

He hesitated a moment, then opened the little bag, and the necklace flowed into his hand like quicksilver. The deep blue stone and the chain of diamond flowers absorbed the light they had missed for a hundred and thirty years and mirrored it back at us a thousand times brighter.

An almost religious hush fell across the assembled group. If nothing good ever happened to me again, at least I'd always have the memory of that moment.

21

The ambulance driver waited until Alice-Ann let me in before he drove off. Filthy, wet, with a bandage on my forehead, Fred tucked under one arm, and the checkered tablecloth still around my shoulders, I knew I had a lot of explaining to do.

As quickly as I could, before Mark came downstairs, I told Alice-Ann of LaVonna's death. Her eyes filled with tears.

"She was such a dear, dear person. Why would anybody kill a harmless soul like her?"

"Because the murderer was afraid of her. I think she knew who killed Richard, or had suspicions, and that was what she wanted to talk to me about on Thursday morning. She must have been overheard talking to me. Right then, she was destined to die. Damn! If only she'd told me then, she'd still be alive. And the judge, too."

I plopped down on one of the wooden benches in the living room, and while Fred toiled with his raspy tongue to turn his feet white again, I told Alice-Ann about the cavern, my discovery of the long-lost jewel, the vicious attack on my person, and the recovery of the Edison machine.

"What an amazing adventure," she said when I finished. "I can't wait to see Sylvia's Star. It must be fabulous. Do you think all this is tied together somehow?"

I nodded. "It's got to be. Listen, Alice-Ann. Are you absolutely positive there were no research notes in with Richard's personal papers?"

"Tori, you know I searched everywhere. The only thing I didn't do was unroll the toilet paper."

"Mom, isn't it time to go?" Mark entered the living room, bouncing with excitement. He stopped bouncing for a minute when he saw me. "Gee, Tori, you sure look funny."

"I had a little adventure with a runaway cat."

Fred paused in his pedicure to meow his corroboration.

"We need to get going," Alice-Ann said, glancing at her wristwatch. "I thought you could ride with us, but you obviously need a shower and a change of clothes. Will you be able to get downtown to see the ceremony?"

"I wouldn't miss it for anything. Garnet's coming over in a little while. He can give me a lift."

They left in a panicky flurry of last-minute adjustments: "Where did you put it?" "Better brush your hair again." "Didn't I tell you to wear a . . .?" "Aw, Mom!" "Your shoes!" "Has anyone seen my . . .?"

Alone at last, I filled the bathtub with water as hot as I could take it and lowered my aching bones, watching my skin gradually turn bright pink from the heat.

When the water began to cool, I climbed out and was drying myself with a soft, white towel when, to my horror, the bathroom doorknob began to turn. I grabbed the bottle of bubble bath and held it over my head. If I was going to go, I was going to go fighting. The door opened.

"Hey, hey, Tori. Put that thing down. I come in peace."

"Garnet! You scared me half to death." I dropped the bottle—luckily it was plastic—and clutched at the towel in an inadequate attempt to preserve my modesty.

He blushed almost purple, slammed the door shut, and

yelled through it, "Sorry. When you didn't answer my knock, I was concerned you might have fallen asleep. That could be the sign of a serious concussion. Are you okay?"

"I'm fine," I yelled back at him.

"Then why the hell didn't you lock the front door?"

I was struggling to pull on my underpants. Not easy when one's body is still warm and damp. "I thought it locked automatically."

"You really need someone to take care of you."

I froze in the middle of hooking my bra. *Don't go serious on me, Garnet. Please don't.*

"I could use some coffee," he called. "See you downstairs."

I blow-dried my hair and dressed with extra care in navy linen slacks and a red-and-white-striped blouse with a long red silk scarf. Garnet's admiring look when I walked into the kitchen affirmed that I looked as good as I hoped I did.

He put his big hands on my shoulders, bent down, and kissed me gently, so as not to dislodge the bandage on my forehead. "Tori Miracle, you've got me coming and going. When I'm with you, all I can think of is protecting you. When I'm not with you, I'm worried that you're getting into some sort of trouble. What are we going to do about it?"

He must have felt my body stiffen, because he dropped his arms.

"Let's have some of that wonderful-smelling coffee you made," I said as I scooted around him to look for the coffee mugs.

When I turned around, I saw his mouth was screwed up in a little half-smile. "I wish I knew what you were thinking right now. I wish I knew where you go when I try to tell you how I feel."

"I'll see if I can find us something to eat."

His voice was cool. "Good. I missed breakfast this morning."

Feeling like Old Mother Hubbard, I searched the near-empty cabinets until I found a box of saltines and a jar of peanut butter. I placed them on the table along with a knife and a couple of paper napkins.

There didn't seem to be anything else in the kitchen that would be good for breakfast except for a Snickers bar, and I was determined to save that for myself.

"Is this your idea of breakfast?"

"We're lucky to have it," I said staring at the congealed spaghetti in the refrigerator left over from last night's dinner. "Neither Alice-Ann nor I have given any thought to going grocery shopping. Look! Jelly! It's a feast."

We managed to devour half the box of crackers and an enormous amount of peanut butter and grape jelly, too hungry even to talk. When we were full, we moved out to the back porch with fresh mugs of coffee.

"Time for me to be a policeman again," he said. "Tell me what happened to you in the cave, and how you found the diamond and your notorious black box."

I related the whole story, starting with Fred's impromptu attempt at cave exploration and ending with Michael's rescuing me. Well, almost the whole story. I didn't mention finding the directions for building a spirit communicator— said papers now hidden safely away in my underwear drawer.

I finished with, "And I really do think it was Praxythea who knocked me down."

"Explain, please."

"Because of the box. I think she took it down there to test it. Maybe she'd heard about the dead soldier and thought the cave would be haunted. And after I was hit, I smelled her perfume."

"Tori, how would she have known about the dead soldier?"

I hadn't thought of that. "Maybe someone told her about him?"

"Even if someone had, there's no way she could have

found her way down there by herself. Not without a map, and the only ones I know of are what Michael and I drew when we were kids."

"Then someone else is helping her. Someone from the castle who knows about the maps. Of course. How stupid of me. She'd have to have a partner."

There had to have been someone else down there with her, someone who knew his way around. Michael had arrived awfully soon after I was knocked down. Could he be the partner? He knew his way around in the caves. He could have plotted with Praxythea to steal the machine from Richard, and as big and strong as he was, it would have been much easier for him to kill Richard with a blow to the head than for Praxythea to do it. He had a motive to kill the judge, too. It was quite possible that he knew the judge was his father and wanted revenge for all the years the man had ignored his existence. So he took his power nailer and . . . No! No way could I believe Michael capable of that. I hoped it was because of my innate ability to judge people's character and not because he was the most gorgeous man I'd ever met.

"Do you really think that stupid-looking box is important enough to kill for?"

"I really do, Garnet. People have been trying to find the plans for it for years. As I told you yesterday, I'm positive Edison tested it in your very own Historical Society building."

"It obviously didn't work."

"What makes you so sure?"

"Because if it had, everybody in the country would have one sitting next to their VCR and compact-disc player. Think what fun it would be to talk about the good old days with Great-Grandpa on a dull Saturday night."

"Maybe it did work. Maybe something happened that made Edison realize it was too dangerous to use again."

Garnet shook his head. "I just can't buy this supernatural stuff. It's the same kind of garbage Praxythea talks about."

"Exactly. And that's why I think she was the one who took it down to the cave to test. Just think what this discovery could do for her career."

"So you're still saying Praxythea killed Richard?"

"It's entirely possible."

"She's a dingbat and an opportunist, but I don't picture her as a murderer."

"Then who can you picture as a murderer? Rose? Alice-Ann? Michael? Me? No one *looks* like a murderer." I asked him if he'd had a chance to question Rose.

"For about two minutes. Getting information out of her is like trying to take a bone away from a dog. All she admitted to is that Judge Parker was the father of her child. However, she says that had nothing to do with her going to talk to him the night he died, and she says it's none of my business why she went there."

He sipped his coffee. "We found traces of blood on the power nailer. As expected, it matched the judge's."

"Prints?"

He shook his head.

We took our empty mugs into the kitchen and placed them in the dishwasher.

"I've got to stop by the clinic and talk to Doc about LaVonna's murder. I'm also going to make arrangements to recover the Union soldier's body this afternoon and have it buried properly. Do you want me to drop you off downtown? You might as well see the Rose Rent ceremony."

"Thanks."

I grabbed my purse, made sure the front door was locked behind me, and stretched gracefully into the front seat of his truck.

"Aw shucks," he teased, "I wanted to grab your bottom and push."

At least he was in a good mood again.

"You'll never catch me climbing into this truck in a tight skirt again," I warned him, but with a smile, trying to make up for my earlier rejection. Damn it, anyhow, I really liked the man, his crooked grin, his concern for me, his eyes that could switch from the color of summer sky to ice in an instant, his gregariousness, his sexy body. I could go on about what I liked for a long time. I just didn't want to be rushed.

❧ ❧ ❧

Great timing! The Rose Rent parade was heading down
Hemlock Street toward Main Street and the square, and of
course, the cross street we were on was cordoned off and
guarded by two volunteer firemen, who were taking their
official duties very seriously.

"Might as well relax and enjoy it," Garnet grumbled as he
turned off the engine.

From the cab of his truck, we had a great view of little
girls doing gymnastics accompanied by the silver tinkle of
the glockenspiels. I was glad to see that someone had been
assigned to march ahead of them shoveling up the poop
from the horses of a dozen or so men dressed in Civil War
uniforms.

After the girls came a covered wagon, pulled along by
more horses. A bearded, young man in jeans and a plaid
shirt waved his whip at the crowd while people cheered.
Garnet informed me that this was an almost exact replica of
the famous Conestoga wagon that had fallen into the Lickin
Creek, along with the town's illustrious founder.

"After the ceremony, they'll drive it on down to the Creek
and push it in . . . that's the brilliant reenactment put on by

the Lickin Creek Community Theatre every year."

"Amazing," I said dryly, shaking my head.

A seemingly unending procession of Scout troops—boys and girls—came along, interspersed with marching bands from the Lickin Creek High School and several neighboring towns. The musicians looked miserable in their wool band uniforms, designed for winter football games, not July parades.

Along came the VFW, DAV, American Legion, AMVETS, Elks, Moose, Owls, Odd Fellows, Soroptomists, Optimists, DAR, Caven Countians for Choice, and other groups I'd never heard of. To delight the children, there were clowns, jugglers, balloon tiers, and more Teenage Mutant Ninja Turtles than should have been allowed. Even Ronald McDonald was there, throwing out coupons for free burgers.

Near the end of the procession came the contestants for the Best Pet Award, according to the banner that preceded them. At least a dozen adults and children were carrying or pulling animals, most of which looked as if they wished they were anywhere else. A Gila monster glared at me through the wire mesh of his cage.

"Ugly beast," I commented. "I think the black kitten should win."

"Like the looks of that Doberman myself," Garnet remarked.

The parade ended with about twenty men dressed in suits of armor and a few women in long, tattered dresses—the camp followers.

"What on earth does that have to do with Rose Rent Day?" I asked.

Garnet shrugged. "They show up for everything around here. Apple Fest, Corn Festival, Civil War battles, supermarket openings, you name it. I guess it's okay as long as they think they're having fun."

"What will they do after the parade?"

"They'll camp in back of the Holiday Inn and hold a jousting tournament later in the day. The people who are too poor to go to the Mystery Dinner at the castle and too sophisticated for the Monster Tractor Pull will turn out for that."

Finally, the parade was over, and Garnet turned on his engine. He dropped me off behind the courthouse, and the last I saw of him was his truck cutting down a one-way alley the wrong way.

Mark had already taken his seat on the platform when I reached the square. He was watching the last of the paraders march by, their armor, which I suspected was mostly made of recycled beer cans, clanking, and their swords raised in salute. He graciously acknowledged them with a royal wave that King Arthur would have approved of.

I pushed forward until I was standing right in front of the platform and next to Alice-Ann. Her eyes grew misty when she saw me.

"Wouldn't Richard be proud of him," she whispered.

"I'm sure he is." I squeezed her hand.

"Look, here comes Sylvia. The ceremony is about to start."

"I can't believe she's recovered enough to be here."

"Recovered from what?" Alice-Ann asked curiously.

"I forgot to tell you, but after LaVonna's body was found, she collapsed. She had a high fever, and Dr. Jones wanted to put her in the hospital."

"But naturally, she wouldn't go because of the Rose Rent ceremony."

Sylvia was helped onto the platform by Praxythea and began a long-winded speech reminding everyone there that it was due to her efforts that the Rose Rent ceremony had been reinstated after having been forgotten for nearly a hundred years. Then she suggested a moment of silent prayer for the recently deceased Richard MacKinstrie, Judge Parker, and

LaVonna Hockenberry. Most of the moment was far from silent, since not all of the spectators knew of Judge Parker's death and word hadn't gotten out yet about LaVonna's demise. Questions buzzed like bees through the crowd.

Sylvia finally stepped down from the platform and came to stand between Alice-Ann and me. Her face was flushed.

"You belong in bed," I whispered to her.

"Later. This is far more important." As she spoke, her knees buckled, and I seized her arm to keep her from sinking to the pavement. She let out a small cry of pain and pulled away from me. "Don't grab me like that!" she said nastily, rubbing her arm.

"Sorry. I was just trying to keep you from falling."

"Next time, mind your own business," she hissed.

A chorus of *shhhh*s surrounded us, so I turned away from the grumpy old woman to watch the activity on the platform.

Three adorable little girls, wearing old-fashioned white frocks, ascended the stage, each carrying a beautiful red rose. Fowler's Flowers must have come through with some new ones, since I knew where two of the original ones were.

Mark stood and accepted their tributes, one at a time, bowing politely to each of them as they curtsied. Then it was time for the formal serving of doughnuts and coffee. As soon as Mark had been served, people began lining up at the tables on the sidewalks to receive their snacks.

Alice-Ann brought Mark down to earth, literally and figuratively, wiping the grease off his fingers and taking the roses before they were completely crushed. "I'm proud of you, honey. And Daddy would have been proud, too."

Mark beamed. "I was good, wasn't I?"

"You sure were," I put in.

"Can I go play now?" Mark asked his mother.

"Run along. I'll meet you down at the Creek in an hour to watch The Accident."

He took off with the three little girls close behind.

A quavering-voiced woman from the Ladies Poetry Society was reciting "Ode to a Rose" on the marble steps of the Lickin Creek National Bank. I grabbed a doughnut, and we moved out of listening range, where we narrowly missed being run down by a horde of skateboarders preparing for their competition.

"We'd better get out of here before the bed races start," said Alice-Ann, laughing. "Do you want to come watch The Accident?"

"I think I've had all the excitement I can handle. Since everyone in town appears to be here, I'd like to borrow your car and do some uninterrupted investigating. I want to look through Richard's office myself and then go out to the castle. It still worries me that we haven't found any of Richard's research papers. Sylvia claimed a couple of days ago that the project was hers, and Richard was only assisting her. That's just the opposite of what he claimed. I want to poke around and see if I can't turn up something."

Alice-Ann handed me her keys and told me the address of Richard's office. "We'll get Mrs. Seligman, or someone, to give us a ride home."

"Thanks," I said, then noticed Sylvia leaning against one of the bank's Doric columns. She was clutching Praxythea's arm and looked as if she was about to collapse.

"Sylvia," I said, hurrying to her side. "I think you'd better see the doctor."

She didn't argue, which was proof to me that she was really sick. I ran back to the parking lot behind the courthouse and found Alice-Ann's disreputable VW.

Main Street was blocked off to traffic, so I tooted at the fireman manning the barricade and convinced him to let me drive onto Main Street. A lot of happy celebrants grudgingly moved out of my way. It took two strong men to load the almost unconscious woman into the car. She insisted Praxythea come with us.

"I'm taking you to the clinic," I said.

"Nooo," Sylvia protested weakly.

"Yes," I said firmly as I guided the Bug safely through the crowd—just in time, the beds were lining up at the end of the street.

Praxythea guided me through the maze of one-way streets to the clinic, which was a low, modern building of brick and glass, devoid of character and hideous in contrast to the neighboring Victorian buildings. I pulled up at the ambulance entrance, where an orderly yelled at me to move. Once he saw who was in the car with me, though, we were immediately surrounded by attentive men and women in white, and Sylvia was efficiently spirited away in a wheelchair, still clutching Praxythea's hand in a death grip. As soon as she was out of sight, the orderly grew surly again and ordered me to move my car at once.

I circled the clinic for about twenty minutes looking for a place to park. Finally, desperate, I gave up trying to be ethical and pulled into the only empty spot, which was marked MINISTERS ONLY.

Garnet was standing in the lobby talking to Dr. Jones.

"How is Sylvia?" I asked them.

"She's got blood poisoning," the doctor said. "I discovered it this morning after she collapsed at the castle. I gave her a penicillin shot and told her to stay in bed and not go to the ceremony, but naturally she didn't listen. Now she's had a serious relapse.

"She got some nasty puncture wounds on her arms from the thornbushes the night Richard's body was found. If she'd shown them to me then, I would have started her on penicillin right away, but all I saw were the scratches on her hands, and I thought simply treating them with an antibiotic ointment would be sufficient. With all those people wandering in and out of the bushes, about half the town got scratched. We're lucky no one else got that sick."

"Is she going to be all right?" I asked.

"Oh, she'll be fine, no doubt. Tough old broad. Now, if you'll excuse me, I have patients to attend to. LaVonna's autopsy took up most of my morning. Several people at the Rose Rent ceremony passed out from heat exhaustion, and I have to get to them."

He disappeared through the emergency room doors.

"Garnet, I didn't get to finish telling you what I learned yesterday. I talked to Mrs. O'Brien and she said she saw the judge, alive, when Rose left his house."

Garnet's jaw clenched. "I thought I told you . . ."

"There's no law against asking questions."

"All right. Here's something for you to stew about. I've learned Alice-Ann had another motive to kill her husband."

"Like what? I thought you were through with suspecting Alice-Ann."

"I'm never through suspecting anybody until I have a crime solved, Tori. Richard had a large life-insurance policy. Enough to cover most of his debts. If she collects, she won't have to lose the house."

"What do you mean 'if she collects'?"

"She can't collect if she's convicted of murdering him."

The hair on the back of my neck bristled. "And what motive do you think she had for murdering the judge?"

"Tori, how many murders do you think were committed last week in New York City?"

"Twelve? Thirty?"

"Do you think all those people were killed by the same person?"

"I get your point. Does this mean you're looking for two murderers?"

"One, two, ten; I don't really know. But I won't stop till someone's behind bars."

"I see. Thank you for sharing that with me."

I wasted no time saying good-bye. Somehow, I had to prove to him that Praxythea, not Alice-Ann, was the murderer.

I stopped at Richard's office and let myself in with Alice-Ann's keys. Like Garnet and Alice-Ann, I didn't find anything there about his research project.

I was positive the answers I needed were to be found at the castle.

23

🌹 🌹 🌹

So far I hadn't done a lot of good in proving Alice-Ann's innocence. She was depending on me, and I was letting her down. I had to find the real murderer—and I had to do it soon!

It seemed that every time I came up with a likely suspect for Richard's murder, there was no reason for that person to have killed the judge, and vice versa. LaVonna, I figured, was an innocent bystander who was killed because she was in the wrong place at the wrong time, but the other two . . . there had to be a connection that I wasn't aware of. Garnet had suggested the murders might not be connected. But then why the roses near both corpses?

I parked by the castle's kitchen entrance and walked in without knocking. George was supervising several people busily chopping vegetables and didn't look at all pleased to see me.

"Oh, no! Don't tell me Fred's on the loose again?"

"I won't get in your way. I had promised LaVonna I'd help do some housecleaning. Now that she's . . . gone, I figure I'm needed even more."

He gestured somewhere over his left shoulder. "Cleaning

supplies are in that closet. Keep out of the kitchen."

"No problem," I said cheerfully.

I grabbed a lamb's-wool duster and the first few cans and bottles I saw, without paying attention to what they were, and headed up the stairs to the first floor. Good. No one in the front hall! I climbed the great staircase to the second floor for the first time.

I turned left, into the north wing, and opened the door closest to me. The room obviously had not been used in years. Same with the next. Puffs of dust rose from the hall carpet with every step I took.

The third room, I guessed, had been Michael's since childhood. Built-in shelves contained such boyish treasures as a rock collection, trophies for swimming and football, and a photo of Michael and Garnet, about age fifteen, dressed in identical plaid shirts, holding a trout between them. Odd that the years had led those two boys in such different directions.

A silky white nightgown folded on the pillow was the only sign that the teenager had grown up and married a beautiful TV star.

Another door, and I found a room full of costumes and props. Several more doors and this was where the actors were staying. I backtracked and tiptoed across the gallery to the south wing. This was a little cleaner, as though people really lived here. I put my ear to the first door and, hearing nothing, took a chance and opened it. It was a nightmare of pink froufrou, from the silk-covered walls to the fluffy pink canopy over the bed. Even the windows were covered with layers of pink chiffon, so the very air looked pink. It was every little girl's dream bedroom, right down to the white French-provincial furniture, although I was pretty sure this was the real stuff and not the Sears catalog variety.

There was no doubt in my mind that this was Rose's bedroom. I pulled open the drawers in the bedside table and dresser and did a perfunctory search through them. I didn't expect to find any papers about the Edison project; no one ever claimed she was involved with it. As a matter of fact, I didn't see any papers at all, then I remembered she kept her desk in the library. I'd check it out when I went downstairs.

I continued opening doors until I found the room that had to be Sylvia's.

Unlike Rose's pink passion pit, Sylvia's bedroom was furnished tastefully with walnut and mahogany antiques. A worn but still-beautiful Oriental rug lay on the floor, the original colors faded to soft, muted shades of rose, blue, and green. Because the room stood at the end of the hall, there were windows on three sides, gold draperies drawn back to allow light to stream through the leaded glass. A person could feel like a queen in such a room.

I hastily rummaged through the drawers of Sylvia's bedside table and dresser, spent more time searching her desk. I had no idea what I was looking for, but it seemed to me if she and Richard had been doing research about Edison's spirit communicator, there should be something about it in her desk.

There wasn't.

The bottom drawer was full of old, used manila envelopes. The kind we save thinking we'll use them someday, then never do. But underneath them, probably long forgotten, was an eight-by-ten folder full of yellowed typed pages. On the front someone had written in elegant script, *The History of Rose Rent Day.*

I opened it to the first page. And stared with bewilderment at what was typed there. It slowly dawned on me that the discovery of Edison's invention had only been the catalyst that had led to the three murders. The real reason lay buried deep in the past.

I stuck the folder down the front of my slacks and tried to hide the bulge by letting my shirt hang out over my hips. It was time to take another look at Edison's infernal machine.

To my great surprise, Rose was sitting at her desk in the library, writing in a small, red, leather-bound notebook.

"What are *you* doing here?" she asked as she closed the book and slipped it into the top drawer of the desk.

"What are *you* doing here?" I echoed idiotically. "I thought you'd be at the Rose Rent celebration."

"I have far too much to do to get ready for the Mystery Dinner. And my health . . ."

I picked up on that. "That's why I'm here. I came to help with the cleaning. I told LaVonna I would. And I knew you weren't feeling well."

"Funny," she said wryly. "You don't strike me as the domestic type. But, thank you. Why don't you start with the bathroom down the hall."

Bathroom! Yuk!

"Be happy to," I said, forcing a smile. "Where is it?"

"To your left. Second door. And Tori, you'll need more than furniture wax and silver polish to do it."

"Right . . . I know that." I headed down the hall to the bathroom, which had fixtures old enough to have been brought over from jolly old England when the castle was first built. It didn't appear to have been cleaned since then, either. I stayed there, rubbing the faucets with a washcloth, until I heard Rose leave the library, waited a good five minutes to make sure she wasn't coming back, then headed directly for her desk. I wanted to see what she'd written in that book.

The drawer was locked, but it had one of those old-fashioned keyholes, like the kind kids draw. When I was about eight, I'd discovered my parents kept a raunchy (at least I thought it was) sex manual locked in a nightstand. The key to my father's desk had opened the nightstand as if it were made for it, and also just about everything else in the embassy that had an old-fashioned lock. I looked around, and sure enough, there was a glass-enclosed bookcase next to the fireplace, with a small brass key protruding from the lock, and sure enough, it opened the desk as if it were made for it.

I removed the book from the drawer, but before I had a chance to open it, the doorbell rang. I heard the tippy-tap of Rose's feet heading down the stone corridor and the creak of the great door as she pulled it open. In a panic, I stuffed the little book down the front of my slacks, next to the folder I had stolen from Sylvia's room. I managed to close the drawer, lock it, and put the key back in the bookcase before Rose appeared in the doorway accompanied by Briana.

"Finished with that bathroom already?" she asked me suspiciously. She walked over to the desk and tried the drawer. Apparently she was satisfied that I hadn't opened it because she smiled graciously at me. "Would you be able to dust the front parlor?"

"Of course, but I just remembered I didn't feed my cats this morning. I'll be back in just a few minutes."

I couldn't wait to get out of there and look over my purloined material. I was almost certain that what I had taken from Rose's desk was a diary, and I had the feeling it would explain a lot of what had been going on.

At Alice-Ann's, in my room, I pulled the loot out of my pants and dropped it on the bed. I picked up Rose's book first, and as I did, it fell open to a page near the center. What a disappointment. Instead of a diary full of secrets, it was only an appointment calendar. Under today's date, it simply said *Rose Rent Day* and *Mystery Dinner.*

I flipped ahead. She had a doctor's appointment scheduled for next week—probably what she'd been writing down when I barged into the library. I flipped backward. Under Thursday's date, she had penciled in *5:00—Visit Ben Parker.* The poor judge's appointment with death!

The first time I'd been in the library, I'd seen the appointment book lying on Rose's desk. She had probably kept it there for years—where anyone could have picked it up and looked through it. It slowly dawned on me that the murderer had probably seen that entry, preceded Rose to the judge's house through the tunnels, waited there to hear what she told him, and then, after Rose left, killed him to keep him from telling anyone else what they had discussed. The fact that the murderer had taken the power nailer along meant the murder was most definitely premeditated.

I knew I should call Garnet and tell him of my suspicions.

I rang his office, but got "Hoop's Garage." The bored female voice on the other end had to be the teenage manicurist. He'd been in for a few minutes, she told me, but got a call and went out.

"I'm at Alice-Ann's," I told her. "Please have him call me as soon as possible."

I sat in the kitchen, ate the Snickers bar, and waited. And waited. No call. I tried Hoop's again. She would give him the message when and if he called in, and would I please stop phoning because she was very busy.

Alice-Ann and Mark came home, bursting with excitement and full of stories about their wonderful day. Garnet still didn't call.

It didn't occur to me until later that I never did get to examine Edison's machine when I was in the library. In fact, I couldn't even remember seeing it.

Chapter

24

❀ ❀ ❀

I looked at myself in the full-length mirror and had to admit the white Victorian gown was flattering.

While I waited for Alice-Ann and Mark to finish dressing for the Mystery Dinner, I wondered offhandedly if it was a smart thing to go to the castle tonight. I decided it would be wise to go, because Garnet was expecting me to be there, and if he didn't get a chance to call me at Alice-Ann's before it was time for us to leave, he would assume I was at the castle and go directly there. If he was late, at least I could keep an eye on the people I suspected of murder.

Almost time to go, and still no call. Alice-Ann and Mark came downstairs. The Rose Rent honoree's face was twisted into a petulant sulk. "I hate it," he cried, stamping on the floor with his little feet. "I look like a dweeb."

He was dressed in short wool pants with suspenders, a once-white—now aged-yellow—shirt with a round collar, and a big red bow tied at his neck. On his feet were brown, high leather boots with buttons. He did indeed look like a dweeb.

"It's traditional. Every MacKinstrie boy wears it on Rose

Rent Day," Alice-Ann told him, ending the argument right there.

I called Hoop's one last time. A different woman answered. She was the night shift, and she hadn't been told of my calls. Garnet had checked in once and was now over at the Civil War battlefield where some "soldiers" had drunk a little too much homemade moonshine and were attempting to reenact Pickett's Charge against the medieval encampment in the next field. I explained I was going to be at the castle, and it was urgent that Garnet contact me.

"I'll do my best," she promised. "He's got a beeper, but if things are really rowdy out there, it may be a while before he can get to a phone."

We walked down the footpath to the castle. There must have been a hundred cars there. Most of them looked abandoned rather than parked. First in would definitely have to be last out.

The woman who admitted us into the castle looked vaguely familiar. "Hi. Remember me? I was at the station when you'uns came in on the bus."

"Of course. Janet. It's nice to see you'uns . . . I mean, you again."

"I'm helping out tonight, since LaVonna . . . well, you know. I'm kinda scared. With all these murders, I don't know if it's safe to be here."

"Don't worry. There's plenty of people around. Nothing's going to happen."

I certainly hoped I wasn't lying!

Almost everyone had shown up at the castle in costume. Most wore Victorian garb, but some wore the earlier clothes of the pioneers, and a few were in Civil War uniforms, both armies represented.

Michael approached me as soon as I walked in. He was dressed in white tie and tails and looked stunning. He lifted my hand to his lips as he bowed to me.

"My heroine! I've great news. The Smithsonian already has

found a person who is willing to buy Sylvia's Star from us and donate it to the museum. The jewel will be on display for everyone in the world to enjoy, and Silverthorne is saved."

"I'm thrilled for you, Michael. I hope you put that necklace in a safe place. You don't want it to get lost for another hundred years."

"Don't worry. It's in a box at the Old LCNB."

"Old LCNB?"

"Old Lickin Creek National Bank. Sorry, I keep forgetting you're not a native. It seems as though you've always been here."

Several guests had been listening to us and were saying things to me like *ooh* and *aah* and *weren't you brave.* I was thoroughly enjoying every bit of it when the spell was broken by the arrival of a man in a trench coat and a brown fedora.

His hands were trembling, and perspiration beaded his upper lip. "Michael," he said. "Problem. The countess can't find her gun."

"She had it at rehearsal. Where did she leave it?"

"She said she put it back in the prop room."

Michael sighed and grinned at me. "Something always goes wrong on opening night." To Trench Coat he said, "She'll just have to improvise. Get her a knife."

"But I'm supposed to accuse her of murder because she's holding a smoking gun. Whoever heard of a smoking knife?"

"Shit!" Michael muttered, and hurried off.

Alice-Ann and I helped ourselves to champagne, and Mark ran off to join a small group of children.

Father Burkholder walked in, spotted us, and came over. "Sorry I'm late. The traffic is unbelievable. I think everyone in southern Pennsylvania is heading into Lickin Creek tonight." He grabbed a glass of champagne from a passing waiter.

"What on earth for? Certainly they can't all be interested in a medieval jousting match," I said.

"Don't forget the Monster Tractor Pull. That always draws a big crowd," Alice-Ann put in.

"Just what is a tractor pull?" I asked.

"Farmers hook their tractors up to sleds weighted down with heavy objects and pull them," Father Burkholder told me. "The tractor that pulls the heaviest load the farthest is the winner. Obviously."

I shook my head. What a strange place this was!

Another waiter, dressed in an impeccable black tuxedo, came by bearing a tray of fluted champagne glasses. I put my empty glass down and took another, and as I did, he leaned close to the three of us and whispered, "Did you hear the countess was seen kissing the ambassador in the library?"

"Huh?" was my intelligent response.

He was already serving someone else, and I noticed he whispered a message to them also.

A hand touched my shoulder, ever so lightly. I jumped a mile and turned to find myself nose to nose with Praxythea.

"You startled me," I gasped, heart pounding.

"Where's Garnet? I need to—" she began. But she didn't have a chance to finish because Sylvia descended upon us, a Valkyrie without her spear.

"Praxythea, I need your help." She took Praxythea's arm and they sailed away in a cloud of Bellodgia.

What was that all about? I wondered. I took a sip of my wine, and a maid in a Victorian servant's uniform—long black dress and white apron—appeared before me with a platter of hors d'oeuvres. I helped myself to some caviar on toast and heard her say, sotto voce, "The detective is not what he appears to be."

I thought for a second she meant Garnet, then I got it. "It's part of the play."

"Brilliant deduction," Alice-Ann said.

A woman in a Jean Harlow–style skintight white dress slinked up to us, tapped Father Burkholder with her whitefeather fan, and told him that the Orient Express was late in arriving.

I caught her arm before she had a chance to ooze toward the next couple. "What's the point of all this?" I asked her.

She looked shocked but stepped out of character for a minute. "We talk about the different characters to each group of people, dropping clues that will help you solve the murder later on."

"What murder?"

"The murder that's going to take place during dinner. Then each table will discuss the clues they saw and heard and will write the name of the murderer and his motive on a piece of paper. The winning table gets a prize."

"I remember now. A season's ticket to the Whispering Pines Summer Theatre."

"Toodle-oo," she said, tickling the priest's nose with her feathers. She was back in character.

It was an absolutely bizarre situation. Here we were up to our necks in real murders, and a bunch of fruit loops were running around pretending murder was fun. I excused myself to go to the bathroom, but what I really planned to do was look in the library to see if the Edison machine was still there.

I barged into the room and surprised Sylvia and Rose, who were engaged in a quiet but intense conversation. The sisters stared at me like panicked rabbits. As usual, Rose was wearing something pink, and Sylvia was in her black mourning gown.

"Oh. Sorry. I didn't realize there was anyone in here."

"We're quite finished. Aren't we, Rose?"

Rose nodded. Her eyes and nose were red, as if she had been crying.

"I'm glad you're feeling better," I said to Sylvia. "I thought the doctor might keep you in the clinic overnight."

"He ordered me put on an IV, but I had too much to do

here, so I called Uriah's Heap and came home. It was really just exhaustion, my dear. Rose Rent Day always takes so much out of me. I feel fine now."

I glanced quickly around the room. No black box in sight. "Did either of you see where Garnet put the Edison machine?" Both shook their heads.

"Haven't seen it since you dragged it out of the basement," Sylvia snapped. Rose blinked. They left the room together but went in opposite directions when they reached the hallway.

I checked every corner, but the box I'd risked my life for was gone. Maybe Garnet had taken it with him, I hoped, but doubted it, since he didn't really think it was anything other than a curiosity.

Chimes rang out, the signal that dinner was ready. I picked up the telephone in the hall and tried to call Garnet again. As far as the receptionist at Hoop's knew, he was still out at the battlefield, and she was still trying to beep him. I told her it was a matter of life and death. She didn't sound impressed, but promised to keep trying.

I walked into the ballroom, studied the seating chart, and located my table. I joined the mayor, the Seligmans, Alice-Ann and Mark, and three people I hadn't met before. It turned out they were all winners of some of the day's special events. The owner of a two-headed snake was proudly displaying her pet's first-place medal. I prayed she didn't have her pet with her, too. The two muscle-bound young men were the winners of the bed race, having represented the Old LCNB in that competition. They were both from the accounting department, and conversation with them was as fascinating as watching an industrial training film. I was just thankful that the teenage winners of the skateboard race were seated elsewhere.

I sipped champagne and looked around to see who else was there. Twanya Tweedy, looking virginal in a white dress similar to mine, was seated on the other side of the room.

Tactful planning by someone! She was having a lively conversation with a good-looking Union officer—the king was dead, long live the king!

The Thorne sisters were at a table near the entrance to the front hall. Rose looked upset. Sylvia, pale and fidgety. Seated with them was Praxythea in a black dress she'd spray-painted on.

At another table, Maggie, the librarian, waved at me. The nice-looking man on her right must have been her fiancé. Dr. Meredith Jones was there, of course, positioned where he could keep an eye on his favorite patient, Alice-Ann. His dinner companion was the editor, publisher, reporter, etc., of the Lickin Creek *Chronicle*. She nodded graciously in my direction and coughed.

To give the waiters credit, they kept the wine flowing, and I was having trouble concentrating on the confusing, complicated mystery plot. The pretend one, not the real one. People in strange costumes kept appearing, making dramatic speeches or bursting into tears or threatening to kill themselves or someone else.

Michael was apparently the comic relief, showing up every few minutes in a different costume, starting with a Lawrence of Arabia outfit, and most strangely, during the shrimp-cocktail course, wearing a pink satin negligee and what must have been one of his mother's Lucille Ball wigs. I don't know if it was his intent, but he looked a lot like Rose.

In a loud "intimate" conversation with a bespectacled man, Michael explained he was a princess from a Balkan country who needed to marry for money before her country was sold to a Japanese businessman for a ski resort. Everyone laughed a lot as he swished around the room, so I suppose it was funny.

Suddenly a shot rang out, and you could hear silverware dropping all over the room. A moment later we heard a woman's scream from the great front hall.

Everyone at our table jumped up with much excitement.

Not me. I took another tiny sip of wine and told Alice-Ann, "Some guy gets shot by the countess and rolls down the steps. I watched the rehearsal."

But it was happening differently this time. The woman who ran into the dining room, screaming, was not the French maid in her skimpy costume, but Janet in her sensible shoes and plain dress.

"Help, someone, please. There's a dead body in the hall." She sounded convincingly panic-stricken.

Everyone laughed and clapped, and about half the people in the room followed the trench-coated detective into the hall. The rest stayed behind to eat.

"Let's go see," Alice-Ann suggested. Mark didn't want to, so she and I went together to watch the show in the hall. I couldn't see a thing over the heads of the people in front of me, so I took Alice-Ann's hand and we weaved our way to the front, where we saw a woman, dressed in pink, lying facedown in a pool of blood. Her bright red wig was slightly askew.

"They changed the plot," I whispered. "It was supposed to be a man that was killed. I guess Michael decided to be the 'corpse' after the countess lost her gun. She must have found it though, or she couldn't have 'shot' him."

"Are you making any sense or is it me?" Alice-Ann asked, obviously confused.

Before I could explain further, Trench Coat, who had been kneeling next to the "body," got to his feet and turned to face us. "Everybody go back to your dinners, please. We'll be solving the murder right after dessert."

We all cheerfully did as we were told and headed back to our tables for more fun, games, and wine. Not to mention baked Alaska. Except me. I waved Alice-Ann on back, but I remained there.

I waited till they were all gone and stage-whispered to the body, "All right, Michael, you can get up now. The others have left."

He didn't move.

"Boy, that fake blood sure looks real," I said.

"Mother!"

I spun around and saw Michael, still dressed in the pink dress and red wig, running toward us.

He knelt down and gently turned the body over. It was Rose, blood pouring from a gash over her right eye. Her red wig fell off, revealing the few straggly wisps of white hair left after her cancer treatment.

I didn't want to look, but I had to. "Is she dead?" I asked fearfully.

"No. Go get Doc Jones," Michael ordered.

I managed to fetch the doctor without alarming any of the partygoers.

He examined Rose quickly but efficiently.

"Head wounds bleed a lot, but this one isn't fatal. It would have been if it had hit her straight on. She must have ducked just in time."

"You mean someone really shot her? She didn't just fall?" I asked.

"Yes, she's been shot," the doctor said. "I want her carried upstairs, please. It's going to be a while before we can get an ambulance out here. I don't think she's in any danger. The bullet just grazed her head."

"You're right." I'd been checking around while he talked. "Here's the bullet. It was stuck in the banister."

Michael picked up his mother and carried her up the staircase as though she weighed nothing.

Trench Coat followed him, wringing his hands. "What do I do now?" he wailed.

"You're an actor," Michael called over his shoulder. "Improvise."

25

❦ ❦ ❦

The doctor and I walked back into the dining room, where the noisy guests were feeling no pain.

"I was afraid of this," I said. "They're gone."

"Who's gone? For God's sake, Tori, stop the Nancy Drew stuff and tell me what's going on."

"Sylvia and Praxythea. Can you get Alice-Ann and have her meet me in the next room, the one they're using for a pantry?"

His eyes brightened at the sound of her name, and he did what I asked without arguing. I walked through the room trying to look casual, smiling at the people I recognized. I ducked behind the screen Michael's set designers had built and found myself in a room full of waiters, actors, and food, lots of it, on steamer tables.

Janet was shaking in a corner, where several young women were trying to comfort her.

"So much blood," she kept repeating.

"Janet, where were you when you heard the shot?" I asked.

"At the hall closet. Some people wore capes, and they needed hanged. I ran out when I heard the shot."

"Did you see anyone?"

"I seen her lying there. I thought I heard someone running down the hall. I was scared to go after them."

"Them? Do you think it was more than one person?"

She nodded. "Oh, yes. I could hear their high heels clickety-clacking on them stones. You'd think people lived in a castle would put rugs down," she said with a sniff.

The doctor then came in with Alice-Ann.

I held my hands up for silence and raised my voice. "Did any of you see Praxythea and Sylvia anytime in the last twenty minutes or so?"

"I did," George said. "I was down in the kitchen putting the baked Alaskas in the oven when the two of them came charging through. They went down the basement stairs."

"Was either one of them carrying anything?"

"Praxythea had something like a black suitcase with her," George said.

I had to find them before someone else was killed. Until just about an hour ago, I thought they were accomplices. Now I was pretty sure that only one of them was involved in the murders, and the other was in serious danger of becoming the next victim.

"Come on," I said to Alice-Ann and Doc Jones. I ran down two flights of stairs to the basement with the two of them close behind. Sure enough, the kerosene lantern Michael had said always hung on the hook by the cave entrance was gone. I knew I was on the right track.

"Damn!" I said. "It's all so obvious. Sylvia was the one who knew about the dead soldier and took the machine down there to try to communicate with his spirit. If they want to test the machine again tonight, why go into the caves? Everyone knew Garnet had the body removed this afternoon."

Then my mind cleared, and the answers to my questions came to me. "The Historical Society headquarters—that's where they went!" I exclaimed. "Garnet told me that if there were such things as ghosts, that's where they'd be. They're going to try it out there, while everyone in town is away at one of the Rose Rent activities. I'm following them."

"Through the caves?" Alice-Ann said, golden eyes wide as bottle caps. "You'll get lost. I'll go with you."

"No. You stay here and keep trying to get hold of Garnet. Tell him where I am. I won't get lost. Garnet showed me the secret markings on the cave walls. All I have to do is follow them." I wished I felt as self-assured as I sounded. "Keep calling until you get Garnet, please!"

"Then I'll go with you," the doc said in a Dudley Doright voice.

I shook my head. "Rose might need you. And Alice-Ann." That got him. He put an arm around her shoulder.

"I'll take care of them," he said.

I ran upstairs to the kitchen and found one of those great big flashlights with a long handle. I also grabbed a butcher knife. It would be better than no weapon at all, although I was positive Garnet would get to the Historical Society before I did. Cursing at the lost time, I headed, once again, into the darkness of the caverns below.

The magic of the caves overwhelmed me anew. In the dim glow of the flashlight, the walls of the tunnels reflected back glints of gold, while embedded crystals flashed all the colors of the rainbow. And always, there was the slow drip, drip, drip of water, leaking through the limestone crust above.

I passed the entrance to the crystal cave and underground lake and saw several tunnels veering off in different directions. I moved the flashlight beam around until I spotted an arrow carved into the stone. Under it was scratched the letter T.

Praying T stood for *town,* I moved along the tunnel quickly but cautiously, remembering the cave-in we'd encountered the day Garnet first took me down. The long white skirt on my dress kept wrapping itself treacherously around my ankles, threatening to trip me, and finally I gave up and ripped it at the waist. Once out of it, I felt much safer if colder.

When I started encountering the skeletal remnants of old ladders and even some shelves still holding long-forgotten jars of preserved food, I realized I was under the town. Above me I could see outlines of the trap doors that would lead into the basements of the oldest buildings in town.

At last, I came to the caved-in area and knew I was close to my goal. I tried to skirt it carefully, but my heart did a quick double-time beat when my foot slipped a little on some loose stones. How easy it would be to lose one's balance. Could an old woman like Sylvia have maneuvered around it? I shuddered at the thought of falling and falling into unending blackness.

After a few moments that felt like hours, I was standing at the foot of the ladder that led up into the cellar of the Historical Society. The trapdoor was propped open, and from the other side came a dim, orange-gold glow. It had to be coming from the kerosene lantern they'd carried from the castle. A high-pitched hum filled the space around me and increased in volume even as I stood there. The air in the tunnel seemed to vibrate in response to the sound.

I turned off my flashlight and placed it on the ground, then, clenching the butcher knife between my teeth like Douglas Fairbanks, I climbed the rickety ladder until I could peek through the trapdoor. The little secret room where the slaves had died was empty; the flickering light was coming through the archway from the large utility room next to it. I pulled myself out of the hole and lay prone on the earthen floor. If I could have burrowed into the dirt to hide, I would have. *Garnet. Be here. Please, be here.* I inched forward, leaving the skin on my knees behind, until, crouched next to the arch, I could see into the other room.

The kerosene lamp was suspended from a hook in the ceiling, illuminating the room. I could see Sylvia and Praxythea from my vantage point, but they couldn't see me. I hoped.

Praxythea was on her knees in front of the Edison machine, and Sylvia was leaning against one of the wooden posts that supported the floors above. A gun dangled from her left hand.

"Find someone," Sylvia ordered, her voice quavery. "Damn it, you've got to find someone."

Praxythea slowly turned a knob and the sound intensified. "Sylvia, please, let's stop," she pleaded. "It's not going to work."

"It's got to work. Three people have died for it. Make it work!"

Praxythea wiped her forehead with the back of one hand and bowed her head for a moment, as if in prayer. With a quick twist of her wrist, she turned the knob all the way to the right.

The humming noise changed to an ear-piercing whine. Around me currents of air swirled, cold as wind from a graveyard. Cold as the wind that only I had felt during the séance at the castle. Cold as the wind in the Mark Twain House.

The whining sound changed again and filled the room with a thousand tortured screams, and the wind blew with the fury of a tornado, spinning old newspapers and trash around the cellar like a carousel gone mad.

I covered my ears, trying to block out the malevolent noise, and I thought of the Mark Twain House, where I had first felt the tangible pall of evil—evil so strong it had come to life. Evil so terrible that I had sworn never to enter that building again. Evil so persistent that I would never be able to escape from it. It had followed me here. To Lickin Creek. And once more it caressed me, loved me, enchanted me, enticed me to kill for it—as it had made others kill.

You can't run from me, Tori. There's no place in this world you can hide from me. I will be with you always. I love you,

Tori. Do what I ask and I will give you everything you ever wanted.

I saw Billy—waiting for me, happy, not blaming me for what I'd done. My mother—whole and well again. My father—able to smile once more.

The machine—I had to turn off the machine!

I lunged into the room, knocked Praxythea over, grabbed the black box, and flung it as hard as I could against the wall. The noise stopped, and so did the obscene voice in my head.

Sylvia was stunned into immobility by my sudden entrance, but now she swung the gun up and pointed it at me. Praxythea lurched forward and grabbed Sylvia by the ankles, pulling her to the floor, and the gun discharged with a roar. The bullet hit the kerosene lantern, which crashed to the floor and shattered.

As the two women wrestled, I groped around on the floor, in the dark, trying to find the gun. Where was the damn gun?

Unnoticed by any of us at first, the flame from the broken lantern was following small rivulets of kerosene; little fiery fingers reached eagerly for the old newspapers piled against the wall. And suddenly we weren't in the dark anymore. The heavy stacks, dense and damp from years in the basement, smoldered slowly at first, then began to burn around the edges, as clouds of thick, inky smoke whirled up from the fire, sucking the oxygen out of the room. It wasn't exactly comforting to remember that more people died from smoke inhalation than from burns in a fire. There was supposed to be more air near the floor, so I dropped to my knees. Not only could I breathe better, but I could see Praxythea and Sylvia both crouched on the floor.

"Let's get out of here," I croaked to them. The smoke was filling my lungs and it was hard to talk. "The stairs are behind you. Crawl. Don't try to stand up."

We had almost reached the door at the foot of the stairs when I heard Garnet's voice coming from behind it. "Tori, are you in there?"

He flung the door open, and black smoke was sucked up the stairwell with a whooshing sound. I saw Garnet fall to the floor as flames rolled up the stairs, fed by the oxygen-rich fresh air. They spread out across the ceiling, ignited the dry, old wooden beams, cut off our escape route. And I couldn't see Garnet.

I screamed his name, choked, and found myself gasping for air.

"I'm okay," he called back.

A shot rang out, and Garnet yelled, "Geez, my leg!"

"Garnet!" I coughed. "Are you all right? Damn it, answer me!" My throat felt as if someone had poured lye down it.

He groaned. At least he was alive.

I was looking at three walls and the ceiling on fire. We were almost surrounded. The only escape route was behind me through the tunnel, if the fire hadn't already spread there, too. A piece of the ceiling collapsed. If we were going to get out, it had to be now!

How bad was Garnet's wound? Could he crawl? I inched forward, following the sound of his groans. He had to be close. Sylvia appeared before me, rising out of the smoke, silhouetted against the flames like a creature from hell, the gun pointed directly at my head. Out of the corner of my eye, I saw Praxythea crawling in Garnet's direction.

"Sylvia, put the gun down, please," I croaked.

"Bitch!" she spat at me. "Everything was okay till you got here. You had to go sticking your nose into everybody's business. I left that note to scare you away—you and your stupid cats."

I had to keep her talking. Keep her from pulling that trigger. "Sylvia, Why? Why did you do it?"

From her seventy-year-old mouth came the voice of a young girl. "It was Rose's fault. Rose was the oldest. Rose was the prettiest. Rose was the smartest. Rose was Daddy's favorite. Rose had the boyfriend. Rose had the beautiful little boy. Rose made Daddy hate me. Rose made me kill Daddy."

"Oh, God!"

"She told him I made her stay away and not tell him about the baby. He got mad at me. It was her fault."

Praxythea was dragging Garnet across the floor. He was on his back, trying to help by pushing with his good leg.

Keep talking, Tori. Keep her from noticing them. Tears streamed from my burning eyes. "Richard? Why kill him?"

"It was Rose's fault. She was going to tell everyone she did the Rose Rent research. They would have kicked me out of the Society. I needed the Edison machine to get back in, and Richard wanted it for himself. Then I had to kill the judge because Rose told him. And poor LaVonna because she knew. It was all Rose's fault."

She started to cry. "All I ever wanted was for people to like me."

She was a monster, but I couldn't help but feel compassion and sympathy for her. That was all I'd ever wanted from my family and never got. I gasped, "Put the gun down. We'll get help."

Sylvia raised the gun, calmly placed it in her ear, and pulled the trigger. Praxythea screamed.

I took one last look at Sylvia's body, then seized one of Garnet's arms, wincing at his moans of pain. "We've got to get out of here before we suffocate."

Praxythea grabbed his other arm, and we half-carried, half-dragged him across the room. We were bent almost double, trying to stay as close to the floor as possible. It felt as though he weighed as much as both of us combined. The muscles in my back screamed in agony. Sooty sweat poured into my eyes, nearly blinding me. I prayed we were going in the right direction.

A red cinder dropped from the ceiling onto the skirt of

Praxythea's long, black dress, and the flimsy material flared up at once. She dropped Garnet and ineffectively attempted to snuff out the flames. I grabbed hold of the cloth on either side of her cleavage and pulled. The dress ripped down the middle and she wriggled out of it. I was glad I'd shed mine earlier.

Garnet was attempting to stand, not very successfully, on one foot. The fire hadn't spread to the secret room, yet, and we were close to the entrance. We draped Garnet's arms over our shoulders and made a dash for it.

"You go down first," I told Praxythea. "I'll help him get on the ladder. You try to keep him from falling."

Garnet lay facedown on the floor, and I helped him swing his legs into the hole. He used his muscular arms to lower himself down the ladder, one rung at a time.

I yelled for Praxythea. "There's a flashlight down there. Near the ladder."

I saw the light come on. As soon as Garnet was far enough below me, I turned around and let my legs find the ladder. The last thing I did before climbing down was to slam the trapdoor shut above my head.

Garnet was leaning against the damp cave wall, blood pouring from a wound in his thigh. Praxythea, flashlight in hand, was examining his leg. "Give me your shirt," she said to Garnet. "We've got to put pressure on it to stop the bleeding."

I helped him get it off, and Praxythea wrapped it around his leg. "That should hold it for a while," she said. "Do you know how to get out of here?"

I wanted to scream out of frustration and pain. I was just beginning to feel the burns on my hands and legs. "I do, but there was a cave-in just a few feet from here. I don't know how we'll be able to get him past it. We're going to cook down here."

Indeed, smoke was seeping through the trapdoor into the tunnel. How long before we were asphyxiated?

"Then we'll go in the opposite direction," Praxythea said

practically. "There have to be entrances to other houses."

She was right, of course, and a few minutes later I was hauling and she was pushing Garnet up a ladder into another dusty cellar. One that was free of smoke and fire.

We staggered up the stairs into a large, old-fashioned kitchen, horrifying the family gathered there for a late-night snack.

"Call an ambulance." I sounded like a crow. "And the fire department. The Historical Society building's on fire."

"My word," the woman said. "It's Chief Gochenauer, and he's hurt." She ran for the telephone while her husband assisted Garnet to a chair and unwrapped our makeshift dressing. He replaced it with a clean towel and applied steady pressure while we waited for help.

The Historical Society building surrendered to the fire, and when the trucks from several volunteer fire departments all showed up at the same time with sirens screaming and lights whirling, there was nothing left but smoldering ruins. The firefighters concentrated on preventing the fire from spreading to nearby buildings.

I learned later that no trace of Sylvia was ever found.

Sunday

🌹 🌹 🌹

Chapter

26

❀ ❀ ❀

I awoke to the ringing of bells. The local churches, their Rose Rent paid for the year, were celebrating the Sabbath. I could hardly believe it was Sunday, and that I was really alive. So what if my throat felt scorched, my head throbbed, and I had some burns on my hands and legs? I was alive!

Praxythea and I were sharing a room at the clinic. We were both hooked up to IV bags, dripping a clear solution into our arms.

"Hi," Praxythea said with a grin. "Helluva night, wasn't it?"

"I'll say. I wonder what those poor people thought when three half-naked, bloody, soot-covered people came staggering into their kitchen?"

"We sure looked a fright. You in that frilly Victorian blouse and cotton underpants . . ."

"And you in that black satin thingamajig. Is that what they call a teddy? I didn't know people really wore those things."

The door opened and Doc Meredith entered. "Good. You're awake at last. Let's just check you out." He listened to my lungs for a long time with an ice-cold stethoscope and studied my burns, then did the same to Praxythea. "You're both in good shape. You can go home anytime you like."

He turned to me. "You certainly do have a brave friend," he said enthusiastically.

I thought he meant Praxythea, but he went on, "Alice-Ann has been here half the night just waiting for you to wake up."

I lay back on my pillow and grit my teeth. That's what infatuation does to a man—I was the one who rushed through the tunnels chasing after a dangerous murderess, I stopped her from killing again, I almost lost my life saving two people from a burning building—and Alice-Ann was the "brave" one because she'd survived a night on an uncomfortable hospital chair. Men!

Alice-Ann came in carrying a nylon gym bag. "Thank God you're all right," she cried. "I was scared to death. I brought you both some clothes. They said you were almost naked when you came in."

Meredith unhooked us from our IVs. "Garnet's in his room dying to ask questions. Are you up to it?"

"You bet," I said.

After getting dressed, we followed a nurse down the hall to Garnet's room. He lay with his leg bandaged from ankle to hip. His smile, when he saw me, was worth all the danger I'd been through. I bent over and kissed him gently. He put his arms around me and kissed me back, not so gently.

"Thanks for saving my life," he said, still holding me.

"Anytime," I said as I managed to disentangle myself from his bear hug. Then I saw there were others in the room. Luscious was leaning against the wall, and Michael was there with Rose, who was seated in a wheelchair wearing a fuzzy pink robe and a bandage wrapped around her forehead.

"Now," Garnet said, "you are going to tell me what happened last night and explain why." He sounded tough, but I was learning that it was just his way of expressing concern.

"I will, but I think Rose should start. It's really her story. Will you, Rose?"

"I think I'd better. It's all been inside me for so long . . . then I told Benjamin . . . and . . . and it killed him."

I took her withered hand in mine. "Go ahead, Rose."

"I killed them. All three."

"Is this a confession?" Luscious asked, pulling out his notebook.

"Put that damn thing away and don't be ridiculous," Rose snapped. He sheepishly stuffed the notebook back in his shirt pocket. "Where should I start?"

"Start with your father's death," I suggested. "Sylvia admitted she killed him."

Rose gasped. "I always thought she had. The whole thing began more than thirty years ago. I was happy here, piddling around with the local history stuff, and taking care of Father. And I was in love with Benjamin Parker. He wasn't a judge then, just a lawyer, and he used to visit the castle and discuss history with Father and me. Sylvia was never interested in history, but she always hung around when he came over. Later, I learned she was in love with him herself and had deluded herself into thinking the reason he came to the castle was to see her.

"When I became pregnant, she was furious. Benjamin wanted to get married at once, but she swore she would kill herself if we did. She told me lies—that she and Benjamin had been having an affair, and that it was really her he loved.

"I was confused and scared. Things were different then; unwed mothers were not glamorized like they are now. Sylvia convinced me that Father would disown me if he knew about my wicked behavior. She talked me into leaving town to have the baby. She made up a lie that I had a job at the Smithsonian in Washington, and she sent me money every month to cover my expenses. Her idea was that I would put the child up for adoption, then 'quit' my job and come home.

"Like a fool, I refused to see Benjamin again, believing that he had betrayed me with Sylvia, and I left the state. Everything went as Sylvia planned, but when I held Michael in my arms for the first time, I knew I could never give him up."

Rose looked up at Michael and smiled. "I brought Michael home. I didn't care if my father kicked us out or disowned us, I wanted him to know he had a grandson. He was delighted and never even asked me to tell him who the father was.

"Sylvia was horribly jealous of me and Michael. She went to Father and told him I was wicked and immoral and a disgrace to the Thorne family and should be sent away. Her plan backfired. Father grew angry with her and drew up a new will, disowning her and leaving everything to me and then Michael.

"When he told her what he had done, she went crazy. That's the day Father died. I guessed that she had killed him, but I couldn't accuse my own sister. I knew he would have forgiven her if he had lived.

"I always treated her as if we shared everything equally. I even enjoyed watching her become the town's social leader. She never mentioned our father or the will again, and I thought everything would be all right."

Rose took a few sips of water. "Now we come to the terrible thing I did. A few months ago, I started having headaches and blackouts. Meredith diagnosed an inoperable brain tumor. We do a lot of stupid things when we stare death in the face. What I did was to kill three people."

Luscious pulled out his little notebook again, convinced he was finally going to get his confession.

"I can't go on," she said tearfully.

"I can," I said.

Everyone stared at me in astonishment, including Rose.

"Sylvia didn't just send you money out of the goodness of her heart. She demanded something from you, and you gave it to her, the results of the research you had done about the history of Rose Rent Day—and allowed her to pass it off as her own. She used the 'borrowed' research to gain member-ship in the Historical Society, hoping to impress Benjamin and her father."

"Is she right?" Garnet asked.

Rose nodded.

"It was obvious to me that the roses found with the bod-ies linked the murders together, and that they represented a connection with Rose Rent Day. That's why I was sure both men had been killed by the same person."

I paused and looked pointedly at Garnet. "But who? I knew Rose had the motives, but she also had an alibi for the judge's death. Sylvia was the one person most closely associ-ated with Rose Rent Day, but she had no motive to kill any-one. Or at least that's what I thought until yesterday."

"How do you know all this?" Garnet asked, sounding none too pleased.

"I did a little snooping around the castle and found the original Rose Rent research paper in the bottom drawer of Sylvia's desk. She must have forgotten it was there after all these years. On the title page it said 'by Rose Thorne.' That meant Sylvia had been living a lie all these thirty years. Her motive was to protect herself from being exposed as a fraud. And she had the opportunity to kill them both."

Garnet's eyes were that icy-cold blue again.

"Garnet, I tried all afternoon to get hold of you to tell you, really I did."

I helped myself to a sip from Garnet's water glass. My throat was raw from all the talking. "Sylvia learned Rose was going to talk to the judge, and she feared the worst."

"How did she know about the appointment?" Garnet asked.

"I 'borrowed' Rose's date book yesterday and saw she had

written down her scheduled meeting with the judge."

"I knew you didn't come over just to clean bathrooms," Rose said, smiling just a little.

"You made an appointment to meet the judge at his house and you wrote it down in your book, which you kept on your desk where Sylvia could read it. When she saw you had a meeting scheduled with the judge, she guessed correctly that you were going to confess the fraud you'd been a party to."

Rose nodded. "I wanted to die with a clean conscience. I didn't think about how telling the truth would hurt Sylvia. It was terribly selfish of me."

I continued, "Sylvia realized her time was running out. Not only would she be exposed and look like a fool in front of those people who admired her, but when you died, the estate, what was left of it, would go to Michael. She would lose everything that had been important to her for the past thirty years.

"Some time ago, Richard had found the Edison spirit-communication machine in a house he was selling and brought it to Sylvia, thinking she could help him get into the Historical Society. When she felt threatened by Rose, she must have regarded the machine as a godsend—something she could use to retain her own Society membership and social position.

"The first night I was here, I went to the Rose Rent meeting at the castle with Alice-Ann and her husband. As we were leaving, I overheard Sylvia telling Richard to bring 'it' over early the next night. They seemed to be having a disagreement. When she noticed me listening, she explained to me she wanted Richard to tape-record the séance. Later that evening, Richard stormed out of the house, carrying the Edison machine with him, although I thought, at the time, it was a suitcase.

"As we know, he went to the castle and was killed there. I think he probably decided to drop the machine off, and they had an argument about what they were going to do with it.

She let him in, and while he was putting the machine in the library, she picked up Alice-Ann's hammer. When they went out on the terrace, she struck him with it. Then she strapped him on his motorcycle and drove it out towards the highway."

"But she was seventy years old," Garnet protested.

"Yes, but in good health, and a lot bigger than Richard. I don't think she would have had much trouble dragging him around. She probably meant to drive the motorcycle out to the highway and make it look as though he'd had an accident. I don't think she meant to ride it into the firethorn hedge. Most likely she lost control of it. Richard had joked with her earlier about giving her stopping lessons next.

"That's how she got the puncture wounds on her arms. She had to wear long sleeves at the séance to hide them. And she made Rose wear a similar outfit, so she wouldn't look out of place. She got frightened when she heard the doc say that firethorn wounds could cause blood poisoning. She pretended to get scratched after we found Richard's body in order to get some antibiotic ointment, which she thought she could rub on her arms to prevent infection. But as the doc said, deep puncture wounds are far more serious than scratches and require treatment by penicillin injection."

"What happened to Richard's helmet?" Garnet asked.

"She found it on the terrace, when she came back to wash the blood away. The simplest way to get rid of it would have been to throw it in the pond. I'll bet a nickel you'll find it there. And LaVonna's missing purse, too."

Luscious licked his pencil lead and made a notation in his little book.

"Why did she leave the rose with Richard?" Alice-Ann asked.

Rose spoke up. "Remember, Rose Rent Day had been the most important element of her life for thirty years. She must have wanted Richard to receive his due, even in death."

"I think poor LaVonna must have looked out her window

281

and seen Sylvia riding off on the cycle," I went on. "It must have seemed strange at the time, then the next night, when Richard's body was found, she realized it had to have been Sylvia who had killed him. Maybe she went to Sylvia with her suspicions, or maybe Sylvia overheard her earlier telling me she had something she wanted to talk about. Later that night Sylvia lured her down to the kitchen, stabbed her, and stuffed her in the oven. She probably meant to move the body later, but never found a convenient time to do it.

"And, she still had to worry about Rose's appointment with the judge. She had seen the power nailer earlier and realized it could be a deadly weapon, so she swiped it from the ballroom and took a shortcut through the caves to the judge's house. She waited, and just as she'd feared, Rose told the judge the truth about Rose Rent Day. Sylvia used the power nailer to keep him from talking."

Michael asked, "What was the point of leaving a rose with the judge?"

"She left it as a warning to me," Rose said, "knowing I would realize she had killed Benjamin and why. Tori, when you walked in on us in the library, just before the Mystery Dinner, she had just told me that if I exposed her, the third rose would be for Michael. She knew I would keep quiet to protect him."

"Then why did she try to shoot you last night?" I asked.

"I can tell you about that," Praxythea said, speaking for the first time. "When Sylvia invited me to come to Lickin Creek to help her with her 'special project,' I was quite excited. I had no idea that she had acquired the invention illegally, and truthfully, I was fascinated by the idea of trying to get it to work. She and Richard made me promise not to mention it to anyone—so the news would be even more astounding when we finally broke it.

"Sylvia wanted to test the machine at once. She scheduled the séance to try to find a ghost in the castle to talk to—pretending to look for the necklace was just an excuse. I was surprised when Richard didn't show up, but I figured he and Sylvia had probably had another disagreement. They'd been arguing about the project ever since I became involved. Couldn't agree on what they were trying to accomplish—or who should get credit for what. But I never dreamed she would kill him. Not even after his body turned up. After all, half the people in town hated him for one reason or another.

"Ever since I came to town, she'd been begging me to go down to the caves with her to test the spirit communicator. I wanted to wait until I felt the vibes were right and kept putting her off. When Tori came out of the caves on Saturday morning with the machine and said she'd been hit by someone and smelled my perfume, I was sure Sylvia had done it. My perfume had been missing since Thursday morning, and I began to smell it on Sylvia after that. It's hard to accuse one's hostess of stealing, so I hadn't mentioned it."

"Of course," I said. "I was the one who pointed out to her how distinctive it was. That it was your trademark. She must have stolen it to sprinkle on the cat-threat letter she left at Alice-Ann's house. She thought I'd blame you. And she was right. I did suspect you. In fact, I believed you were her accomplice, right up to the time of the Mystery Dinner."

Praxythea smiled. "I understand. After she hurt you, and LaVonna's body turned up, I realized she was the killer. I was terribly afraid of her. She sensed my nervousness and wouldn't let me out of her sight. She even made me go to the clinic with her.

"She insisted we were going to test the box at the Historical Society Saturday night while everyone was involved with the celebration. She was acting terribly irrational, and I couldn't get away from her to tell anyone. Once, at the dinner, I did slip away—remember, Tori?—I started to ask you where Garnet was, but she stopped me."

"I remember," I said. "And that was when I realized you weren't wearing perfume. You were able to come up behind me without my knowing you were there. But I did smell it when Sylvia showed up, and it dawned on me that for the past few days I only smelled it when she was near. I knew then that it was she who had hit me and left the threatening note. That's why I stopped suspecting you and realized you were probably going to be her next victim."

"How could she have found her way through the caves the way she did?" Michael asked.

"Probably the same way she knew there was a body in the crystal cave. She found your old maps. You had a set, didn't you?"

"Years ago. I haven't seen them in ages. But when you live in a castle, you never throw anything out. She could have found them in my room."

Rose started to cry. "She was so strange, all during dinner, wild-eyed, hands shaking. She told Praxythea it was time to go, and Praxythea tried to talk her out of it. She said she had Father's gun in her purse and would kill anyone who tried to stop her. That's when I jumped up and ran out to the hall, thinking I could yell for help. She followed me and shot me. My own sister shot me!"

"I'm so sorry," I said. I was never going to tell Rose of Sylvia's lifelong jealousy of her. There was no reason to cause her any more hurt.

Praxythea sighed. "If only I had tried to use my powers. I might at least have saved Judge Parker."

"I don't think anything could have stopped her at that point," Rose said. "The time to stop her would have been after she killed our father, and I'm the one who should have done it. But I never imagined she would try to hurt anyone else."

Garnet cleared his throat. "I think we can declare the case officially closed. Three of us heard her confession in the basement of the Historical Society. Her actions will be judged by a higher court than any we have. There's still one thing that really puzzles me, though. As I was getting out of my truck outside of the Historical Society, I heard a sound, a high-pitched whine, that I couldn't identify. Tori, do you know what it was?"

I nodded. "Remember what I told you about Edison trying to communicate with the dead? He believed he could use something like radio waves for reception. Probably the machine was picking up a whole bunch of radio signals at once. What do you think, Praxythea?"

"Could be," she said noncommittally.

Garnet sank back into his pillows. "Well, even though it didn't work, it was an instrument of evil. Because of it, four people are dead. I'm glad it was destroyed in the fire, so no one can ever again be tempted to fool around with it."

I thought of the plans hidden in my underwear drawer. Anyone with a basic knowledge of electrical engineering could build another one, using the diagrams. "Yes, thank God, it's gone," I murmured.

"Thank God," Praxythea echoed, her green eyes boring holes into my skull.

She knows. Somehow, she knows.

We all started to push our chairs back, getting ready to leave, but Garnet reached out and took hold of my wrist. "Stay a bit, won't you please? Any minute now my sister, Greta, will be marching in here with all my relatives in tow. I'd like to talk to you privately before they get here."

When the room was empty, he said, "Following them down through those caves was a dumb thing to do."

I didn't say anything.

"And very brave. You could have been killed."

"I really did try to call you all afternoon. I had to do something when I couldn't get you. I couldn't let Sylvia kill Praxythea, and I was sure she would to cover up all her other crimes."

"You saved my life. There's no way I can ever thank you for that."

I blushed. "It was no big deal."

"Like hell, it wasn't." He twisted his fingers through

mine. "Tori, there's something I wanted to ask you last night,"

Oh-oh! Too soon, Garnet. It's too soon.

I stiffened and pulled my hand away. "My burns . . . ," I mumbled.

Much to my surprise, he laughed. "I wish I knew why you've built that wall around you. But I promise you I'm not going to even make an attempt at breaking through it until you're ready. What I was going to ask was if you'd like to go to Hershey Theater with me Friday night. I've got two tickets for the road show of *Les Miz*. I thought we could have dinner first—at a real restaurant, maybe start getting to know each other a little better. But you'll have to do the driving."

I breathed a huge sigh of relief. New York, my second book, job hunting—they could all just wait a little longer. "I'd like that very much," I said. "Very much."